PLEASURES OF THE *Flesh*

Laurence Haloche is a journalist for *Figaro Magazine* in
Paris. This is her first novel.

LAURENCE HALOCHE

PLEASURES OF THE *Flesh*

Translated from the French
BY RORY MULHOLLAND

PAN BOOKS

First published 1999 by Macmillan

This edition published 2000 by Pan Books
an imprint of Macmillan Publishers Ltd
25 Eccleston Place, London SW1W 9NF
Basingstoke and Oxford
Associated companies throughout the world
www.macmillan.co.uk

ISBN 0 330 35351 9

1 3 5 7 9 8 6 4 2

A CIP catalogue record for this book is available from
the British Library.

Typeset by SetSystems Ltd, Saffron Walden, Essex
Printed and bound in Great Britain by
Mackays of Chatham plc, Chatham, Kent

FOR MY FAMILY

Chapter One

'Let's see them swing!'

The cry went up a hundred times, fuelling the crowd that swayed the Grand Place in Figeac. Like corks on the tide, a wave of heads surged towards the gallows where the hangman strutted. Men stood on tiptoe, jostling to get a better view, while women elbowed their neighbours to avoid being suffocated. Not since Capeluche was hanged was there such a throng. Processions of onlookers had come scurrying in from the Gramat plateau, from Capdenac and from Limogne. An entire region, alerted by hawkers, was here to attend this free spectacle of public punishment. The common people, of course, but also the lords and ladies had hastened to Figeac, seizing vantage points in the town's houses as though they were the tiers of an amphitheatre. For three sous they could squeeze up against a window, cling on to a balcony or crowd on to a roof. Hundreds, thousands merged in the town. An icy, driving rain drenched their frantic faces, their damp shoulders and their dripping cotton smocks. After a six-month sensational trial the justice of King Louis XV was to be carried out at last, and carried out as ruthlessly as the crime committed by the condemned couple in their blood-soaked inn.

A growing murmur bore the news that the cortège was beginning to make its way through the crowd. It progressed with the rhythmed pace of a funeral march. There came a procession of twenty black-cowled penitents preceded by a man bearing a magnificent crucifix that almost touched the sky. Then came the bishop, Monseigneur de Nicolai, crosier in hand and mitre on head, accompanied by intendant Lescalopier, the comte de Plas de Taines and the seigneur de Bessonies. At the rear of the cortège came the magistrates, followed by the cart bearing the prisoners. This was escorted by thirty archers and mounted provosts. Drenched and shivering, Gabert and Marie Raynal stood in woollen shirts, their wrists bound behind their backs as they drew closer to their deaths.

The people's fervour, numbed by the cold, was suddenly reawakened. They broke down the slender wooden barriers erected to contain them. The cavalry held them back for a moment, reining in their mounts in a vain bid to inspire obedience, but hysteria prevailed. Like furies, the villagers hurled themselves at the cart and snatched the bridle from the driver's hands. A chorus of insults flew up into the sky as the air of revolt intensified. The people's mouths were locked in grimaces and their faces contorted. They were possessed by rage and ready to take the criminals' execution into their own hands. The knight and the soldiers protecting the prisoners brandished their weapons at the crowd, but again, their gestures went unheeded. Consumed with hatred, the rabble was a mass of invective and violence by the time the convicts arrived at the steps of the gallows.

Marie Raynal was the first to be led onto the scaffold. Her hair was drawn back under a white bonnet and a cord tied around her knees gathered in her full clothes. Her face bore no expression save for its usual tenseness. Her silhouette offered no more than a fleshless mask, emaciated by the weeks she had languished in a dank dungeon. The most ghastly forms of torture had extracted no confession from her. Nor had they brought her to ask for the forgiveness that Père Fournier besought her to seek. No, death would not rob her of her soul! Limpid was her look, her body diaphanous. Around her wrist she wore a blue cloth, the kind newborn babies are wrapped in. She climbed the six steps of the scaffold, refusing all help. Proud, with her chin held high, she displayed a courage that said death, for her, was a merciful deliverance. The serenity of her features earned the respect of the mob that had come to watch her die.

Their roars abated and the square fell silent. The hangman took hold of the rope, checked the noose, placed it around Marie Raynal's neck and pulled it tight. The pressure caused the young woman's veins to swell and her breast to heave rapidly. She scanned the crowd for the one person in the world that she loved. Marie Raynal sought to glimpse her only child: Malvina, her nine-year-old daughter.

The judge had insisted the sullied child be present so that she too could atone for the crime. 'Let her watch, and let her remember.' This day was designed to burn into the girl's memory just as the branding iron marks the flesh of the damned. Thus Malvina stood there, a grey silhouette, slight and fragile, her complexion pale with terror, her mouth clenched purple. She was immured in her silence, her senses deadened.

A shudder ran through the assembly. A rope tautened, legs tightened, jerked, then stiffened. The muffled sound of a suspended weight told the girl it was done. Her mother swung back and forth, her head hanging to one side. The cloth on her wrist had fallen to her feet. It bore the imprint of the fingers that had gripped it in fear. But already a second thud shook the platform as Gabert Raynal fell to his knees before the corpse of his wife. He let out an endless wail, struggled, sobbed and screamed out his repentance.

'A farthing for a stool to get a better look at the beast,' came the reply from a man in the crowd.

'Evil scum!' yelled another.

Abuse poured out from all quarters: 'Death to the Devil's henchman,' 'Death to the cannibal of Assier!' . . . The mass of evidence had shown it was his hand that carried out the crime, that robbed and killed, without a tremble, more than ten foolhardy travellers.

The hangman shoved the villain off the scaffold to join his hanging wife. The crowd applauded as he shook the dangling bodies to make sure the life had gone out of them. On the balcony of the provost's residence, the nobles and the clergy congratulated each other, agreeing that the event had indeed gone smoothly. The Lord of Bessonies stood up to declare in a loud voice:

'Justice has been done. The Devil is dead and so, too, is his wife.'

His words drew a loud cheer.

Their appetites sharpened by the day's emotions, the noble guests proceeded to the chateau of Balène where a feast, games and a ball had been arranged for them. The assassins' remains were to stay hanging in the wind and the storm until they disintegrated. Their rotting corpses were to serve as a warning to those tempted to abandon God and his laws to satisfy their natural instincts for crime and savagery.

*

While the curious crowded round the dangling bodies to look for signs of contrition on their lifeless faces, a peal of thunder rumbled, followed by a sudden hailstorm. Night engulfed the town, and the Grand Place emptied. The throng raced for the shelter of nearby trees, porches and alleys. Windows were slammed shut. Alone before the scaffold, Malvina stood motionless, her eyes dilated with horror. Rain and tears flowed down her cheeks in unremitting sobs and her throat was a knot so tight that only in painful gulps could she draw the tempestuous air into her lungs.

'Come, you can't stay out in this deluge.'

Père Fournier, the parish priest of Assier, had insisted on being the one to accompany the girl to her new home at the only lodging house in Figeac that would take her in.

'Come on! There is nothing more we can do for them.'

The girl didn't move.

'There is no sin so great that God in his bounty cannot

forgive. Listen to me. I tell you that the Lord will save them from eternal damnation.'

Malvina did not hear him. With her head down and with the rigid gait of an automaton, she approached the gallows to pick up hesitantly the muslin cloth that had fallen from her mother's body. She looped it round her neck and drew it tight. Blackish water streamed down her limbs as she tightened it still further. Her heart beat violently under the pressure of the garrotte, her lips turned blue and a mist formed around her eyes. A frenzied impulse took hold of her, urging her to free herself from the misery of the life that lay before her. She did not want to be what she knew she was and always would be: the tainted progeny of murderous parents.

The priest rushed to remove the bind. The child's clasped hands tensed still more before finally ceding to the man's superior strength. Malvina tottered, her mouth gaping open, then fell down in a spasm. Her chest heaved as she slumped to her knees and stared at the ground as though it were about to swallow her up. For a long time she groaned, holding her right hand over her stomach, her left clenched on her thigh. A sudden cold had descended on the town. Everything around her was whirling. The square vibrated beneath its cobblestones, and the grey wavering houses that lined it plunged deep into the earth, their roofs soaring towards the heavens. It was neither day nor night, this single moment suspended in nothingness.

'Taking your own life will bring no relief,' cried Père Fournier. 'Lucifer possessed your father – do not let him take *your* soul.'

Malvina abruptly raised her head to look the priest in the eye.

'It was only him that should have died. Not my mother. You knew that and you said nothing.'

Père Fournier recoiled from the dark eyes scowling at him. They were forlorn, but hardened with a ferocious hostility. Never in so young a person had he seen such a wicked glare. It was the Devil he now saw on this face suddenly dry of tears.

The priest frowned as he wiped his brow. He had always sought to dispel popular superstitions, and was outraged to see such beliefs still in existence after more than a millennium of Christianity. He would never dare deny the existence or even the power of Satan, but his reason would not permit him to read it on the face of a child.

'You must trust me,' he said. 'Your mother wanted it that way.'

'She told you that?'

'The poor woman confessed to me the day before she was arrested. She knew what was going to happen. She was thinking only of you.'

'You're lying!' screamed Malvina. 'You did nothing to defend her.'

How could he explain to her? How could he explain that it was jealousy that had made the gossips lie about her mother, made them say that Marie Raynal was a witch, a servant of the Devil, that she had turned the cows' milk and had made barren the women in two households? He had, of course, tried to reason with them, but the rumours still spread. Everywhere the story was told that travellers were disappearing at the inn at Assier. The young wife of the innkeeper had not been able to prove her innocence simply because she too was guilty. She was an accomplice because of her silence and because of her acts, because she prepared soups laced with sleep-inducing herbs to alleviate the suffering of the unfortunate ones chosen by the master of her house. How could he explain to Malvina that, in the logic of her madness, her mother used her husband's crimes to buy liberty for the both of them? She was much too young to understand.

Strengthened by this conviction, the priest took his ward by the arm and drew her quickly into the nearest alley, the Rue des Échevins. The people scurrying for shelter there had to negotiate both the torrent of mud that flowed along the open drain in the middle of the narrow lane and the water gushing from the gutters of the houses. Malvina realized she could take advantage of this scramble to make off. She knew that the habit the old man wore would give him no hope of catching her. But like a cowering animal that can hear the hounds approaching, she was incapable of action.

*

They passed through the tanners' quarter and took a path round the town battlements that ran along the Célé. The streets were deserted and silent, for by now the townsfolk had shuttered themselves in their homes to hide from the tempest. What little light the night afforded was soon swallowed up by the tall buildings. The house where Malvina was to be lodged overlooked the river on Rue de La Fosse-aux-Chiens, a lane as dark as could be, barely wide enough to let two people pass. An entrance opened on to a series of arcades leading to a back courtyard. As the man and the girl plunged into the dark, four figures emerged from the shadows to block their path. They bore steel-tipped bludgeons and had pistols tucked into their belts. One carried a long pitchfork.

'We've been waiting for you,' bellowed the tallest of them. 'Don't you know, priest, that we can't let vermin grow? Just like her mother, she is – possessed by the Devil. Can't you get the stench of sulphur off her?'

The clergyman gave no reply. The face of the man addressing him was not unknown to him. On its right cheek, a broad scar gleamed from the corner of the eye all the way down to the nostril. Only one person in the village bore such a mark. It was the brother of Gabert Raynal.

'It was her that gave them away,' he said, growing more excited. 'She's got to pay for that. We're going to hang her on this here hook. See it? She'll struggle and wriggle just like a chicken. And we'll make her scream. And then you'll hear it – she'll confess!'

'Stop!' cried Père Fournier, stretching out his hands to try to calm the men. 'She has done no wrong.'

He knew he had to speak, had to find words to make them listen to reason. They now formed a tight circle around the child.

'I beg you,' he repeated, 'spare her! The customs men

from Villefranche are after you already. And what they want you for is nothing compared to what you're about to do!'

'Enough of your preaching, Fournier. You're no better than her! Let's string the bitch up by the armpits. Right, lads.'

The blows began to rain down upon Malvina. She tried to struggle but could not free herself from the powerful arms that gripped her. Each man was keen to have his part in this act, and like hyenas they attacked her, lifting her up by the ankles and wrists. They tossed her to this side and that, and then dropped her. Her head thumped dully on the ground. The youngest of the four then pinned her to the earth with his knee. Grunting, wine-stinking breaths scorched her neck and ears as clumsy fingers tried to lift up her dress. Malvina screamed in rage. She clawed and bit the cheek of her adversary, tearing off a piece of flesh. Warm blood flowed onto her tongue. The youth cried out in pain as he clapped a hand to his face. Père Fournier tried to come between them, but, gripped by blind violence, the other three brigands threw themselves upon him. A cudgel caught him on the shoulder. The priest fumbled on the ground for a stone, but the cobbles would not come loose.

'Run!' he managed to shout, before collapsing under the gang's onslaught.

*

Malvina ran, falling several times in her haste. Her feet, cut by her clogs and frozen by the cold, pained her cruelly.

But she knew she had to flee, to run and run, to keep on running. She needed to find the shadows, the nooks and crannies, the places where only a child could hide. Only when the town lost her in the labyrinth of its lanes and its badly lit quays did she slow down to look around her. Under the arches of a church door a group of beggars was sleeping; they were piled on top of each other as if engraved on the stone. A statue of Saint Agnes, the child martyr, with her palm leaf and her lamb, seemed to watch over them. Malvina approached slowly. She knew she would not sleep, but she would be better off here than wandering aimlessly through the night.

Reassured as much by the celestial protection as by the warmth of her fellow creatures, she slipped in among the bodies. But, displeased at being shaken from their sleep, her companions in misfortune insulted her and threatened to knock her senseless. Malvina clenched her teeth to stop herself from crying and got up to resume her flight. Her despair grew with each passing second. Did people reject her because she was bad? She wanted to ask pardon of someone, anyone, so that somebody would love her. She was so alone, so bewildered. She wanted with all her heart to be with her mother. 'Mama—' She choked back the cry. She looked around to get her bearings and saw, on the other side of the square, a light gleaming in the darkness.

It came from a building whose outline could scarcely be made out. The grey façade, pockmarked with lichen, was hemmed to the ground with ivy. Only the sign – The Gouty Rat, written in big red letters – gave a hint of colour. The top half of the sign depicted a plump creature hung upside down with its hind legs tied to a spit. It also showed four quails and two pigeons, all ready to undergo a mysterious culinary torture. Malvina's heart beat faster. From the outside, the inn resembled the one she had grown up in.

She was about to go up to one of the windows when a long spidery silhouette thrust itself towards her. A man, bent under shapeless rags, grabbed her, brandishing a wicker hoop from which hung ten dead bats.

'You want one? One sou each, just one sou!' he cried with his pink tongue between his stained teeth.

Malvina recognized him as one of the tramps from the cathedral. She elbowed him away but he continued to come towards her, still holding his string of bats with their pierced necks, their throats crimson with blood.

'The wings of the denizens of hell! But don't be afraid of these poor fallen birds,' he said, caressing the hairy membrane of one of his catch.

He gestured recklessly, his rags flailing in a wild dance. Terrified, the child hammered on the inn door until it eventually creaked open to let out a customer. Malvina, in her terror, clutched at the departing man's legs and clung to his clothes.

'The man with the birds,' she blurted out.

'What?'

'Dead birds. Lots of dead birds . . .'

'But there's nothing there!'

'He was there, right there . . .'

The man unhooked a lantern, picked up a nail-studded cudgel that lay on the doorstep and went out to have a look around. Malvina gave a start when she saw his shadow loom inordinately large on a wall on the far side of the street.

'Over there, that's where I saw him!' she screamed.

'I've looked everywhere. There's nobody there.'

Then he held the lantern up to the girl's face and asked, 'What are you doing here all alone?'

She shoved her chin further down into the blue cloth tied around her neck.

'Where are your parents? What's your name? You're not from Figeac, are you?'

His questions received no response and he made as if to leave her. But at that instant, Malvina collapsed, exhausted, in a heap on the cobblestones. The innkeeper, who had come to stand on the doorstep of his establishment, took the lantern from his customer and invited him back into the inn.

'You can take your walk later,' he said. 'She'll catch her death if she falls asleep there!'

Malvina put up no resistance when they picked her up off the ground. The landlord closed the door while his companion carried his burden across the room to the hearth. He was like a giant whose long strides made his torso appear to lean forwards and sway jerkily as he moved. The light in the room revealed a high forehead, narrow to the point of almost spoiling the effect of his imposing corpulence. He could not have been more than thirty years of age, but a hideous ugliness made him seem much older. His bony face was divided into two ovals that stretched up towards his temples. The right eye was brown, the left scarred by an opaque spot ringed with green. His cheek-bones jutted out, which had the effect of raising up and hollowing his cheeks. A short forehead, supported by the pillar of his strong nose, suggested a headstrong man who did not like to be crossed.

There were no customers left in the inn at this time of night and the fire was almost dead. Just a few pinkish filaments still glowed amidst a pile of grey ashes. The man grabbed some wood shavings and spread them over the embers, bending his shaved head to blow vigorously on the grate. One of the slender ribbons of wood reddened and a flame appeared. The little girl moved closer to the heat and felt her numbed legs sting as the blood began to flow through them again. She shivered as she opened distraught eyes to bring her petrified gaze towards the ground, and clasped her right hand against her chest.

Her benefactor sat opposite her on a stool and watched her come back to life. A strange charm emanated from the child. Her dress, made of a good-quality material with a saffron sheen, was ripped in several places. Those tears could not have been due to the ravages of the weather. They were clearly the signs of a fierce struggle. The flesh on her upper body was covered with bruises, and blood-stains marked the scarf she wore around her neck. The hawker wondered how a child who appeared so fragile could have survived such an ordeal. A closer inspection provided the answer. The girl's eyes were a sombre grey colour speckled with black. They were the colour of the storm, the colour that peasants believe to be a sign of special powers. And in these eyes could be seen a supernatural strength. This strength came not from the girl's character but from an impossible harmony between two opposing wills. He could not tell if they sought to strike you down or gain your sympathy. At that precise instant, the play of the flames in the hearth gave them the cold brilliance of a knife blade. Or perhaps it was the brilliance of her tears, tears that were empty of emotion, pearls of glass which neither flowed nor gushed, like those of a porcelain doll. Her face was marvellously delicate. Her fine, straight nose created a perfect balance between slightly slanting eyelids that lengthened out into the form of butterfly wings. Her candid mouth appeared ready to bite or to beseech. Her dishevelled copper-coloured, honey-tinged hair rolled down over her shoulders to the small of her back.

'Where are you from?' the hawker asked. 'What's your name? I'm Rougemont.'

Malvina became even more alarmed when he spoke, and kept turning her head as if there were someone spying on her from behind.

'Why are you frightened? Don't you want to tell me? Maybe you're hungry. Tavernier, give her something to eat. Give her some soup with a bit of bacon in it.'

'And who's going to pay for that?'

'Don't you worry. You know me.'

'Yes, I do. So that'll be three sous, in advance.'

From Beaulieu to Montauban, the hawker's reputation preceded him. He kept up a dubious trade in regional wines with the north of the country as well as selling some to be shipped out to the West Indies. But this was never enough for him. He was always boasting of some new business venture or other that was sure to bring him enormous profits. His unshakeable belief in his own power made him impervious to morality, and he liked to make use of the lowest tricks to swindle those who had the misfortune to cross his path. Rougemont would use his smooth tongue and feigned affability to quickly assess an individual's gullibility before exploiting it ruthlessly. His wealth resulted directly from his complete lack of scruples, and this fact made him despise those who praised honesty.

'Eh! Isn't it our Christian duty to help our neighbours?' he asked as he poured himself a glass of Cahors wine.

'So you're playing at being a priest now, are you?'

'God renders a hundredfold the alms given to the poor. My dear and sweet sister Hubertine told me so.'

'You're one to talk about charity!'

'You doubt my generosity?'

'Don't patronize me. How much will you get for handing her over to the police?'

Rougemont feigned surprise.

'The latest royal declaration promised a reward to anyone helping in the arrest of vagrants. And you know as well as I do that the place where they lock up tramps is a lot nearer to here than the Griffoul poorhouse.'

'Who says she's a vagrant? Why don't you just give her a bowl of soup, instead of letting your imagination get the better of you?'

The innkeeper grumbled, but obeyed.

*

Malvina, shaking so much that she almost missed her mouth, lifted the broth to her lips and gulped it down. She choked in her haste. Rougemont again noticed that she only used her left hand, and that her right remained pressed against her body. He thought that perhaps she was injured.

'Are you hurt?' he enquired. 'Don't be afraid. Let me have a look, my love.'

He went to take hold of her, but the child struggled against him. As she resisted, her elbow came away from her chest, and a book she had been hiding next to her skin slipped through a rip in her dress. She tried to snatch it back but was too slow and stood with her fists clenched in anger as she watched the man take it in his hands.

'*Le Secret des secrets de la nature*, par Jean-Baptiste Dandora de Ghalia,' read Rougemont. 'Never heard of it.'

Unlike the chapbooks he was used to reading, which were sloppily printed on poor-quality paper, this one had some thirty well-bound pages bearing a strange script that the profane Rougemont took for the formula of an alchemist. Astonished to find such a thing in the hands of a little girl, he hurriedly skimmed through it.

'God knows what it is! It could be a book of medicine, a cookery book or an astrology almanac. It's impossible to decipher!'

But a smile appeared on his lips as he scanned the last pages of the volume, where a child's hand had drawn plants and insects. The enthusiasm of the illustrations gave them a seductive appeal. Proportions were not respected in these feverish drawings, as if the paper were not big enough to meet the demands of the artist. What sort of imagination could have produced such works? Nature was here misused, relations inverted, logic contradicted. On one plate, a praying mantis with a disproportionately large body was rummaging through what appeared to be the remains of a human skeleton. Rougemont shivered and grew pale when he read the dedication: 'He who masters the secrets of nature masters the hearts of men and rules the world. From Marie Raynal to Malvina, her beloved daughter.'

'Marie Raynal? The witch of Assier!' he roared.

The discovery brought him a joy so unwholesome that he could not hide his excitement.

'Who gave you this? Where did you find it?'

Then, in a more reserved tone, almost in confidence, he went on, 'In the name of all the saints! Do you know what a risk you're taking, walking around with a book of magic on you? Nobody knows what these formulae could do. They might be powerful! Once you start believing in them, you're lost. Marie Raynal read this book and look what happened to her – she was hanged this very day. But then Raynal was the daughter of a whore. They should have burnt her alive and scattered her ashes in the four corners of the town . . .'

At this the girl cried out in a wild rage, 'My mother did nothing! Nothing!'

And in a strangled voice she began to blurt out incoherent sentences about a town square, two bodies, a clergyman and a young boy who had attacked her.

Rougemont stared at her, flabbergasted.

'What are you saying? Your mother?'

'They didn't steal anything from anybody. But me, I've had everything stolen. Give me my book back!'

She became suddenly animated in her indignation. A flow of blood swelled her slender neck and she rose up onto the tips of her toes and twisted her tongue into a viper's hiss.

'You're a nasty piece of work!' said Rougemont. 'I only wanted to look.'

As he closed the book to return it to the child, she snatched it from him and ran towards the staircase. She sat down on the first step and put the book back under her dress, next to her skin. With her face between her knees and her chin jutting out, she looked like a gargoyle atop an ancient cathedral.

'She's a creature of the Devil,' interjected the inn-keeper, who had been watching the scene from the other side of the room.

'A little witch,' agreed Rougemont.

Troubled by this strange encounter, he sat down again at the table. He poured himself another glass of wine and drank it down in one gulp. He could, of course, sell the book at a good price. It would also be easy to get a reward for handing the girl over to the police. But he began to think of an old tale he had often heard recounted in the taverns of an evening.

The story told of how Jacques Joli Coeur's ingenuity had enabled him to purloin a fabulous diamond that could transform lead into gold. The precious stone belonged to a serpent-woman who lived near a pond. Jacques spent all the money he had in the world – which was no more than two crowns – on materials to build a barrel. He left the nails of the barrel sticking outwards and rolled it along the bank of the pond where the serpent-woman had made her home. He then placed it at the centre of a forty-foot-long white sheet to entice her to come and sleep on top of it. As soon as the monster had dozed off, the young man seized the diamond from her and rushed to hide inside the barrel. The trap was set. Scenting the flesh of a good Christian, the serpent-woman quickly coiled herself around the cask and just as quickly died from the wounds caused by the sharp nails on which she had impaled herself. And thus was born the legend of Jacques Joli Coeur, a simple artisan who became the richest man in the kingdom, richer even than the king.

The voice of the innkeeper shook Rougemont from his thoughts.

'This child came out of the night, and only bad things come out of the night. Take her to the poorhouse tomorrow. Her parents can go and fetch her from there!'

'I don't think so,' replied the merchant.

'Did you get any clues about her from the book?'

'No, nothing. It was just some sort of almanac.'

Rougemont's mind had turned to money. The more he thought about it, the more he realized how much he could profit from this child. The fortune the Raynal couple had amassed had never been found. It was doubtless buried somewhere in their house or garden. The girl must have seen something. She would inadvertently yield up to him some memory, some detail that would lead him to the hidden riches. He had to think of some way of gaining her confidence, of making this half-wild child believe that he was only trying to help her. The merchant smiled to himself, but then, worried that his smile might reveal his ignoble intentions, changed the direction of the conversation.

'This wine is marvellous!' he said. 'Our lovely Cadurcie region produces the best in the world. Much better than that Gaillac and Madiran stuff that only imbeciles prefer.'

Rougemont duly polished off the bottle, and then took from his pocket a bulging leather purse. He undid it nonchalantly and with two fingers drew out a newly minted louis.

He threw it onto the table in front of the innkeeper, who quickly snatched it up for fear that this might be some malicious trick and the coin would be taken from him again.

'I'll give you the room in the attic,' he said.

'Good. I'll be leaving tomorrow, at dawn. The girl will sleep with me.'

'Then that'll be five sous more. Payable now.'

'Here, there's two sous. She can sleep on a straw mattress.'

Rougemont looked around for Malvina. The child, still sitting on the step, was biting her cheeks to stop herself falling asleep.

He stood in front of her.

'Come on. You can't stay here!'

The little girl drew back mistrustfully but the weight of her drowsiness was too much for her. She obediently followed the two men towards the loft. The nauseating stench and humidity which impregnated the air on the stairs left no doubt as to the insalubrity of the hovel. The narrow wooden staircase was rotting and trembled under every step they took to reach the top landing. The breathless landlord handed his customer the candle stub he had been carrying, opened a door for him and withdrew without further comment. The room appeared to be quite clean, but it was no more than three feet in height because of the slope of the roof. Rougemont pushed Malvina forward and pointed to the place where she was to sleep. The child did not move and appeared ready to attack him if he tried again to touch her. So he let her be and, without bothering to undress, stretched himself out on the bed.

Malvina waited until she heard his snores before believing he was asleep. She then moved towards a corner of the room where, like a dog crouching in its kennel, she curled up underneath a low table. She raised the cloth she wore around her neck to her mouth and began pressing lightly on it with her lips. This she did to calm the anguish she felt every evening as she drifted into sleep. It was always the same nightmare – a group of travellers sat around a table, but these travellers had no contours and no consistency. Their animated gestures, their darting elbows and the tray piled high with delicacies showed that they were feasting. Malvina's father sat enthroned in the middle of his guests. Her mother stood a little back from them. Her face seemed blurred, perhaps because of the odorous vapour that rose up from the soup she was serving. The diners, gentlemen whose clothes were trimmed with braid and whose scarves were made of silk, came from distant parts of the country. The late hour and the wine and the intoxicating flavours of the food had had their effect, and tongues were loosened. The travellers' voices had become loud and strong. One man excitedly told his companions how he had made his fortune, while another was exhilarated by the prospect of starting a new life in the locality. Malvina spent hours spying through a crack in the floorboards on this spectacle to which she was not invited. She would have liked to have joined the revellers. But suddenly, a macabre scene paralysed her. She saw her father frenziedly bashing a body with a mallet.

The profound fear this vision inspired in her shook Malvina out of her sleep. Panting, she listened for the muffled beating of her heart and waited for the image to fade and for her breathing to become calm and regular again. Her own breath came in short gasps, but that of Rougemont stretched into long, noisy rumblings. She wiped her cheeks. They were still wet with kisses, the abominable kisses of her father.

Chapter Two

All Malvina could later remember about the journey to Cahors was the jerks and jolts she was subjected to as she sat huddled in the back of the cart, shaken like a sack of walnuts by the rutted, frozen roads. But neither Rougemont nor the rigour of the trip could bring her out of the silence in which she had immured herself. In Quercy, the first region through which they travelled, there were still numerous Roman roads in use, but the lack of maintenance meant that there were many stretches where the ancient, regular flagstones gave way to what was little better than a dirt track. The roads in Cadurcie were just as hellish as those in Périgord, and the route through the Célé valley was even worse. The river wended its way along to Boussac, its wide, heavily cultivated banks lined with poplar hedges and studded with saffron plantations. A dense and humid fog subdued all but the brightest colours of this winter morning. Through the mist, the nearby chateau of Saint-Dau could be glimpsed, with its narrow mullioned windows. A little further away, perched on the hillside, was the pretty village of Béduer. And then came Espagnac-Saint-Eulalie. Its nunnery could be seen from a distance of several leagues because of its peculiar steeple, which was crowned by a square, half-timbered structure that was itself topped by a pyramid-shaped roof.

But Malvina saw none of these things. Only much later, when the approaching cliffs made the road narrower, did she finally come out of her torpor. The limestone plateau she now looked upon was similar to that of Gramat, where she had lived with her parents, where the worn-out land was like a scrawny skeleton wrapped in a scabious and leathery skin. The region was too barren to support meadows or orchards. Here, as in Gramat, the maddening wind screamed violently over the plateau. Here the first heat of spring wrenched rocks from the plateau and the intense cold of winter splintered stones from the cliffs. What lay before Malvina was an immense chaos, a vision of the world in its first ages.

She saw herself wandering happily through this sepulchral landscape. Nature was her accomplice. One day she would take refuge up here, she would live alone in an abandoned shepherd's hut. For there was no one left in this world that she wanted to be with. Vengeance was the only sentiment she now knew. And to wreak her vengeance she must not be disturbed, must be under no obligations to anyone. She was like a tick that would wait a year for its prey to come within range.

'Are we near Cahors yet?' she asked.

'Ah, found your tongue again?'

'Are we nearly there?' she said.

'What a lazybones you are! Sit up a little and you'll be able to see its roofs and vineyards.'

Clasped by a loop of the River Lot, the town appeared

before them. They entered by the Tour Saint-Jean, also known as the Tower of the Hanged. But they had no sooner paid the toll than Malvina began to feel ill at ease. The ramparts seemed to be bigger than the town itself. Everything here appeared poised to attack her, particularly the severe, fortress-like cathedral of Saint-Étienne. A law student might well have boasted to her about the beauty of this massive edifice, the symbol of power for bishops, seigneurs and counts of the region. But the university had been closed since 1751, and there were no longer any law students here. The only person who approached their cart was a tramp seeking alms, whom Rougemont pushed aside with a curse. It was true that there had been four poor harvests in a row, but the government had at great expense brought in foreign wheat and distributed it to the needy.

'Nothing but good-for-nothings here,' he said as they arrived at Dames de la Charité hospice.

The porch was this morning besieged by a group of beggars, just as it was every morning. The number the Sisters could accept each day depended on how many beds had been freed by people dying during the night. Those they turned away got a bowl of hot soup or a slice of bread and would return the following day at dawn to be first in the queue. The travellers made their way through the wretched throng to reach the postern, where the merchant pulled on the bell.

'We've no room left. Come back tomorrow,' said a sister as she peered through a gap in the door.

'Don't you recognize me, Sister Clotilde? It's Rouge-mont, Hubertine's brother.'

'God forgive me, but my old eyes are failing me,' said the nun as she moved aside to let them in. 'I'm sorry, but I have to be vigilant,' she explained. 'We just can't take in every orphan who turns up on our doorstep. The winter has been hard on the poor. The ones that have come here for treatment have to sleep three or four to a straw mattress. And that's not to mention the newborn babies! We don't have enough wet nurses to feed them.'

'The Lord gives us children, and the Lord takes them away again,' replied Rougemont. 'It's his way.'

'Are we so wicked that we deserve the punishment the Lord God above sends down to us?' she asked as she invited them to follow her. 'The poor little things are just dumped at church doors or left by the side of the road. Do you know that three out of four infants die before they are a year old?'

'But they would also certainly die if they were not helped by kind souls like yourself,' replied Rougemont.

'You yourself were only eleven months old when we took you in after your poor parents died. Well do I remember the day Hubertine arrived here holding you ever so tightly in her little arms.'

Sister Clotilde became silent as she dwelled nostalgically on the scene. How time could gobble up the years with the insatiable hunger of the starving! Thirty long years separated the face of the child she saw in her memory from that of the man who now stood before her. She knew she would not live to see the fresh young face of the girl Rougemont had at his side reach maturity. More and more people in the hospice were falling ill. Those who were not

yet contaminated feared they would be the next to succumb. None of the nuns had yet been afflicted, but it must
surely be only a matter of time.

Sister Clotilde told Rougemont that the Mother
Superior was the only one who could officially register the
girl as a ward of the hospice.

'I found her in a street in Figeac,' the hawker explained.

'Figeac? That's a fair distance from here. I hope we'll
be able to take her. Just yesterday I was told of some new
cases of cholera. That's how the Black Death starts. I've
seen it before.'

Malvina shrank back from the nun and stared at her as
if she had the plague. The woman's sunken eyes were like
the empty sockets of a skeleton. Her youth was far behind
her now. Her skin was grey and the lips of her thin mouth
were dry and blanched. A serenity lay behind Sister
Clotilde's austere appearance, but the girl was much too
young to be able to recognize it. The nun carried on
talking to the newcomers as she walked, but exhaustion
and illness made her step unsteady. Her slow, troubled
breathing also revealed her debility.

'I get weaker with every passing day,' she admitted.
'But I'm not afraid. I've come through many an illness in
my time. Now I have only one wish – that God grants me
a few more years to look after all these poor people we
have here.'

'You're not well, Sister Clotilde?' enquired Rougemont.
'But you do know that Hubertine has many herbs in her
garden whose powers would be a lot more effective than
your prayers. You may well think it's some sort of witch-

craft, but your stubbornness will only bring your end closer. You'll die, with the help of God, when you could have been cured.'

'Be quiet, or you'll bring down the Lord's anger on our heads.'

*

Malvina had stopped listening to their chatter, for she was busy observing the buildings through which the nun was leading them. She had never seen anything like them. The convent began its life in the fifteenth century, but was rebuilt two centuries later by Bishop Alain de Solminihac. Wherever the eye wandered it was confronted with the grossly exaggerated proportions of monumental architecture. In the centre, a Gothic chapel soared majestically above the houses of the town. The four two-storey buildings that surrounded it had roofs of pink slate quarried in the valley of the Lot. From the courtyard one could glimpse through large, arched windows the wimples of the nuns who beavered in the convent's many workrooms and wards. To Malvina, it all looked little different from the gaol where she had been kept during her parents' trial. Tall, imprisoning walls hid the horizon from the girl, and a maddening brouhaha of shouts and groans filled the air. To her, there was no difference between the tramps locked up in her former prison and the poor who queued here for a bowl of soup.

'I'll leave you here, Rougemont,' said Sister Clotilde as she took Malvina by the hand. 'Hubertine will be pleased to see you.'

'As for you, my girl, you shall come with me,' she said. 'At this time of the day we can be sure to find Mother Superior doing the accounts.'

They climbed up an exceptionally wide staircase in a building on their left and then along a corridor that led to the head nun's office.

'Go on in,' whispered Sister Clotilde as she pushed the girl forward. 'And stand up straight.'

Malvina stumbled inside. She had seen the austerity of the exterior buildings and thought the entire hospice was constructed with the same rigour, the same delusions of grandeur. But here an atmosphere of serenity reigned. The silence and the light softly filtering through stained-glass windows heightened the feeling of well-being the room induced. Bookshelves lined the walls and books were piled on tables and scattered across the floor. Perhaps there was a reason for this shambles, this exception to the rule of religious order, but the visitor could not see it.

The books were such a prominent feature of the room that Malvina did not at first notice the Mother Superior. She eventually spotted her, sitting behind a mound of papers and holding a goose quill that darted between the scrolls and ledgers on her desk.

'Please forgive me for bothering you, Mother Superior,' ventured Clotilde.

'If you've risked disturbing me, then it must be for a good reason,' came the reply. 'At least, I hope so.'

'I've come to see you because the brother of our cook arrived here this morning and he had with him an orphan he found in Figeac.'

'Figeac? The Benedictines in the Daurade convent would have been just as close for him. And what about Notre-Dame-des-Incurables? Is there no room there? Do you not think we have enough unfortunates in our own parish?'

She addressed the child as she stood up.

'Come here so I can get a look at you. Are you ill?'

Malvina said she was not ill.

'Good. But we'll still have our doctor examine you, just in case.'

Then she turned again to Sister Clotilde.

'You didn't find anything on her? No name-tag, no letter? Nothing to tell us who she might be?'

'Rougemont didn't give me anything, Mother Superior.'

'Stop talking to me about that blackguard. I'd like to know just what he's up to. It's not in his nature to do good deeds, is it? I think we can safely say that there's something he's not telling us.'

She took up her goose quill and went back to her work. Then, without raising her head from the papers that lay in front of her, she asked Malvina her name.

'Your name?' she repeated more firmly. 'If you can't tell us your name, we'll have to give you a new one. It's January, so let's see. You can choose between Saint Agnes and Saint Martine.'

The Mother Superior stared at Malvina with her metallic-blue eyes, eyes that were barely softened by the little wrinkles that ringed her eyelids. The starched grey hair pulled back over her forehead and the dour mouth suggested a woman little given to pleasantries.

'Malvina,' muttered the child.

'I can't hear you.'

'Malvina.'

'She said Malvina, Mother Superior.'

'Malvina is not a name,' said the head nun after a pause. 'Indeed, the peasants in this region have strange ways about them. But I suspect you were given a proper name and you don't remember it any more. Do you even know your surname?'

The girl hesitated, then remembered the priest who had died trying to save her.

'Fournier,' she said.

The Mother Superior wrote the name down with a flourish.

'Fournier. Good. Where were you born?'

'I live in Assier.'

'So you're not from Figeac like Rougemont told us! But then he never was one to be frightened of a lie. He was certainly a handful during his time here at the hospice,' she added wearily.

'We'll send you to our school, even if you are too young,' she went on. 'Some of us teach the poor. It's our duty to educate youth, for youth in its natural state is ignorant and disobedient. But I'll have you know that we have no room here for mediocrity or rebellion.'

She drew a long line under the information she had noted down to signal that the interrogation was at an end.

'Sister Clotilde will take you to the doctor for your examination, then you'll go to the kitchen for a bowl of hot soup. As it was Rougemont who brought you here, it'll be his sister who can look after you. She could do with a hand. Come on, come on! Don't stand there gaping!'

Sister Clotilde and Malvina withdrew. They went along a corridor which led to the main ward where the sick were housed. Here uninterrupted rows of straw mattresses on thin wooden frames lined the room. Two, three and sometimes four women were stretched out head to foot on each mattress. The bedclothes that covered them were stiff with dirt. They were ageless creatures with bloated, chapped and pockmarked faces. Malvina was horrified.

'Watch where you're walking,' shouted a nun who was struggling to clean the floor with a bucket and broom.

'Don't stand there!' scolded another who was dispensing medicine.

The nuns' task was not made any easier by the children who ran amok, barefoot and barely dressed despite the cold.

Sister Clotilde stopped when she reached the far end of the room, where she found the doctor operating on a girl. Malvina thought at first that he was doing some carpentry. A brace and bit, a hacksaw and a large rasp were laid out before him, alongside other fearsome instruments she did not recognize.

'I've brought you a new resident. Could you please check that she's not "spoiled"?'

'I'll finish here and then I'll see to it.'

This was the third person in the hospice to whom Malvina had been introduced. Aubin Donatius was of a particularly unstriking physique. He was around fifty years old, small, thin, with a bony face and a hooked nose from which hung a drop that gleamed like a pendant on a chandelier. From where she stood, there was nothing Malvina could see that distinguished him from a journeyman or an artisan. When he turned around she saw that his apron was smeared with blackish stains and that his hands were a crimson colour. These hands were not working with wood. They held a needle and thread which they used to stitch together blood-smeared flesh.

Aubin Donatius knew well – knew far better than the boors who boasted of their medical qualifications – how to sew up wounds or lance boils and abscesses. But it was not from books but from practical experience that he had acquired his surgical skills. He had first begun to wield the scalpel on board the ships of the great explorers. Malvina would later learn that the nuns regarded him as an eccentric character with a great natural gift for medicine. From Asia and other far-off lands he had brought back new treatments. He had a passionate desire to understand the causes of pain, and he did not hesitate to use very personal methods to overcome it.

Thus was he able to sew up the leg of the girl he had just operated on without so much as a scream or groan from her, because he had given her a special brown paste to chew on.

'That's it,' he said as he wrapped the limb in a canvas dressing. 'Don't get up. I'll be back to see you in a moment.'

He then turned to Malvina and said, 'Let's find a place where I can examine you.'

The girl was petrified by what she had just seen and

was about to flee when the doctor stopped her short, saying, 'If you have gangrene, it will eat away at your limbs. You see your little friend here? She waited too long.'

Malvina realized there was no point in resisting. She did not have the strength to try and escape from the hospice. She would wait until she was calm again and had time to put together a plan.

She got undressed alone and hid her precious book under the mound of clothes she left on the floor. Her body was covered in scratches. In some places the skin was swollen and yellowish, serous fluid seeped from it.

'The main thing to look out for is St Anthony's fire. Move your fingers,' he said softly.

Malvina obeyed.

'Good. There's no palsy.'

'So she can't infect anyone, can she?' asked Sister Clotilde.

'No, but we need to treat her all the same. Hubertine has some plants that should do the necessary. And you could ask her to give the girl double quantities of soup – she's got nothing in her stomach.'

'No need to worry about that. The cook is the one who's going to look after her.'

'Well, you couldn't do better than that,' Aubin Donatius told Malvina. 'As for the scars on your body, you'll just have to be patient. They appear as quick as a flash but can take an eternity to go away again.'

*

A slightly acrid smell of smoke told Malvina she had arrived in the kitchen. A pile of embers glowed in an immense oven, in front of which bustled a portly woman. Hubertine, dripping with sweat, sleeves rolled up to her elbows, was preparing a batch of bread. The heat made the logs in the fire sputter and transformed the dry wood into effervescent displays of carmine red and golden yellow. In a corner of the room Rougemont sat and watched.

'Come on in and sit down,' said the cook as she pushed aside some wicker baskets to make room for the girl.

Hubertine went to the fireplace, lifted the lid off one of the pots that bubbled there, had a taste and shook her head. She added some salt and had another taste. The soup she then served Malvina was in no way comparable to the watery gruel the girl had been given at the inn. It was thick and in its depths lurked ample portions of corn and chunks of bacon as big as your thumb. Its lardy aroma made her stomach rumble as she drank it down greedily.

'Aha! You're just like the sailors who arrive back on land after months of eating dry biscuits,' said Hubertine as she watched the colour return to the girl's thin cheeks. 'Go on, have another helping.'

Malvina looked at the oven which lay open like a large, lolling mouth. She imagined her own tongue was the long paddle on which the cook had just placed a knob of decorated pastry as though she were making an offering. Bread and flesh, milk and mother – all the signs there for Malvina to read told her to accept Hubertine.

Everyone in the region knew of Hubertine and her singular ability to take the most contemptible ingredients and make of them the most delicious of dishes. Her whole life had led her to this culinary alchemy. Nature had bestowed upon her a body ample enough to incorporate her great weakness for good food. When she was still very young, she acquired the plumpness that is the sign of a happy child. She blossomed into a ripe, round fruit and her body quickly took on its magnificent proportions. The death of her parents did nothing to diminish her vigour. She came to live at the hospice where she soon grew fond of Mamoune the cook. The old woman, in turn, began to regard the girl as her own daughter and taught her all the recipes and culinary secrets she knew. The old cook's talent lay in being able to make a remedy of any food that was available to her. With the precision of an apothecary, she would weigh and blend her ingredients and then mix them with herbs she had distilled to produce soups that helped restore the health of the ill or eased the agonies of the dying. Mamoune did not seek to replace medicine, but to complement it. And when she died, two years before Malvina appeared at the hospice door, Hubertine realized she had no other ambition in life but to carry on her mentor's work. For her there was nothing more Christian than the act of giving food, and her only weakness was that she wanted the good she did also to taste good.

'I'll give you a nice little bread roll as soon as this batch is baked,' said Hubertine. 'Would you like that?'

There was no response.

'Don't be afraid. No one's going to send you away from here.'

Malvina looked down at the ground.

'You're not much of a one for talking, are you?'

The chair on which Rougemont was sitting creaked as he tilted it back to look inquisitively at the child.

'She never speaks when she's forced to,' he said.

'My name is Malvina.'

'You see, Rougemont? She speaks to me!'

'My name is Malvina Fournier.'

'Fournier?' said a surprised Rougemont.

'That's right. That's the name we've entered in our register,' confirmed Sister Clotilde, who had just rejoined them.

The hawker got up and began to pace back and forth. He stared at the girl with distrust. She had not said her name with the usual insouciance of a child of her age. No, she had said the word 'Fournier' with the clear intention of repudiating her past. Troubled by her precocity, he wondered what to do. Was he making a mistake? What if this assassins' daughter had inherited the perfidy of the Devil? Would she not be the source of great troubles for him, troubles he could well do without? He knew that if he were to reveal her true origins, she would immediately be expelled from the hospice. Rougemont considered the matter as he lumbered around the kitchen. But he eventually decided to keep silent, and to keep to himself his secret hope of finding the place where the innkeepers had hidden the money they had stolen from their guests.

'So Mother Superior is letting her stay?' he asked.

'She thought the child might be able to help out here in the kitchen,' replied the nun.

'Perfect,' he said. 'That's put my mind at rest. Hubertine, I'll leave my little protégée in your safe hands. Take good care of her! As for me, I must leave today. I have to see some merchants in Cantal who are interested in my Crespiat and Souleilla wines.'

'But you've only just arrived,' said the cook as she dried her hands on her cotton smock.

'I really must leave. This detour to Cahors has already made me late.'

'Very well, then. But wait a moment and I'll get you some provisions for your journey.'

'You're too good to me.'

Then he turned to Sister Clotilde to say, 'Keep a close watch on Malvina. She's a right little hussy. You'll see that soon enough.'

'Don't you worry,' said the nun. 'My eyes may be weak but I shall be uncompromising in punishing any bad behaviour from her!'

Rougemont felt he could trust Sister Clotilde to keep the girl's rebellious spirit in check.

Hubertine came back with the provisions. Into a brown hemp bag she placed some rye bread, a rind of bacon and some apples.

'Here you are,' she said. 'That's for the road. How long will your business keep you?'

'I've heard that the engraver in Montauban has just made a job lot of artificial pearls. Aristocrats are wild about such cheap rubbish, so I was thinking I might buy a few trunkfuls of the stuff. Buying and selling wine doesn't bring in that much, you know.'

'It's food, not jewellery, that we need here,' said the

cook as she kissed her brother goodbye. 'Take care of yourself and come back to see us soon.'

'I'll be back next winter.'

Before leaving the room, Rougemont knelt down beside Malvina. They said nothing as they looked each other in the eye, but their silence was eloquent. The child felt the man's breath on her cheeks. She knew intuitively that he posed a threat to her.

Chapter Three

As soon as Rougemont had left, Malvina began to impose her will on her new companions. When night came, she refused to sleep in the children's dormitory and instead settled down on the hard floor of the kitchen. She curled up under the table like a hunted animal, puckered her mouth into an aggressive pout and stared out at the room. Even Hubertine could not make her see reason. The following day, Malvina hid in the wine cellar and resisted Sister Clotilde's attempts to dislodge her. Anyone who tried to enter her lair was repulsed with a cry of 'Go away!' resonating from the depths of the girl's distress. Hubertine then tried being firm, but that also met with failure. Threats appeared to have no effect on this wild child.

'She's just like a viper. She slips through my fingers and bites if I go near her. I don't know what to do with her,' the cook confided to the Mother Superior. 'She hasn't eaten a thing in the last three days. Just keeps on saying that she wants to leave. But where would the poor thing go? Where on earth would she go?'

'Do you want me to deal with this?'

But Hubertine did not like to admit defeat and asked for some more time. She had to find the words and gestures that would make the girl happy. She remembered an old adage about vinegar not being the best lure with which to catch flies, and suddenly realized she had found the solution to her problem. Malvina would probably have a sweet tooth, just like any child her age, and this was what Hubertine would use to mollify the girl.

She went to the attic where Malvina was now ensconced and found her sitting sulking cross-legged in the middle of the room.

'Can you just have a little taste of this for me?' Hubertine said.

'I'm not hungry!'

'It's lettuce preserve. You really should try it. The sugar in it eliminates the sourness.'

'I want to go home.'

'Go on, try some. I bet you've never had it before!'

Malvina hesitated, then snatched the pot from Hubertine's hands. Her suspicion made her sniff it, but her curiosity made her plunge her index finger deep into the concoction and then into her mouth. In a flash her face lit up and her smooth cheeks were filled with the tender happiness that good food can bring to one who knows how to appreciate it.

'So you can smile,' said Hubertine.

'I did not smile!'

'Not with your lips, but with your eyes. A fine big smile. I knew you weren't bad. I even think you might be quite a clever girl.'

The cook had noticed that while Malvina had refused all the soups that had been brought to her, she had nevertheless not stopped feeding herself. The room where she had taken refuge was used to hang plants out to dry, and the girl had been able to find enough to eat there. Bouquets of flowers had been torn from their hooks on the ceiling, and the floor was strewn with dried leaves, berries and crushed seeds.

'How do you know which plants are edible?' she asked the child.

'I just know.'

'Can you tell by smell?'

'No, by using my tongue. My tongue never lets me down,' she said as she proudly stuck it out for the cook to see. 'I chew herbs and then taste the sap to see if they're good for calming you down or if they will stop you falling asleep. It was mother who taught me how to do it.'

'So you know the virtues of the simple.'

'The simple? It's not at all simple. In fact, it's quite complicated.'

Hubertine moved closer to the girl, touched by her ingenuousness.

'Would you like to help me?'

'To do what?'

'You could learn how to handle herbs, how to sort them, how to put them in little bags to make tisanes and remedies. And when April comes, you could go and look for mushrooms that grow in hidden places that I could show you.'

To be able to get out of the hospice, to escape from the watchful eyes of the nuns – this was more than Malvina had expected.

'I want to pass on to you all that I know,' explained the cook. 'And you can tell me what you know. Will you agree to that?'

The girl gave her assent.

Hubertine took her to see the two gardens she was in charge of. The first, in which she grew medicinal herbs, was beside the infirmary. The second was next to the kitchen and was for aromatic herbs.

'It's a pity it's not the spring. You could have found your way here just by following the scent of the plants. Basil, thyme, mint – these are the savours of paradise. You must come to know this place very well indeed before you can learn the art of taking what the earth has to offer and using it to make food that can fill us with pleasure.'

The cook suddenly stopped, as if an invisible hand had been placed on her shoulder.

'Because never forget,' she continued in a pompous tone. 'Never forget that your nose is just as important as your mouth. We have five senses: sight, hearing, touch, taste and smell. If you want to know the world, you must develop them all. To neglect one would be like depriving yourself of an arm or a leg.'

Malvina nodded, more from a desire to please Hubertine than out of conviction. For she was still certain that she would never be able to judge things other than by their taste. The tongue could produce sensations that no other organ was capable of arousing. Only by tasting, only by way of one's mouth could one totally give oneself over to something outside of oneself. Smell, in comparison, was insignificant. For Malvina, only what was eaten could have any value. This was because she consumed, destroyed what she ate, but above all, because once eaten, the thing also became a part of her. And she judged people by the taste that appeared in her mouth when she was near them.

Sister Clotilde's physique and her pockmarked and goose-pimpled, grey-green skin made one think of a gherkin, but for Malvina the nun's dominant trait was the bitter taste of rhubarb she evoked. Whenever she saw the old woman her saliva would take on a bitter and thoroughly disagreeable flavour. Her tongue had judged. Just as Rougemont made her feel nauseous, the nun made her shiver. And that was that. Nobody could do anything about it.

But Hubertine, on the other hand, was a source of pleasure. She was a juicy apricot, or perhaps a luscious pear, whose plump and velvety skin was like a cheek offered for a loving kiss. Malvina would never forget that their first meeting had been marked by the sweetness of bread and sugar, the very same taste she associated with her mother.

The cook had the same kindness, the same comforting, protective voice. But above all, she was full of the same overflowing love. For Marie Raynal had given her daughter all the love that was in her heart, and her love was devouring, desperate, almost despotic. An indissoluble link united them, a bond from which the father was excluded. He incessantly reproached his daughter. 'Don't sit there, rooted to the bench. You'll be burnt to cinders. Just look at you! Anybody would think you're raving mad. I'm not surprised your mother gave you that name. The Devil obviously whispered it in her ear.' And when he felt that his words were not strong enough, Gabert Raynal would take the whip to her. He liked to see fear in the child's eyes. 'On your knees!' he would scream as he struck her. Making his daughter yield to him gave him great joy. He loved to see her at his mercy. Malvina opposed her father's rages with silence and feigned imperviousness. She had never once cried out when he hit her. A seal of terror gagged her mouth, and she had not addressed a single word to her father since the night he had tortured and killed her dog.

On one particular evening he had drunk too much, just as he did every evening. His breath reeked of alcohol, and in his eye could be seen a murderous madness, a hatred of everything in this world. Marie Raynal was not at home, and in her absence Malvina had tidied the kitchen, washed the dishes and swept the floor. Her father grabbed her, rubbed his body against hers and then pulled her towards him by the hair to force her to kiss him. He liked to frighten her by tightening his hands around her neck. She had often felt these hands thrash her, beat her as if they would break all the bones in her body. She was almost paralysed by fear, but somehow managed to drag herself away from her monstrous parent, across the room and out into the yard where she crawled into the dog kennel. There she cowered, hugging her beloved dog to try to relieve her anguish. Long and tense minutes went by before she heard her father's footsteps approach. He had armed himself with a pitchfork and began to taunt her. She listened to his sneers and his terrible threats. He would kill the rabid mongrel, he screamed. She believed him, for she knew he was intensely jealous of the affection she felt for the animal. Malvina screamed when she saw her dog raised up into the air on the prongs of the pitchfork. She heard its agonized barks, and saw it jerk a couple of times before her father dealt a final, fatal blow. Then, with a rapid gesture, he cut open the smooth, bare skin on the animal's abdomen. He pulled out the viscera and seemed to take an indescribable pleasure in piercing and crushing the intestines. Blood spurted everywhere, even onto Malvina's face and hands. Her father went back inside the house, leaving the dog at his daughter's feet. She felt as if she were going to die. She wanted to kill this brute she had the misfortune to have as a parent, to wrench out his heart and make him eat it so that he would be poisoned by his own ferocity.

But instead she took the dog up in her arms and began to caress it. Blood flowed from its open wounds. On these she placed her mouth and began to suck up the life that ebbed out of the tortured body in a red trickle. A dull throbbing began inside her head and slowly grew into a heavy rhythmic beat. A hum rose up within her body and filled all her senses. The animal's heart was now beating in every fibre of the girl's body, like a faint rumour infinitely repeated. They were now joined for eternity.

'Why are you so sad all of a sudden?' asked Hubertine.

'I'm not sad.'

'Does the garden remind you of something?'

'No.'

'Was there one like this at your parents' house?'

Malvina did not reply, so Hubertine let it drop and invited her instead to come and see the vegetable garden.

There three nuns were at work, their backs bent as their hands moved through the earth. One of them was spreading straw to protect the vegetables against the cold, while the two others were pulling up leeks and cabbages.

'Sister Marie, Sister Jeanne and Sister Bénédicte,' said the cook. 'And this is Malvina. She's going to work with me.'

'What a charming child,' said the oldest of the three. 'It's still quite early in the year, but in the spring you'll be able to see all the magnificent vegetables that grow here. My favourites are artichokes. Do you know them? They're the big pine cones that have green and violet leaves just like lilacs.'

'But, Sister, isn't it a sin what these plants do?' asked Hubertine.

They looked at her with surprise.

'Don't they steal from each other a little of what God has given them?'

The trio burst into laughter.

'Instead of indulging in such tomfoolery,' said Sister Jeanne, 'perhaps you could tell us if you need anything for supper?'

'I'll take care of that! Don't you worry yourself.'

Hubertine was better versed in the secrets of conservation than anyone else in the hospice. She knew that for grapes to be just as tasty at Christmas as in September one had to place a phial on the bunch as soon as it began to form on the stock. To stop the quality of fruit deteriorating, she would plunge it into boiling water that had honey added to it. She was expert at making poached cabbage and confit of goose soup, azinat, which was a delicious hotpot of pork and vegetable, as well as aigo boullido, a soup made with eggs and garlic.

They arrived at the dispensary, where the Mother Superior was now on duty. She reigned proudly over this large room filled with glass cabinets containing blue earthenware pots decorated with mysterious inscriptions. In the centre of the room stood an oak table overflowing with porcelain mortars, stills and copper and pewter containers. Every morning after Mass the head nun would arrive from the chapel, followed by Sister Clotilde. While one of them worked with a pestle to make potions, electuaries and ointments, the other would classify medicines that the other Sisters would later come to collect for their patients.

'Mother Superior is skilled in examining medicinal plants. She touches them, smells them, crumples them between her fingers. Simply by their smell she can evaluate their worth. When I find the time, I provide her with plants, fruits, buds, leaves, bark, stalks, roots, gum and seeds. Everything she needs to make up her recipes. Theriac, for example, contains seventy substances including wine, honey, viper flesh and opium . . .'

Malvina looked at the cook, impressed by her talk.

'You know a lot of things,' she said.

'I know that you may not like her very much, but Sister Clotilde has taught me a lot.'

The girl made a mental note of this. She, too, wanted to learn and she wanted to learn quickly. To do so, she knew she would have to make some concessions.

*

Thus, in the months that followed, Malvina obediently carried out the nuns' orders. The most diverse of duties took up all her time and energy. She would rise at cockcrow, say the Angelus and dress in silence. Hubertine made her a jerkin of blue serge, a dress of the same colour, a red apron and a muslin bonnet. Malvina wore this outfit when she went to Mass every morning before her classes began. The schoolmaster taught piety and virtue to his pupils. On Monday, prayers in French and in Latin were memorized. Mistakes made in the recitation of these prayers would be corrected on Tuesday. On Wednesday, the pupils would practise reciting from *The Life of Jesus*. On Friday, they were taught how to pray correctly and on Saturday, they went over the articles of faith in the catechism. This was the week's schedule. And Malvina submitted docilely to this discipline because she knew that when the classes were finished for the day, she would be able to help Hubertine prepare dinner.

'Use the nail of your thumb for the salt, two doses for each plate. Go on, count.' Here in the kitchen the girl was learning as much about arithmetic as she did in the classroom. The table was covered with peas piled into pyramids and grains of corn divided into dozens and classed by colour. Bowls were piled up in fours or fives. Although she had little free time, Hubertine would never refuse to help her ward. She herself had learnt to count with tokens before the Mother Superior had let her use the books in the library.

'Will I be able to see the books myself one day?' asked Malvina.

'We'll have to ask for permission.'

'When?'

'After your tenth birthday. Now, describe agastache. Let's see if you can remember.'

'One form of it has white flowers, but in general it is red.'

'And what does it smell like?'

'It smells of mint and liquorice.'

'Excellent memory.'

She cut a slice of bread for the girl and asked, 'Did you put away the herbs and spices as I asked you?'

For two weeks now, Malvina had been entrusted with this task but already she was becoming tired of it. Even playing at the cupboards where the herbs were kept or screwing on and off the tops of the cylindrical jars no longer amused her. She wanted to be able to use the mortar, the mill and the chopping knife that were reserved for more expert hands.

'I can't learn anything new because I'm not allowed to touch anything.'

'Would you be able to use a hoe? You know how difficult it is to break up the earth and make furrows.'

'I know how to do it,' she said. 'Thyme, savory and sage go in the furrows and you put the flowers in gaps in between.'

The gardens were laid out in the English style of a succession of intertwining decorative motifs.

'You're a brilliant pupil, Malvina, but it's not good to move ahead too quickly. Go and get the glass cloches from the greenhouse and put them over the cuttings.'

'To protect them from the cold and the frost?'

'Frost is the enemy of nature.'

'So why aren't there any cloches in nature?'

Having no answer to her pupil's question, Hubertine sidled over to the stove to add some more water to a bubbling pot.

'Don't forget to bring me the shallots,' she said. 'My vegetables are overripe. I need to take the bitterness out of them. Go on. Quickly, or I'll have to send you to help Sister Clotilde.'

*

For Malvina, this simple sentence was the most terrible of threats. She was not repelled by having to clutch the hand of a patient when master Donatius was lancing a boil, nor when she held the bowl to catch the liquid when he was blood-letting. But she had a strong feeling of aversion whenever she saw, or even thought of, Sister Clotilde. She detested her because she represented authority and, more-over, because she paid no attention to the girl. She had not commented on the progress Malvina was making. She had paid her no compliments, had given her no encourage-ment. And when the girl had asked one day if she could go into the Mother Superior's library, she had simply laughed in her face.

Malvina was seized by a fit of rage and began running from one end of the hospice to the other, screaming and shouting out how much she hated God and the Sisters who were his helpers. She was shut up in the attic for two days as punishment. She refused to eat anything during this time.

A muffled noise woke Hubertine on the second night of her ward's incarceration. She heard footsteps whirling above her in what seemed like a wild dance, then she heard the thump of a body falling to the ground. Hubertine feared the worst. Malvina was not an easy child. The Sister had not failed to notice her strange behaviour. She never, for example, shared the games of the other children. When she came near them, they would huddle together as if they were suddenly cold. They were clearly afraid of her.

Hubertine quickly climbed the steps that led to the attic. She found the girl sprawling on the floor, staring wide-eyed ahead of her, with a blue scarf stuffed into her mouth. She was biting the blue cloth so hard it seemed she was trying to suffocate herself.

'My God, what are you doing?' she said as she rushed towards the child.

She gently removed the cloth from her mouth. Malvina coughed and caught her breath.

'What took hold of you, my poor darling? Why do you want to hurt yourself like that? Sister Clotilde will show you the books one day. There's no need to get into such a state!'

Malvina was like a fish out of water, with her mouth gaping open and her chest puffed out.

'Come on. Breathe, breathe.'

'I want my mother,' the girl finally blurted out.

'I know. I know,' replied Hubertine as she took her in her arms. 'But I love you, too.'

Malvina began to cry. She had for the first time realized that she missed her mother. She wanted to smell her, touch her.

Often, when she closed her eyes, forms would appear to her. She remembered how she had seen a tiny speck, far off in the distance but bright with the brilliance of precious stones. She saw a dancing line, a pastel cloud and then, closer, a face full of grace and mystery. She saw warmth in her mother's smile and on her lips she saw love. A blind love that would do anything to prove its grandeur. Marie knelt down, stretched her arms out and called her child. 'Come, my angel. Come, I have a secret to tell you.'

Yes, now Malvina remembered. Her mother had spoken just a few days before she had been taken away from her. 'Above all, say nothing of what you saw in the inn. Only by forgetting can you save yourself. We have ruined you. I'm going to go to the police and confess the crimes your father and I have committed. And we will be punished. I don't want evil to take you as well. I want our deaths to pay for your freedom, my sweet. I want them to bring you redemption. Because I have already paid a price that is high enough for two people.'

Malvina was silent, surprised by this memory, her eyes unmoving, pensive but happy. With all the wisdom of her nine years, she now understood why she must carry on living. The words of Père Fournier rang out again in her head. 'Your mother was thinking only of you.' Yes, that was it. Marie had sacrificed herself to save her daughter. It was the same type of sacrifice that the nuns spoke of when they talked of Christ. Malvina knew she must now forget. From now on, she must forget everything. She must suppress her blood-splattered memories.

What cannot be seen does not exist, Malvina told herself. She would make her past disappear just as easily as she used to hide her doll.

'I won't get like that again,' she told Hubertine. 'You needn't be afraid any more.' Then, worried, she asked, 'But do you still love me?'

'Of course, my child. Of course I do.'

'You'd do anything for me?'

'What funny ideas you've got in your little head!'

'You'll always protect me, won't you?'

'Good Lord, of course I will! But against whom?'

'I don't know.'

'Instead of all this nonsense, you should be thinking about tomorrow.'

'Tomorrow?'

'Have you forgotten that it's already springtime?'

'Tomorrow is Friday, the first day of May . . .'

'And the moon is waning,' added Hubertine. 'That means we're going out to the country to see what herbs and plants we can find.'

'So I don't have to go to school?'

'It's me who'll be giving you your lesson tomorrow, mademoiselle. I've arranged it with the Mother Superior.'

'Thank you. Oh, thank you,' was the girl's reply.

And then she whispered in her friend's ear, 'Can you give it back to me now?'

'What?'

'The scarf. My mother used to wrap me in it when I was little.'

Hubertine took the piece of cloth out of her pocket and ran it through her fingers. Its exquisite motifs showed it was the work of a talented artisan. As she handed it back, she noticed the initials M and P embroidered in one corner.

'Go to bed now,' she said. 'We have to leave at dawn.'

Malvina had difficulty getting to sleep. She sat at the window to follow the course of the moon. She prayed and begged this adored star, this heavenly body before which she would gladly prostrate herself, to hasten towards the end of its nightly journey. She eventually rolled up in a ball on the doorstep and fell asleep. Tomorrow there would be no more buildings, no more enclosing walls. No, there would only be a rocky landscape, a landscape of liberty.

*

The song of the birds woke her. She jumped up and began untangling the knots that had appeared in her hair over the last two days. Despite the season, she chose to wear a dress made of thick wool. Its spiky stitches would catch the down of dandelion flowers as she walked through the fields. Malvina spun herself around to make her dress billow. Then she headed for the kitchen, where a steaming bowl of soup awaited her.

'Are you ready for your big day?' asked Hubertine.

The child barely took the time to answer. She rushed to the table and began to wolf down her broth.

'Have some white bread. You'll need all your strength today because we'll be doing a lot of walking.'

The girl reached out to grab a couple of slices without even lifting her head from her bowl.

'What restlessness!' remarked the cook. 'Don't forget that patience and observation are two of the qualities required to be a good herbalist. They enable you to appreciate the treasures of nature, for which the ordinary person can only have an ignorant admiration.'

Malvina was no longer listening.

'Shall we go?' she said.

The cook smiled and nodded.

It was as if they were setting out on a great expedition. Each carried a walking stick, bore a basket on her arm and wore a linen bonnet on her head as they marched out through the gates of the hospice. This was the first time the girl had left the grounds of the establishment since her arrival there. Watching the hustle and bustle of the town gave her an immense joy. She would have loved to have gone to the port to see the gabbarts docking there – the nuns had often spoken to her of this spectacle – but the little time they would have in the countryside permitted no detours. They had also decided to leave the banks of the Lot to take a path that led straight up into the hills.

Brilliant, chalky-white clouds blurred the horizon and veiled the sun. The air was fragrant and birds in the trees and hedgerows warbled out their shrill, amorous trills. Malvina pressed ahead with no regard for Hubertine's fatigue, undaunted by the mounting morning heat. She marched, free, bold and radiant.

'Come on, quickly,' she ordered as she held the bottom of her dress just above the grass so that it would brush off the tips of the stalks. 'I'm in a rush to see everything.'

'Well, then, stop charging around and just open your eyes!'

Malvina stopped for a moment to look at the flowers that grew along the side of the path. She plucked the largest one. She observed its bright yellow colour, breathed in its orange scent then rubbed it across her mouth.

'It's sweet,' she said.

She greedily licked the golden spangles the pollen had left on her lips.

'These are forest daffodils,' said Hubertine.

'I like them,' replied the girl, who by now had opened the stem and was sliding her tongue inside to lick the sap.

'I like the whole thing,' she added. 'Inside and out.'

'What a funny little girl you are!'

'But that doesn't matter because you said you loved me.'

Malvina had started walking again. Every step provided her with a fresh joy that made her cry out in admiration. Here she found meadowsweet, which was perfect for curing stomach aches, and there she discovered rue, which could be used to combat fever or nausea.

'God made everything for the benefit of Man,' said Hubertine.

'But there is so much to learn.'

'Of course, but I sense that you have the ability to do

it. I know that, like me, you are able to make the plants yield up their secrets to you.'

Malvina asked Hubertine to explain.

'Every element in nature,' said Hubertine, 'is linked with other elements. Thus plants with yellow flowers cure illnesses of the urinary tract, the sweet violet soothes sore throats and the autumn crocus is used to treat gout. You see,' she said as she plucked one, 'its bulb looks just like a deformed toe.'

Without knowing it, Malvina was learning the theory of humours. If there was too much or too little of one of the humours – blood, phlegm, choler and melancholy – this could be resolved by absorbing substances which combated or corresponded to it. It was necessary to distinguish between the cold herbs such as sorrel, chicory or lettuce, and the hot herbs such as sage, fennel, mint or parsley. And to make the best use of their virtues.

*

This lesson interested Malvina so much that she soon became obsessed with the study of plants. She would squat for hours in the garden of the hospice, observing and touching them. Her fine fingers sprang like field mice from one leaf to the next. 'Laurel helps breathing problems,' she repeated to herself. 'Thyme is good for asthma.' Her favourite game was to make bouquets of love and of repulsion. She had no doubt that flowers evoked ferocious sympathies and antipathies. Thus, for Sister Clotilde, she did not hesitate to mix apparently opposed plants such as olive and cabbage, or cucumber and vine.

The girl and the cook often went walking in the forest that summer in search of one specific thing, such as flowers, herbs or mushrooms. Sometimes the excursions were the pretext for more serious lessons. Malvina would then fill her notebook with drawings of the plants she examined. She would often imitate the pictures she had seen in her mother's notebook. But she never let herself be carried away by her imagination, preferring to limit herself to simple reproductions. Nature was presenting itself to her to be deciphered and the child never tired of unravelling its mysteries. When they returned to the hospice and deposited their harvest in the dispensary, Malvina would watch as the Mother Superior prepared her concoctions. She was interested in all things in both the dispensary and the kitchen. She learnt how Hubertine made use of scraps and peelings. How she used turnip roots, stalks of lettuce that had gone to seed and fresh radish leaves to make delicious purées.

The girl was clearly happy, and nothing could have pleased Hubertine more. Nature had helped her reconcile herself with her life. After almost a year at the hospice, Malvina was at last beginning to lower her guard, to let herself go. She no longer had the evasive look of an unhappy child. She no longer lowered her head when spoken to. Sometimes she even ventured a smile. But Hubertine had not taken into account the fact that Rougemont was due to visit soon. The first cold days of winter announced his return. And Malvina had not forgotten him.

Chapter Four

The night before the hawker arrived, Malvina awoke with her cheeks on fire, burning with fever. Her blood was beating at her temples and her heart was racing. Neither master Donatius, the doctor, nor Sister Clotilde could find out what was the cause of her trouble. They tried blood-letting and gave her infusions of valerian. Hubertine also administered a tisane of lime blossom. But nothing worked. The girl spent the day sitting in front of the fireplace, shivering.

She had been sitting there when the hawker left her a year earlier, and it was in this very same position that he now found her.

'What's wrong with her?' he asked Hubertine.

'I don't understand it. Everything was fine until now . . .'

'Do you really want me to believe that it's my presence that's frightening her?' he said as he crouched down in front of the child. He lifted up her chin and stared deep into her grey eyes, eyes that were cold with suppressed rage.

'You're not happy here?'

Malvina was disgusted by the rancid taste on his lips

and by the acidity of his skin. When she saw him move towards her, she gave a start and felt like vomiting. She was about to fall, to collapse into those detested arms. But the very thought of it was enough for her to regain her strength. She heaved herself up, knocked the man over and ran towards the door.

'What a welcome,' said Rougemont as he picked himself up. 'Have you not taught the girl any manners?'

'She's grateful to you,' replied Hubertine. 'So leave her in peace . . .'

'Well, I like that!' he screamed. 'It was me who saved her life!'

'Calm down. Getting angry will do you no good.'

'Leave us alone. I need to speak to her.'

Although she was the elder of the two, the cook obeyed. She had never dared oppose him.

Malvina huddled, terrified, in a corner of the refectory. Rougemont pulled her up with his brawny arms and sat her down on a table.

'So, you don't like me much?' he asked.

'No.'

'And why is that? Go on, tell me.'

'You're evil.'

'Me? Evil? But who are you to judge me?'

Malvina lowered her eyes.

'I went to your parents' inn. Nothing has changed there.'

He told her how, one evening, he had broken the seals on the doors and gone inside the abandoned building.

'Decomposing bodies, skeletons . . . Over a dozen, can you imagine it? The skulls had been hacked from the bodies and hidden in a corner of the cellar. I bet your mother had to cook the brains of the dead to poison the next victims. That kills you, you know, eating your own kind!'

Malvina was struggling not to cry. A voice, a distant voice, was telling her, 'Forget. Forget everything.'

'Your parents were cannibals,' Rougemont continued. 'And it won't be long before you become one, too. How much longer do you think you can keep on lying?'

'My name is Malvina Fournier,' she said.

His stinging look spat poison.

'Fournier!'

'You know that you have the blood of assassins in your veins!'

'I am not bad.'

'You refuse to understand what I've done for you. But have you thought about Hubertine? Have you thought about the pain you'll cause her when she finds out that you're the child of monsters? The horror, the suffering, the death that your parents caused are like so many seeds that have germinated and whose roots are now crawling towards you. Because you saw, Malvina. You saw those vile murders. Evil will embrace you, just as it did your father and mother. It has already started to wind itself around your ankles, your legs, your hips.'

Rougemont had moved closer to the girl and with his fat hands had taken hold of her body. His arms imitated a serpent that wrapped itself around her throat, took hold of her brow, penetrated her soul. His nails dug into the girl's skin.

'Then one day,' he went on, 'the evil is there, right in your heart. The heart is suffocated, devoured by a poisonous herb.'

'Never!' she screamed. 'Never! Do you hear me?'

Malvina was crying, her hands clamped over her ears.

'Enough!' cried Hubertine, who had returned to the kitchen when she heard her ward's sobs.

Fear and hatred alternated in the girl's eyes. She tried to scream out her fear, but her lips moved silently.

'What have you done to her?'

'Don't meddle in my affairs!'

'I don't want you to touch her. Get out of here. Get out!'

'So you'd throw me out, as if I were a lout? And you the only family I have in the world!'

'I won't think twice about reporting you to the police if you come back. I love this child and you're not going to take her away from me. Understood? Nobody's going to touch her!'

'You're sheltering the Devil! The Devil!'

'Look who's talking! Do you think I don't know about your criminal activities?'

Rougemont turned pale as he sought a reply. He had not inherited the generosity and moral uprightness that were a source of pride to his sister. What could he do if nature had not moulded all men with the same clay? Money helped to make injustice bearable. And that helped rid one's conscience of any pangs of guilt when one took certain liberties.

'Even if I were to disappear, you would not be able to make me die within you!' he told Malvina.

And at this, he walked out of the room and out of the hospice.

It took Hubertine some time to find Malvina, who had finally hidden herself in the greenhouse. When the cook approached her, the girl was crouching among the plants and her head hung forward so that her hair fell down over her face as though she wanted to disappear underneath it. There was no point in asking her any questions. She just sat there, uttering groans that sounded like the whimpering of a pup. Hubertine had little experience of dealing with such distress, but she let herself be guided by intuition. She, too, crouched down and began to make the same sounds as the girl, but her moans were calmer in tone. Surprise shook Malvina from her torpor. She looked out furtively through the undergrowth of her hair and observed the mouth which said to her, 'Don't be afraid. Don't be afraid. He's gone.' Then she timidly reached out to touch this tender and reassuring flesh. Hubertine smiled.

'Calm down, my dear. Come, let me take you in my arms.'

Malvina placed her index finger on the cook's lips, exactly in the middle, just as the angels do with newborn babies to make them forget what nature had taught them when they were in their mothers' stomachs. She then moved her finger down along the veins of Hubertine's neck as far as the top of her blouse. She pressed her hand on to the cook's breast, deep into the material, as though she sought to leave an indelible imprint. She wanted to feel the heat of her friend's heart and in this way to share her love, without the need for words.

Hubertine hugged her. She would have preferred not to say anything more, but, fearing that Malvina's head might become filled with thoughts of hatred and vengeance, she felt she had to put the girl on her guard.

'The Devil takes hold of those who stop believing in God, those who lose their faith,' she said. 'You are much too young to have done any evil, or any good, for that matter. The servants of Satan proliferate on the roads of this kingdom just as they do here in the hospice. They dispossess you of the grace of the Lord in order to subject you to their own domination. And since your soul is already beset by disorder, you must be extra vigilant, for the Devil assumes many shapes. His thunder can take on seven forms to deceive you: iron to break you, fire to burn you, sulphur to poison you, rags to smother you, lightning to daze you, stone to destroy you and wood to sink you. Be careful! He is not afraid of laughter, and can be facetious. It is for very good reasons that we also call him the Father of Lies.'

Malvina listened attentively. Fever was once again causing tiny drops to form on her forehead.

Hubertine thought it wise to bring her back to the kitchen, where she would be warmed by the heat of the fire.

'Come, my angel, come with me,' she murmured as she lifted the girl up by the shoulders.

Malvina was exhausted. When the doctor examined her for a second time, he found her even more perturbed than before.

'Do you know what gave her this shock?' Aubin Donatius asked the cook.

'I believe I know what is wrong with her,' she admitted. 'But I would ask you not to mention this to anyone. She has suffered a lot. But her ailment is more a disturbance of the soul than a physical illness.'

'Then she will need treatment for both aspects of her problem.'

'Love is what she needs, love and rest.'

At these words, she accompanied the man back into the main ward. She told him that for this night the girl would sleep in her bed.

Malvina could feel the softness of Hubertine's skin next to her own, but this did not keep the nightmare of the inn at bay. This time there were twelve men gorging themselves noisily at the table. A dreadful hubbub rose up of exclamations, of coarse laughter, of gaping mouths and stuffed gullets. Each of the men bore hideous wounds. One guest's head had almost been severed, but by a miracle still remained attached to his body. On another's neck could be seen the burn mark left by the rope that had been used to hang him. They were all criminals suffering from fatal injuries, but they all somehow continued to live.

'You've given us a lovely corpse there, my dear! This hawker is not exactly rich, but it's a start.' It was her father who was speaking. 'Come on. Come and join us. We're feasting in your honour!'

Malvina did not dare move. Rougemont's body was laid out on the table like a joint of roast meat. She saw his smoking entrails and could smell the charred flesh. A scar ran around the man's neck to form a thick necklace of congealed blood.

'You have earned your place among us,' her father repeated. 'You, too, have killed and you have seen the birth of death. You can look upon your work. You can be one of us now that you are finally freed from your doubts, from your questions.'

The revellers stood up and in a haunting chorus began to endlessly repeat, 'Kill for knowledge. Eat to discover the truth.'

Malvina awoke the next morning paralysed with fear. Her body was so stiff that she could barely stretch out her legs or arms. Her muscles seemed made of stone, and her bones of glass. The slightest movement and they would break. Her heart began to beat so violently that it hurt. A terrible thought had just crossed her mind, a thought so fabulous that the girl could not yet take it seriously. What if Rougemont were really to die? Death to the blackmailer! Death to the thief of her happiness! Death! Death! Once again, anger had overcome wisdom, resentment had dispelled forgiveness.

The idea would not leave her. Although Hubertine assured her that her brother would never return to the hospice, she was convinced that he would never stop stirring up the mud of her past. She felt nauseous. Was this due to the memory of her father's murders? Or was it her refusal to be what she was, the flesh and blood of this foul beast? Or perhaps the disgust at her own feelings of guilt? Malvina could not tell. But she did know that Rougemont's existence nourished her malaise, made her throat constrict almost to the point of suffocation. Because he had condemned her to crime, there was only one way out – to kill. Not to gain knowledge, but to win freedom.

Prudence was required. She need only be careful so as not to arouse suspicion. Perhaps it would not even be necessary to carry out this dirty task. So God had abandoned her? Then Lucifer would help her. Was he not simply an angel who had rebelled against his creator? An angel who had been cast out but who had been able to create for himself an empire in the kingdom of heaven. Malvina thought of Hubertine's lesson on the many forms that Satan could take and now added a new one that the cook had forgotten to list – pretence. If she showed herself to be how the others wanted her to be, then none of them would suspect what she was secretly planning. Just like the tiny tick that appears lifeless, she would withdraw into herself, swollen with gall. She would lie in wait until the day her prey came within range and then cling on to bite into its despised flesh.

*

Malvina learnt to be patient. Six years passed and still Rougemont did not return. When she asked Hubertine about her brother, the cook would repeat that she needn't worry about him. He was no longer a threat to her because she had chased him away.

'What did you say to him that stopped him from coming back here?'

'One day, when we were still young, we had an argument. Over a measly few coins. He hit me in the stomach. I was fourteen years old and the words of the doctor who treated me were worse than Rougemont's blows.'

Hubertine could not hold back her tears.

'So the reason I put him out was that, for the second time, he was trying to take away from me the child I never had! You see, I think of you as my daughter, my darling daughter.'

Malvina went over to the cook and embraced her.

'Don't worry,' she said. 'Don't cry!'

'How can I explain it to you? You'll soon be fifteen, and I can see you getting into bad ways. Look at you. You're intelligent and you're pretty. In fact, you're very pretty. And you know it.'

Malvina was indeed aware of the influence she had over those around her. Her trips to the plateau had shaped her legs and given her a slim waist and strong shoulders. The celestial elegance of her gait lent her the evanescent appearance of an elf. Her hands and her round cheeks may still have betrayed her youth, but she already had all the signs that promise mature beauty. Her skin was silky, her breasts firm and heavy, and above her rounded hips her stomach was flat. Her hair had a reddish-brown sheen and her pale complexion highlighted the raspberry colour of her full and tender lips.

'But on your lips I do not see the sensuality that

seduces men,' continued Hubertine. 'No. But I do see a pinched expression that speaks of a bitter heart.'

'Why are you telling me this?' asked the girl, annoyed.

'I'm saying this to try to make you understand. But I'm not succeeding!'

'Did you not promise that you would always love me?'

'I can love you but still not understand you. Your soul is in two parts and lies open like a walnut. I only wish I could be sure that the rotten part has not ruined the rest.'

'You don't trust me?'

'I know you better than anyone. I found you out, long ago!'

'So Rougemont told you everything. Is that it?'

'I know my brother – he's not all bad even if his ambitions are not particularly honourable. Money always made him mad. Figeac, Assier – his travels helped me work it out. Everyone in the region had heard about the infamous inn at Assier.'

Malvina took a step back.

'I hate him. My God, how I hate him!' she hissed through clenched teeth.

'It's yourself that you should be wary of.'

'Because I'm the child of a monster?'

'Because you're not doing anything not to become one. When I look at a person, I can see the different things he or she could become. And I can tell you that I've seen a change in you for some time now. Yes, I've seen a change. You often go wandering in the forest, up there near Cabessut.'

'All I do is look. I'm fascinated by creatures that can

metamorphose. Things that crawl, swarm, writhe. The lizard that can squeeze itself into the tiniest fissure, the grass snake whose green and yellow scales change with the seasons. I envy their ability to cast off the skin of the dying year. You just don't know what torture it is to want to be someone else.'

'That is not the nature that I taught you about!'

'So you wanted to tell me about the beauty and generosity of nature? But have you ever watched mating displays? Have you seen the praying mantises that savour the flesh of their males? Or the warrior bees, for whom the bumblebee is but a willing victim? You should see how one bee will saw through the peduncle that holds the abdomen to the thorax, how another tears to shreds the nervures of the wings, while a third pierces the cuirass so as to ram in its poison sting. Well, this spectacle provokes in me an intoxication that is undiluted by any remorse. The nature that I like is the one that teaches me the spirit of domination.'

'Let me give you a warning, Malvina. Every being has within it an accursed part. You can direct your gaze towards the light or towards the darkness, and your life will accordingly become a heaven or a hell.'

'Rougemont has condemned me to be what I am. I often feel I want to kill him and this murderous need has become for me just like the need to eat. A vital need.'

'Then education must curb it and religion curse it!'

'Your God is no better than men. Wars, epidemics, misery are his allies. He gorges himself on people's lives. He cuts them down as if they were a field of wheat.'

'Stop this at once!'

Malvina stopped. She didn't want to anger Hubertine.

'I'm sorry,' she said. 'I didn't mean to hurt you.'

'I'll always be at your side to help you keep evil away, but I want to see you fighting against it too.'

The girl took the cook's hands, raised them up to her lips and kissed each of them in turn.

'Look, I don't bite! What can I do to prove my good intentions?'

'Look after Sister Clotilde. Her health is getting even worse. The doctor thinks it's consumption.'

'I can't bring myself to help her. She rejects me!'

'Then your efforts will be all the more worthy. I want you to look after her. She's been confined to her bed since yesterday.'

Malvina thought for a moment before deciding that losing Hubertine's affection would be far worse than having to put up with the sickly nun.

*

It was the first time that the Mother Superior had spoken to Malvina since her interview when she arrived at the hospice.

'Let's not waste any time,' she said. 'Sister Clotilde is a good and generous woman, I am glad that you are to be with her as she faces this terrible ordeal. Am I correct in thinking that your devotion is a sign that you would like to join our order?'

'I'm afraid that I do not have a vocation. I am more interested in plants.'

'Plants?'

'Like you, Mother Superior, I have a passion for pharmacology.'

'I didn't know that. Hubertine doesn't tell me much about you. But she did say that you show signs of an exceptional intelligence. You are apparently very inquisitive and you always insist on an answer.'

'I believe that knowledge can help me become a better person.'

'Your ambition to be an apothecary will be a hard one to fulfil. For such a profession, one needs to be studious and God-fearing. But Sister Clotilde says you are too spirited and that you are also very argumentative.'

Malvina clenched her fists.

'It's jealousy that makes her say that.'

'Your reaction merely shows that she is right.'

'You're better off having no character at all than having a dull one!'

'I see in you certain traits that no amount of education will erase. Scars are the indelible traces of our pasts. You may not think it, but there are many to be seen on your face and in your gestures! The years you have spent here cannot and will not dispel the suffering that has made you different. I sense that one day you will be taught a great lesson. Not by the sisters here, nor by men, but by the Lord himself. Because it is only the word of God that can reach lost souls! Sister Clotilde has told me that you fight against God by claiming that he is weak. She says that vice lies dormant in you like a smouldering fire. But I have chosen to give you a chance.'

Malvina raised her eyebrows.

'I think,' continued the Mother Superior, 'that we should trust you. If my decision proves to be wrong, you will be sent to the workhouse. But if you measure up to my expectations, you will one day take over from Hubertine in the kitchen. From today on, you are to take charge of the medicinal herb garden. You will be responsible for the supply of plants. And if you have a little time left over, I will let you come and help me in the dispensary.'

'Thank you, Mother Superior. But I may be able to help you more than you would expect. Have a look at this book,' said Malvina as she took out from under her dress the work that her mother had left her. She had of course by now removed the drawings so that the identity of their owner would remain secret.

The nun flicked attentively through the book.

'This is indeed surprising!'

She turned the pages cautiously, but there was no sign in her eyes that she understood what she saw.

'It appears to be in a foreign language,' she finally murmured. 'Undoubtedly Turkish. You see here? The name of the author is engraved in gold letters: Jean-Baptiste Dandora de Ghalia, apothecary of Paris.' The Mother Superior ran her finger over the inscription before adding, 'But where did you find this book?'

'Somebody gave it to me.'

'When? How? Do you know this man?'

Malvina's face immediately clouded over. She snatched the book out of the nun's hands, curtsied and withdrew.

Her head was suddenly teeming with feverish questions.

How had the book got to the inn? Had the author given it to her mother? Marie had often spoken about the childhood she had spent with her parents in Saint-Malo. Perhaps this unknown person in Paris could tell her more about her mother's early life. For a fleeting instant she pictured herself in the capital. There she would be free to do as she pleased. There she could give free rein to her rebellious nature.

Sister Clotilde used what remained of her strength to force upon the girl a strict and constant discipline. When she was not bedridden, the nun insisted that Malvina get her up at five o'clock for early Mass. At five thirty, she would make her visit the wards so that she could be kept up to date with the state of health of all the patients she had ever cared for. At eight o'clock, breakfast. At eleven, high Mass. And also during the morning, Malvina would gather herbs from the garden and deposit them in the dispensary. But she would never linger there, because at twelve Sister Clotilde would demand her dinner. The same rhythm would be kept up in the afternoon. At half-past twelve, Malvina would go to the refectory to help Hubertine. Then she would work again in the garden until five. Vespers were at six. Supper at six thirty. And at seven o'clock, Sister Clotilde would go to bed. It was at this time that the Mother Superior would come to administer a remedy to the ailing nun. Clotilde did not trust Malvina, and would often say that the Devil lived in her.

'You do evil without even trying. It's in your nature,' the nun told her.

'All right, then. Ask the Mother Superior to have a nun look after you instead of me!'

'I will not! God has His reasons for sending you to me. Hubertine has been too good to you. You are a weed that she has allowed to flourish.'

'You have no idea what maternal love is! You're just a jealous, bitter old woman. Your death will mean only that the earth has one less burden to carry!'

These words shocked Sister Clotilde. She raised her hand to her heart as a sudden attack took hold of her. She was almost suffocating and began to cough up blood and, for the first time, pus. Malvina was thrown into a panic and ran off to fetch master Donatius. The doctor, by now accustomed to these repeated alerts, did not hurry.

'I don't know what to do,' he confided to the girl as they walked to Clotilde's chamber. 'My remedies are having no effect.'

'So we can expect the worst?'

'Go and get Hubertine. She has some henbane in her cellar, and I think the time is now right to make use of it.'

'What is it?'

'It contains a very poisonous alkaloid in its spiny heart, but if you dry its leaves and administer them in small quantities, they can strengthen the body's resistance.'

A few minutes later, the cook entered Clotilde's room. She was holding a glass of water in her hand, and into this she carefully added four drops. Not one more, for even the tiniest of errors could prove fatal. They waited for the remedy to take effect. Soon, just as Donatius had been hoping, Sister Clotilde's suffering was eased, her coughing fits ceased and she fell asleep.

After only two days, she had recovered. It seemed that a miracle had taken place. Malvina, however, began wishing that the burden that the nun represented for her would soon be taken away. Could her wish have been so strong that it became a reality? What happened on the day of 2 May 1774 would appear to confirm this.

*

Not in living memory had there been such a drought in Cadurcie. A stifling, oppressive heat had been ravaging the countryside for a month now. The crazed earth wallowed in its misery, its vegetation exhausted. The peasants worried about their vineyards and wheat fields. They weren't sure whether they should sow the precious corn which, if it did not produce a crop, would cause famine and ruin. They waited, as if for a gift from above, for the storm to break. In vain.

The nuns were sitting at table listening to the Mother Superior saying grace before supper when the bells began to ring. The nun cut short her prayer, got up and went to the window.

'Something very serious is happening,' she said.

The sisters looked at each other anxiously.

'Those are the bells of Saint-Étienne. It must be a fire.'

At that moment, three nuns came running into the refectory. Their haste revealed their fear. One said the fire seemed to be quite a distance away, while another insisted that the hospice's own alarm bell should be rung. Huber-

tine turned to listen to them, and forgot the hand that
hovered above Sister Clotilde's glass. The drops of the
remedy she was administering fell into the water, forming
large oily circles before becoming diluted. Malvina, indifferent to the drama, continued serving the meal. The nuns
had by now left the table. Hubertine, too, had hurried into
the courtyard to find out more about what was happening.
The bell was not sounded. Wiping her brow with her
apron, the cook eventually came back inside.

'You were right not to get excited,' she told Malvina.
'The fire was near La Daurade. What with all this toing
and froing, I've forgotten to give Sister Clotilde her
remedy.'

And while she spoke she dropped another dose into
the glass. Malvina knew this would be fatal. But she said
nothing. Sister Clotilde took the glass and drank it down
in one go.

When the meal was over, Malvina took refuge in a
corner of the kitchen, where she lay down on the ground
and propped herself up on her elbows. She waited passively,
silently and fearfully for the events that were to come.
What did she hope for? She did not know, but one thing
was clear to her – she had chosen to remain silent. Master
Donatius stood at the bedside of the vomiting and groan-
ing Sister Clotilde and wondered at the greenish liquid
that was being ejected from her stomach. What could it
mean, this vomit and this unbearable stench emanating
from the nun's body? Despite the treatments they had
quickly administered, Sister Clotilde's condition got steadily worse. She rejected Hubertine's potions, arguing that it

was in fact these that were killing her. She moaned that her stomach was on fire. After several hours of agony, the nun died in Malvina's arms.

*

The next day, the girl attended the Mass celebrated for Sister Clotilde. She knew that a consecrated host could burn the tongues of the debauched, but she still decided to receive communion. The body of Christ had its usual taste of unleavened and unsalted bread. She swallowed it and neither choked nor coughed. So, despite the nuns' repeated claims, it was possible to deceive God, to escape his vigilance and to sin with impunity. She joined her hands to pray, but only for appearance's sake. In her mind she saw the altar transformed into a table around which sat monsters with the wings of giant bats, bearing long serrated lances. Their backs were crested like tritons and they hissed like serpents as they devoured hideous toads. They crunched through the disgusting flesh, their thick tongues drawn far back inside their gaping mouths. Beyond the table she could see angels writhing in agony, their eyes contorted with famine and rage. A shiver ran through Malvina. Perhaps she should make use of the Devil's help? Because it was indeed the Devil who had used Hubertine's hand to poison Sister Clotilde. The nun had paid for her indifference and her pride, just as Rougemont would one day pay for taking advantage of her!

'You look worried,' she said to the cook as they were leaving the chapel.

Hubertine did not reply, but simply carried on walking with her head down.

'What's wrong?' asked Malvina.

The cook could find neither the words nor the courage to speak to her. She had tried several times since Sister Clotilde's death, but a lump would always come to her throat, her heart would begin to beat faster, her blood rise up to her temples and her eyes would stare down at the ground. Her conscience was tormenting her. Master Donatius had said the nun's vomiting was simply caused by her body rejecting some internal putrescence. But Hubertine reproached herself for having used henbane without knowing what the side effects might be. She had caused her colleague's death by trying to play God.

Malvina took hold of her friend's hands.

'You did all you could to save her,' she said.

'My conceit blinded me!'

'You have done no wrong. Only those who still bear original sin are in danger.'

'Evil is not automatically passed on to the next generation. Have I not already explained that to you?'

Malvina drew closer to Hubertine.

'I will naturally come under suspicion,' she said in a low voice.

'Be quiet. I can't bear to even think about it.'

Malvina knew that she had been born into the race of guilty children. She knew that someone marked by crime as she was would easily fall into vice. Her breathing suddenly became difficult, her eyes filled with tears.

'Don't ever let doubt take hold of you,' she told Hubertine. 'Never! You are goodness personified!'

At these words she ran off across the courtyard, screaming out that she was innocent. One by one, the windows began to open. The nuns rushed to see the girl spin around the yard, her head thrown back and her arms held out to form a cross as if she were seeking a blessing from above.

'I've done nothing!' Malvina repeated one last time before running up the stairs and locking herself in the attic. Without knowing it, Hubertine was offering her the chance to perform her very first act of love.

That very morning, Malvina had overheard a conversation between master Donatius and the Mother Superior. Her own name, that of Sister Clotilde and of the cook were mentioned several times. Their talk was filled with mistrust, with terrible suspicions. Their voices vibrated with accusations. Was it an accident, or clumsiness or had it been done intentionally? They spoke of a spell, a baleful influence spreading through the hospice.

'These rumours are doing a lot of harm,' said the doctor. 'The patients are refusing to take their remedies.'

It was master Donatius who had ordered henbane to be given to Sister Clotilde. But he now accused Hubertine of not having followed his prescription, of having doubled the dose without telling him. His fear made him lie.

'Have you considered what would become of the hospice if the provost ordered an inquiry and discovered there had been a crime?' he asked. 'I cannot and will not take such a risk.'

'Hubertine was undoubtedly perturbed,' said the nun.

'Sister Clotilde warned us that we should be wary of the influence her protégée has on her. It would be best for this establishment if the girl were placed in the workhouse.'

Thus was Malvina struck once more by her terrible curse. Her past was catching up with her, ruining this new life she had tried to build for herself. To do anything out of the ordinary was seen, here in the hospice, as tantamount to living in sin. Surely between these two worlds, between good and evil, there existed a third where men had learned to compromise? Paris seemed to her the place where everything could gain acceptance. Its diversity would enable her to pass unnoticed. Perhaps she might even succeed in proving that those who were supposed to set an example were little better than those who they judged?

Malvina stood by the attic window and waited for the day to end. She liked choices made in extreme circumstances. It was indeed tragic to leave Hubertine, but it was nothing less than magnificent that her departure should serve to clear the nun's name. What joy to be able to grant a pardon! To be able to play with the facts, to change the course of history according to one's own desires. The price she would have to pay was, in comparison, insignificant. Because neither silence nor distance was enough to separate those who had once given each other everything. Malvina's bond with the cook was now much more than one of friendship. It had become a unique love, a love that would last for eternity.

The clock had struck two when Malvina decided to leave. Everything around her was swallowed up by the darkness as if to facilitate her flight. She gathered up the few belongings she possessed, tied her blue scarf around her neck and placed the book her mother had given her next to her skin. Then she walked machine-like towards the postern. She looked behind her one last time and a shiver of apprehension ran through her as she closed the door on her former life. She began to walk faster, then to run. Her grief lessened as the distance between herself and the hospice increased. Her tears soon dried up as she concentrated on blotting out memories of her life in the hospice.

Several stagecoaches were preparing to leave from the Grand Place. The few coins that made up Malvina's fortune were not sufficient to convince any driver to take her as a passenger. A merchant, however, was more conciliatory. She found little comfort between his casks and earthenware jars, and his itinerary included a long detour. But she cared little that the journey was slow, for she was travelling to discover a new Malvina in the city where all was possible – Paris.

Chapter Five

Chance had it that Malvina's arrival in Paris coincided with a major historical event. At the very moment the young woman was entering the capital, Louis XVI was succeeding his grandfather on the throne of France. An immense crowd had invaded the streets, the squares and the boulevards. There was joy, and hope, too, for this was one of the few occasions in a lifetime when the most marvellous of dreams seem accessible. The anticipation of change lifted the people's spirits. Many were already hailing the start of what they believed would be the most prosperous and happy reign there had ever been.

'Are Parisians always as mad as this?' wondered Malvina as she watched the crowds streaming past her carriage.

People were leaping in the air, shouting and stamping their feet on the ground to the music of a noisy and joyful dance. The young woman's eyes devoured every single person who paraded before them – the ragged man standing beside her carriage clapping his hands, the merchant selling rabbit skins, the woman who offered old hats as she danced around and the porter who, bent under a burden that looked heavy enough to break a horse's back, had shed his load and was merrily singing. Even the apprentice wigmakers, powdered like whitings, and the bourgeois from the neighbouring quarters had ventured to the Faubourg Saint-Martin to take part in the celebration.

Malvina dared not move, fearing that if she even blinked the spectacle might disappear. She had ample time to observe the scene, for the traffic was so dense it had almost come to a standstill. Nothing could dampen her enthusiasm, but she was still astute enough to note that Paris did not exactly match her expectations. If a stranger to the city were to take a road other than the one from Versailles to the Champs-Élysées he would discover the desolation of the faubourgs. Martin, France's most illustrious saint, had given his name to the dirtiest and most repugnant district of them all. Just as in the poorest provincial towns, here too the narrow, filthy roads were lined with tumbledown shacks and cottages oozing with humidity. It was not difficult to imagine that here, as in mountain gorges, the light fell straight downwards between the rooftops without ever reaching the ground. The façades of the buildings were bare and worn and pockmarked like rock faces. Architecture was not a word that could be used to describe these edifices. The only variety they displayed was the irregularity of their alignment and the shop signs and awnings jutting out here and there. Misery lived here.

Malvina's carriage wormed its way through the city for over an hour before arriving at the Pont-au-Change. Here the merchant helped her climb down from her vantage point.

'I don't think I've asked you what you plan to do here in Paris,' he said as he handed her her baggage. 'I don't mean to play the police lieutenant. I'm just interested in figures.'

'What a strange hobby!'

'Figures are my passion, mademoiselle! Let me tell you about my latest estimations. Did you know that Savoyards are mostly woodcutters, that people from Limousin are masons, those from Lyon are sedan-chair bearers and porters, and Normans are generally stonecutters?'

'Stop there, sir. Do you mean to say that the entire kingdom is represented here?'

'Paris never stops drawing people in. The man from the provinces goes back home once a year, gives his wife another baby, leaves it in the hands of the old women and the priest and comes back to the capital hoping to become rich.'

'And does he?'

'As you've seen, there is as much poverty here as elsewhere. Let me warn you not to venture into the poorer quarters at night, for there you would be in great danger.'

'Perhaps you could help me avoid such an inconvenience by telling me the address of M. Dandora de Ghalia? He is an apothecary.'

'My dear child, there are dozens of apothecaries in Paris! Although I do come here regularly, I cannot know them all by name, as I do in Cahors.'

Then he added after a short pause, 'You should perhaps go to the market at Les Halles. When I sold wine there I saw many apothecaries come to buy their medicinal herbs. That is what you call them, isn't it?'

'It is indeed. What a shame you have so little time. I

would have liked to continue this conversation! For if your passion is for figures, mine is for plants!'

'I cannot linger,' he said. 'But it was indeed a great pleasure to make your acquaintance!'

He accompanied the remark with a bow, then pointed out the road that would take her to the market.

'Be careful,' he shouted as he waved goodbye. 'Crossing Paris is often like crossing a battlefield!'

Malvina thought this comment a little exaggerated, but later realized it was actually quite moderate. In the stale smell of the Marché des Innocents, there was so much activity the noise was deafening. Fishmongers, poultry sellers and butchers cried out from one end of the square to the other. 'Mackerel, fresh mackerel for sale!' 'Veal, lovely cuts of veal. Buy some veal!' Their cries jostled for attention and all tones of the human voice, from the shrillest to the deepest, could be heard. A deaf person would not have wished to regain his hearing in this place. All the senses were assaulted. The din would probably have made Malvina faint if the place had not provided such a marvellous opportunity for her to satisfy her curiosity.

Whenever Malvina found herself confronted with a new situation, her mouth would act as her guide. And today was no exception. She moved her tongue discreetly over her lips and found there an unknown taste. She had never experienced such a mixture. There were fresh fish, bunches of onions, bouquets of flowers and strong-smelling cabbages spread across the stalls, piled up in wicker baskets, sometimes even lying on the ground, where the gutter carried away discarded vegetables and scraps of meat. These smells revealed new tastes to be discovered, to be conquered. So this was the city? A sum of differences where the particular disappeared. The girl was dazzled and aroused by the idea of everything she could learn here.

Malvina had almost forgotten the aim of her journey until she spotted a stall displaying medicinal herbs. Borage, purslane, artemisia, chervil, coriander, hyssop, lemon balm and valerian were all on show there. She had never imagined there could be such a concentration of goods in one place.

'Come and have a gander. I'll certainly have what you're looking for! Some dry root? Sorrel is the perfect cure for the King's evil,' said the old woman who owned the stall.

She held out her goods as though they were silk ribbons. Her gestures were elegant, almost precious. 'It has a lovely colour, a lovely texture. Freshly picked this morning in Montreuil.'

'Montreuil?'

'I see from your clothes and your baggage that you've just arrived and have never heard of Montreuil. But that's where I bought all these nice things. Look at this strange fruit here with a funny crown on it! I bet you've never seen one of these before? A pineapple, that's what that is! And they say it's the English who brought it to France! Go on, have a little taste. It's famous and it grows in Montreuil!'

Malvina stared at her, dumbfounded. She realized how ignorant she herself was. A simple stallholder at Les Halles seemed to know more about plants and fruits than Hubertine and the Mother Superior put together!

'What do you do with lemon balm?' she asked to test the woman.

'It's a salutary herb that comforts the heart and the spirit, and you can make delicious cakes with it to soothe humours. You want some?'

'No,' she replied, vexed. 'But since you seem so well informed, perhaps you could tell me where I can find M. Dandora de Ghalia?'

'The Ottoman? I know him well.'

And, indeed, M. le comte Jean-Baptiste Dandora de Ghalia had become the most celebrated apothecary of the quarter. Some saw him as a genius, others as a charlatan, but he indisputably embodied a man of the Enlightenment. His discoveries were not listed in the *Dictionary of Scientific Revolutions* nor in any other reference work. But he had written over fifty books and manuscripts on medicine, pharmacology, astronomy, ethics and divination.

'His boutique is on Rue Saint-Honoré,' said the woman. 'About five minutes from here. Go back in the direction of the Seine and take the second street on your right. You can't miss it. It's right by the Pont-Neuf.'

Malvina thanked her and promised to come back and buy some things from her stall as soon as she got settled in the city.

*

Rue Saint-Honoré was one of the longest streets in Paris, but it did not take the girl long to reach her destination. The Golden Bee dispensary was in fact nearer to the Palais Royal than to the Place Vendôme. Its unusual frontage was clearly visible from afar. Above the shop sign was a life-size statue of Saint Nicholas, the patron saint of druggists, spice merchants and apothecaries. A thick purple carpet, into which was woven the coat of arms of M. le comte Jean-Baptiste Dandora de Ghalia, was spread out over the doorstep. Malvina, intimidated as much by the name as by the luxury of the façade, drew back a little. She wanted to admire the building's splendour from a different angle. It was three storeys tall and sported a majestic wrought-iron balcony. The blazing midday sun penetrated its immense windows to play on the crystal of the chandeliers inside. Two windows on street level, whose decor was inspired by the theme of the four seasons, played on the greed of passers-by and attempted to dazzle them with their display. Spread across a cloth of shimmering silk were sublime vases of blue faience, amphorae that might have been found at the bottom of the ocean and silver caskets inside which could be glimpsed crystals that were still imprisoned in their gangue. Worktops used by herbalists swung slowly back and forth on their chains. Malvina could not believe that her mother would have known a person of such importance.

An equipage drew up outside the dispensary, accompanied by three liveried footmen and two lackeys. A young woman stepped out of the carriage. She was dressed in a splendid Peking-blue camisole and a skirt edged with lace and embroidered with pink roses. She had to bend double to get though the door of the boutique because of the great height of her hat, a complex structure of cardboard, gauze and ribbons. Parisian elegance did indeed require some curious devices! Malvina smiled to herself at this eccentricity before examining her own reflection in the shop window. Her peasant garb betrayed her rustic origins, but a beholder would overlook this to focus on her slim waist and her breasts that seemed about to burst out of their bodice.

She knew she would fare badly if she were compared to the elegant client now inside the boutique, so she waited until she had finished her business there. When Malvina did finally enter the shop, which was smoke-filled and saturated with indefinable smells, a man who had been sitting behind the counter jumped up and walked towards her. His well-groomed appearance told her that this must be M. le comte Jean-Baptiste Dandora de Ghalia himself. He wore a carmelite jacket with red stripes, an indigo satin waistcoat with polished steel buttons and square-toed shoes. The dandy image was completed by a beard the colour of mother-of-pearl, a fine face and a narrow nose bearing a pair of spectacles.

'What can I do for you?' he asked in an affected voice.

Malvina, unable to decide how to introduce herself, replied that she was thinking.

'An apothecary's shop has never been noted as a place where people come to think, but please do carry on, mademoiselle. The smell of narcotics is undoubtedly most intoxicating.'

'Monsieur, I really do not know how to begin.'

'Begin at the beginning, for goodness' sake, and you won't go far wrong.'

She thrust out her chest, cleared her throat and began, 'My name is Malvina.'

'Malvina?' said the apothecary, raising his glasses up over his forehead. His little blue eyes, beaming with intelligence and malice, stared at the girl. 'No, that doesn't mean anything to me.'

'Malvina Raynal,' she added. 'I'm Marie's daughter.'

The count tried for a moment to remember this name, but in vain.

'I have more memories than a man who is a thousand years old,' he said. 'Perhaps you could relate an anecdote, or remind me of some fact that may have marked our encounter?'

Malvina took her mother's book from her bag and handed it to the count. A look of recognition flashed across his face. He leafed through it, passing his hand slowly over each page as if to absorb its presence. A smile began to play on his lips. He was clearly moved.

'Come over here,' he said, leading Malvina to the counter. 'Sit down and tell me about your mother. Why isn't she with you today?'

'She is dead, Monsieur. She died six years ago.'

The apothecary took her hand and placed it in his own. There was a pause before she went on.

'Disease took both her and my father.'

'I know the sorrow caused by the death of a loved one. Nothing can ease the pain. It is but a poor consolation to think that because the dead are in our thoughts, they can never really die.'

'This book bears your name,' said Malvina. 'I thought it would be a good idea to find you.'

'You thought right.'

He picked up the book again.

'Marie was a strange child. Adorable but strange. I do believe that you look very much like her. She was only seven years old when I saw her last. That must have been in 1739. Yes, that's right. I was playing cards a lot at the time. Your grandfather, M. de Bertignac, was a magnificent player. And an excellent cheat! If I'm not mistaken, it was when I was paying off a debt to him that he invited me to come and stay at his residence in Saint Malo.'

Malvina listened with bated breath. The man's words overwhelmed her. He was telling her story, the story of her ancestors of whom she knew nothing. Her mother had rarely spoken to her about her own childhood or about her parents. And now, suddenly, a stranger was filling in all the things she had never known. To learn that she was the grandchild of a cheat was not something she could be proud of. But she was fascinated to discover that, on her mother's side, was a social status she had never suspected. Only the wealthy could afford to lose at cards or to invite aristocrats to come and stay with them.

'We never saw each other again,' the count went on.

'But I am here,' said Malvina, huddling up as if to take up the smallest amount of space possible. 'I've just arrived in Paris and I have nowhere to go.'

This appeal silenced Dandora de Ghalia. He had always helped out any friend in need, but this girl was a stranger to him. And she was clearly, unlike her mother, a coarse peasant.

'I understand your hesitation,' said Malvina. 'My parents left me nothing, and all I can offer you is the strength of my youth.'

'And youth, little though you know it, is the most precious of all things. Indeed, it is the only thing worth possessing.'

Layers of powder, touched with make-up and vermilion, covered the count's face and masked the ravages of time. Malvina knew that the fire that burned inside her and her thirst for knowledge would seduce this man who still knew passion despite his age.

'I was brought up in Cahors by the Sisters of Charity,' she said. 'The nuns taught me well. And when I worked in the hospice there I learnt all about plants, their characteristics and their properties. I will, if you so wish, allow you to test me on my knowledge.'

The count's eyes sparkled with amusement. 'Perhaps later. Go on, I'm listening!'

'Of course, I still have a lot to learn,' said Malvina. 'And I hope to be able to draw on great experience and wisdom, just like our king, if you will permit the comparison.'

The man smiled. The girl did not lack audacity, but she seemed unaware of two important facts. The first was that the profession of apothecary required a very long training period – four years of apprenticeship under a master, then six more years as a journeyman. The second was that women were excluded from the métier.

'I cannot take you on as an apprentice,' he said.

'But I know how to make preparations. I know the secrets of plants and fruits. Listen! To protect the skin from harsh weather, it should be rubbed with a cream made of apples and ground almonds. It's an old recipe from my region, and just one of hundreds that I know! Oh, master, let me work for you!'

Her tone of voice let it be known that this was not a request, but a demand.

The count settled down into an armchair, crossed his legs and leaned his head to one side before assuming his customary air of false severity.

'Don't think that you've found paradise here. The limits you set yourself will be a lot more severe than any I would be able to impose on you. Your desire for knowledge will make you docile, work will extinguish your idle thoughts and fatigue will stifle your anger. When curiosity is aroused by scientific discoveries, it leads one to seek out that which is marvellous and which is worth believing in. It is in this spirit that I conduct my research.'

Malvina did not know how she could enter the new universe that lay open before her. But she did know that no obstacle would prevent her from carrying out the count's orders.

'I want to work for you,' she repeated.

'Well, then, you will have to amend some of your ways. You cannot work for me if you don't display to the world the honour that has been accorded you. A person's bearing should always have something majestic and grand about it. You must never stoop, but walk with pride. But you must not be haughty. Let us try you out on Alcibiade. If he takes you for a companion of one of the fine ladies who are kind enough to give me their custom, then we will have succeeded. If not, then we will simply have to work to achieve perfection for you.'

'Alcibiade!' he cried. 'Alcibiade!'

There was no reply.

'Alcibiade!'

Disobeying the instructions the count had just given her, Malvina twisted and turned to try to see the person who would respond to this call, which was apparently addressed to the floor. Was someone about to emerge from the cellar through a trapdoor? Dandora's assistant finally appeared from between two lots of boxes piled into pyramids. The girl was well used to the vengeful aggressions of nature, but she could not prevent herself being shocked at what she now saw before her. Not only was Alcibiade minuscule, no bigger than a six-year-old child, but his chest protruded like that of a bird and his back was wrenched up into a hideous hump. A long tunic did what it could to hide his deformed body, but it did not cover his misshapen feet and it seemed that at any moment he might fall flat on his face.

'How can I help you, madame?' he asked after bowing to Malvina.

She could not take her eyes off the dwarf's face. From it shone a powerful, seductive, almost magical charm. It was truly beautiful, it was the head of an Adonis. Long lashes and pearl-coloured lids sheltered its jade green, sparkling eyes. Its high forehead suggested excessive generosity, its firm chin hinted at great strength of will.

'How can I help you?' he repeated.

It was the apothecary who replied.

'Show my new pupil around the dispensary.'

The little man nodded his head, then invited the girl to follow him.

'Are you ready for the visit?'

'Yes,' she replied. 'I'm ready to see all there is to be seen and all that is hidden, too!'

The Golden Bee was divided into sections corresponding to the four cosmic elements: earth, air, water and fire. There was the shop, the laboratory, the stockroom where the compositions were fermented and the warehouse. The cellar and the attic were also made use of, according to whether a dry or a humid place was required, to work in or as an extra storeroom.

'Let me first draw your attention,' said Alcibiade, adopting an exaggerated tone of voice, 'to the room in which we now find ourselves. And let me tell you that, after the Hôtel-Dieu, this is one of the top dispensaries in Paris. Our jars are made in the prestigious factory at Sceaux!'

The walls were lined with dark wooden shelves which held a hundred earthenware jars. The heaviest were stored at the bottom, explained the dwarf, and those holding plants were kept nearer the top. Unlike the more crudely made ones Malvina had seen at the hospice, these were varied in shape and were sumptuously decorated. Some displayed floral garlands, bouquets of cornflowers and friezes of palm leaves and branches. The heraldic arms of the count were painted in celadon on every jar. Malvina drew closer to read the inscriptions that described the nature of the preparations: theriac, damask rose-water, vitriol from Cyprus, bole armeniac, senna, scammony and cassia from the Levant in bottles of burnished metal.

'The master is of Turkish origin,' explained Alcibiade. 'We import most of our goods from the East, from the New World and from the colonies.'

Malvina would later learn that Jean-Baptiste Dandora de Ghalia had arrived in France when he was five years old under the tutelage of the marquis de Bonnac, the ambassador of the Sublime Porte. Bonnac grew very fond of the orphan he had adopted, and never once had cause to regret his act of kindness. The boy lived up to all the expectations the marquis had of him. After a brilliant career as a student of medicine in Bologna, London and later Paris, he went on to become chief surgeon of the hospitals of Antwerp, before triumphantly joining the Berry-Cavalerie regiment as army surgeon. In 1758, Dandora de Ghalia, weary of the army and shattered by the death of his adoptive father, turned his attentions towards pharmacology and opened an apothecary's in Paris. His contacts in high places enabled him not only to retain his titles – his great love of science was enough to convince the king – but also to build up a brilliant clientele that was very much in favour with the sovereign.

'If it pleases you, we can proceed to the laboratory,' said the dwarf as he led the girl towards another room whose entrance was closed off by a red velvet curtain.

A fireplace was the centrepiece of this lair that was kept hidden from the eyes of the public. Around it sat several tables on which were laid out copper and cast-iron cauldrons, tweezers, sieves, steelyards and weighing scales, almond presses, albarellos, and vases used for the making of pills. A man was pulverizing drugs in a mortar, while another was distilling something at a furnace.

'What is the quintessence that is coming out of this retort?' asked Malvina.

'That is "mirabilia magna". It's a liquid produced by the distillation of the human liver.'

The girl could not hide her surprise.

'I cannot yet tell if your palate is refined enough to work here, but your disgust is unmistakeable!'

Malvina hated being laughed at for her ignorance. She made a great effort not to lose her composure as she walked towards a board on which pages ripped out of an old book of magic had been pinned up. She was well used to reading the recipes and formulae of alchemy, but these were incomprehensible to her. Someone had used a pen to correct the printed characters and in many places scribbled notes made the text impossible to read.

'Don't worry,' said Alcibiade. 'Master Dandora is both an inventor and a reformer. He is interested only in experiment and research. He regards the works of his predecessors merely as a point of reference, or a playground.'

Malvina was beginning to get a clearer picture of the count's personality. His extravagance came not from any coquetry, but was simply the expression of his enormous curiosity. The more Malvina learnt about pharmacology, the stronger was her belief that she could find here in Paris all that she had ever wanted – novelty, a world of differences and, above all, knowledge. The thought delighted her. Here she would observe all the city had to offer, and observing would be like drinking the most succulent of elixirs.

They next went to the storeroom which housed the animal matter. Here the bodies of reptiles fermented in stoneware jars and glass flasks, and insects were pinned onto boards around the room. Some of these reminded her of the drawings her mother had made in her book. There was death in their postures of crucifixion! Was it possible that, as a child, Marie had already felt her life was a prison, that she would have to fight to avoid ending up like one of these insects skewered to a piece of cork? Malvina promised herself she would one day ask the count about this.

'Spider purée is much sought after by women who would like to see a slim body when they look in the mirror,' continued Alcibiade. 'They take several potions a day at fixed times. The less desperate prefer a paste that we make up from Indian nuts, almonds, pistachios, pine kernels, melon pips, partridge flesh and sugar.'

'Are there still more wonders hidden in other rooms?' asked Malvina.

'I can, if you wish, show you our collection of mineral

products. But don't mention this to the master. It will be our first secret!'

Her smile reassured him.

The spiral staircase they descended was narrow and shaky. The dripping walls showed that they were now below the level of the Seine. Malvina wondered if it was the damp or a decomposing animal that was the source of the disgusting smell. She was about to ask Alcibiade when she noticed a tiny door set into the stone wall.

'That's where the stench is coming from,' she told herself as she covered her nose with the back of her hand.

'Pray to God that you will never have cause to go in there!' said the dwarf in a tone of voice which showed that he did not seek a reply. His eyes had opened a little wider and his breath had become quicker. 'The master would put you straight out of the door if he ever caught you there. Follow me. Our minerals are kept in here.'

He showed her selenite in whose silver sheen could be seen the different phases of the moon, sunstone studded with luminous yellow dots, and alexandrite whose blue-green colour became raspberry red when a flame was held near it. Malvina tried to show interest in the things he was pointing out to her, but she was so intrigued by the mystery of the room she could not concentrate.

'Are you listening to me? I can stop now if you like!'

'No, please, go on! What are rubies used for?' she asked to encourage him to finish his lesson.

'When they are made into a powder and mixed with water, they can soothe eye complaints or dropsy. Topaz can be used to treat problems with the blood, sapphire elixir eases pain, and hyacinth is said to protect against the plague.'

Malvina was captivated by the beauty of the precious stones.

'You will notice,' continued the dwarf, 'that the master always wears an emerald.'

'Does the colour green have a particular value?'

'Of course! It wards off ill fortune.'

Alcibiade suddenly turned to face her.

'We must go back upstairs now,' he said. 'The master is calling'

They returned to the dispensary, where Alcibiade slipped away.

'Let us finish the tour together,' said the apothecary, taking Malvina by the hand. 'I'll show you to your room.'

A vaulted corridor led to a townhouse of imposing proportions. Its rich decoration, like that of the boutique, was baroque in character. But the style of the opulent furniture revealed clear oriental influences, and there was a multitude of carpets made in the Savonnerie workhouse or imported from the orient. Intricately curved lines domin-ated the rooms. Jean-Baptiste Dandora de Ghalia, a man of taste and leisure, had spared no expense to make his residence into a place to which all those in Paris of wit and learning would vie to be invited. Renowned artists had been employed to help him fulfil his ambitions. The painter Robert depicted his interpretations of mythology, while Boucher painted delightful frescos of country life. A vast gallery was lined with bacchanalian scenes, antique statues and busts of sultans. For the first time in her life,

Malvina saw a dining room. 'Catherine II of Russia used this as a model for her summer residence,' the count explained. On the walls, which were covered in purple silk, hung paintings from the Flemish school. And on the credence tables and dressers, illuminated by a chandelier of Bohemian crystal, sat vases made of porphyry, agate, jasper and rare porcelain.

*

In the next room she saw a marble stove and bookshelves that held several hundred books. She ran her fingers over their shagreen with green and red morocco bindings. Then, without turning to look at him, she asked the count, 'Will you tell me what was in the book you gave my mother?'

Malvina was certain there was a link between this place and the crimes perpetrated at her parents' inn.

'I don't think it was about poison,' she said as if to answer her own question.

'I would not want to imitate Brinvilliers. The art of poisoning is one I leave to women, whose treachery knows no bounds. No, the book was about my research into remedies that lessen suffering. It was particularly concerned with the medicinal uses to which the poppy can be put.'

So Marie was not the poisoner Rougemont had tried so hard to make Malvina believe she was. What harm was there in simply putting customers to sleep? The only choice that Gabert had given her was as to the manner in which she could help him. Malvina remembered that he had often threatened to kill her mother if she did not obey him.

'Why did you call it *Le Secret des secrets de la nature?*' she asked.

'Because the book is about producing wondrous effects using only natural means. In it I denounce the ignoble magic that has recourse to charms and illusions. I prefer to delve into the secret powers of the universe! But how pale you are!' added the apothecary when he noticed the girl's face grow suddenly troubled. 'It is probably exhaustion. We shall leave the tour of my private apartments for another time and go straight to the kitchen.'

The kitchen, thirty feet long and eighteen broad, was laid out like a stage. The daylight that flooded in from on high mingled with the flames of the fireplace which was the centre and soul of the room. To its left were three blue earthenware stoves used for making broths and sauces and for cooking meat or dishes that required close attention. Next to these was yet another stove, this time made of copper, a large mortar, and two taps which drew water from a cistern. Malvina had never seen such an arsenal of kitchen utensils. There were copper and tinplate pots, casseroles, hot chocolate jugs, cutlery and plates everywhere she looked. At one side of the room were two worktables next to which was a pantry that held lard, eggs, cheese, milk, bacon, vinegar and verjuice.

'If Hubertine could see this!' said Malvina as she ran her hand over the furniture.

'Hubertine?'

'She was the cook in the hospice.'

'Was she the woman who taught you about herbs and plants?'

Malvina nodded.

'She also taught me how to cook,' she bragged.

'The two are very closely linked. There are a great many dishes that can soothe the soul as much as the stomach.'

'Hubertine always told me that just as the nightingale can sing without ever having learnt to do so, I have the gift of being able to tell which savours would create the perfect harmony when mixed together.'

The count looked at her, intrigued.

'I've just had an idea,' he said. 'I myself have done a lot of work on savours. My wife, the countess, helped me in my research. But she unfortunately died two years ago when she inhaled cyanide fumes. I found her corpse right where you are now standing.'

Malvina took a step back.

'Don't worry. Her ghost no longer haunts the house.'

Then, almost in a murmur, he added, 'There are many who are driven to distraction by love. You will perhaps learn this yourself one day.'

The girl merely looked at him. Love did not figure in any of her plans. Leaving Hubertine behind her had also meant shutting out the world of the emotions. She now aspired to achieving nothing more than a feeling of indifference towards her fellows.

'Your coming has awoken in me the desire to conclude what the countess and I began. The knowledge that I possess and your culinary gifts would not, separately, result in very much. But together they might revolutionize our epoch. The time will come when I will yield to you my secret, which is the art of cooking the dead.'

What did he mean by this 'art of cooking the dead'? Malvina was desperate to know but dared not ask, especially since the count now seemed to have drifted off into his thoughts. He stood there stroking his beard as if this would help shed light on the mysteries he was contemplating.

'Yes, this is indeed a very attractive prospect,' he said.

He showed her to her room, which was quite spacious, if lacking the luxury of his own apartments. Its furniture consisted of a bed, a table and a chest of drawers on which sat a clock in the shape of a globe. The room's bookshelves were overflowing and on the floor was a pile of books on surgery. On the walls she saw anatomical plates, the largest of which showed an ancient Greek athlete. He was leaning forward and the top of his skull was open, revealing the two hemispheres of his brain. The sight gave the girl a headache, as if her own brain had suddenly felt the need to remind her of its existence.

'This was my son Matthieu's room for many years,' explained the count. 'He's living abroad at the moment. I'll leave you to get settled in. Alcibiade will call you when supper is ready.'

Chapter Six

Malvina had time only to unpack her belongings and look out of the window to see the thousand square foot garden in the courtyard when Alcibiade came to knock on her door. Before accompanying her to supper, he took her to a vast chamber that was used both to store linen and as a changing room. Those who worked for comte Dandora wore a uniform he had designed himself. This was one of the man's whims, of which Malvina was to see many more.

'I'll throw your rags onto the fire,' said the dwarf as he pointed to a screen behind which she was to get changed. 'Take your time. I shall wait for you in the corridor.'

The fine cotton of the green and white gown caressed her skin. It was fastened with a bow high above her breasts, and its sleeves reached only as far as her elbows. The skirt was shorter than usual for the fashion of the time and was lined on both sides with buttons. Malvina twirled around like a peacock spreading its tail. Then she looked at herself in the cheval glass and saw that her metamorphosis had begun.

She was led to the dining room, where the count rose to welcome her as though she was a prestigious visitor.

'You look delightful,' he said. 'It is a treat to be able to taste with one's eyes a fruit that has yet to ripen! Please take a seat.'

Malvina felt intimidated. The count sensed her unease and to lessen it continued talking, presenting each of the dishes and wines to her as they were brought to the table. There was cooked Bayonne ham, meat from Vierzon and dates from the Levant, all of which was accompanied by fine wines and followed by delicious desserts. The girl looked at the food but did not dare touch it. She noticed the dwarf sitting in a corner of the room eating a simple bowl of chestnuts boiled in milk.

'Despite being twenty-five years old,' said the master, 'Alcibiade is still quite a child. He lives only off the leaven that governs the mechanisms of birth, growth and regeneration. He believes that milk can both sublimate learned souls and fortify the hypertrophic bodies of the Cyclops. All sweet things are for him the expression of natural forces which man must obey. But you must eat, mademoiselle. You must make the most of the privilege you are being offered here because the task which awaits will plunge you into a universe not quite so pleasing to your palate!'

Malvina frowned.

'Did you not say you wanted me to become your cook?'

'I want no one but myself and Alcibiade to see you, my dear Malvina.'

This was the first time he had addressed her by her name.

'Please don't think I am being possessive. I simply want my efforts to have the greatest impact.'

'Forgive me, master, but I do not understand.'

'You shall remain in the shadows until the time has come for you to take up your position in the world. And this position will not be that of cook, but of culinary expert in the realm of taste.'

Malvina still did not understand.

'You will be an expert on all the possible tastes the human tongue can experience,' he said slowly as though he were reading out a dictionary definition. 'It was your mother who, more than twenty years ago, inspired me with her passion for the taste of things. As for your grandfather, his zeal was reserved for gambling. But I've already told you about that.'

'Tell me more.'

'Your grandmother was a discreet woman. Your grandfather, on the other hand, loved the arts and loved luxury. I never found out what it was that made them leave France – probably their debts – but our last meeting was, and I remember it well, a very curious affair.

'When we arrived,' the count went on, 'our hosts asked us to forgive them for not being able to receive us as they would have wished. They were in the middle of moving and their daughter had just fallen ill. It was only on the eve of our departure that Marie's health had improved sufficiently for her to be able to join us at supper. As soon as she entered the dining room, she ran straight over to me and made me taste her fingers.'

Malvina could feel the salt of tears on her lips.

'A different taste for each finger,' she managed to say despite the lump in her throat.

'Exactly. Her thumb was covered in a bitter jelly that tasted of sorrow. Her index finger was coated with a preserve that symbolized tenderness. And so on until her little finger, which was dripping with fresh milk. She wanted me to adopt her.'

Malvina stared down at her plate and thought of how different things would have been if the count had agreed to this proposition. Marie would not have ended up with the cousins in Quercy who had given her such a harsh upbringing after her parents fled the country. Nor would she have married that cock-of-the-walk Gabert Raynal! He was well off, to be sure, but he was also so violent that no father, however mercenary, would let him have the hand of his daughter.

'For years I was haunted by the image!' said the count. 'I have never been able to forget the look in her eyes.'

He now saw the same look in Malvina. The girl even had the same madness in her eyes, the same sensual lips. Or did the uncanny resemblance merely make him imagine this? The meal drew to an end in silence. The apothecary spoke only to tell Alcibiade to serve the tea.

Malvina observed the dwarf as he strutted about like some high priest carrying out an important ritual. On a wooden stool inlaid with mother-of-pearl he placed a silver tray bearing a teapot, multicoloured fondants, a sugar bowl from which protruded a pair of tongs and a bouquet of roses. The dwarf then began to serve the count and the girl with balletic movements. The elixir flowed in golden arabesques and filled the glasses with the colour of topaz.

'Drink, I beg you. While Versailles has recently become

enamoured of coffee, I find that there is still nothing more exquisite than tea.'

Malvina took a sip. The liquid appeared no different from any other herbal tea, but its powerful flavours penetrated her very soul.

'I feel as though I am in the centre of a whirlwind,' she murmured.

'Enjoy it, my dear, for tomorrow we must get down to business! We have two things to do. The first is to give you an education worthy of your name. And because dear Jean-Jacques Rousseau has made fashionable the natural and the authentic, this task will be far easier. The second is to set up a laboratory for you to work in. There you are to experiment, to research, to find the formula which will enable us to give a pleasing taste to things that are contemptuous and repugnant.'

Malvina could not understand this. The count was about to put her back into a world that was familiar to her, for in the hospice Hubertine had made use of the same techniques in her cooking. But it was unthinkable that a man of quality, a man who was rich enough to buy the rarest, most expensive things, could be more interested in the ugly than the beautiful. The girl had already been dreaming about the wonderful things she would be able to cook here in her new home. She had imagined herself seasoning poultry with lemon-scented radula or perfuming marzipan cakes with daisy petals.

'You must always remember that the simple is immortal, and the complex is but fleeting,' explained the count.

'So you do not hold the art of cooking to be one of life's pleasures?'

'It is not a question of pleasure, but scientific research,' he replied.

*

It was a long, hard month before Malvina grew accustomed to the rhythm of her new life, to the exhausting cycle of deportment and pronunciation lessons, and the perpetual demands of the apothecary. He would make her study late into the night and would often subject her to sudden interrogations on what she had learnt. Malvina's day began at dawn with two hours of natural history and chemistry lessons. As the art of cooking drew from many different sources, her apprenticeship was rounded off by the study of many specialized works: *De materia medica* by Dioscorides, *Regimen Sanitatis Salernitatis* by Arnaud de Villeneuve, *The Chemistry of Taste and of Smell* by Père Poncelet, and the botanical writings of Bernard de Jussieu. She would also frequently consult recipes in the indispensable *Delights of the Countryside* by Nicolas de Bonnefons, *The Royal and Bourgeois Chef* by Massialot, and Menon's *A New Treatise on the Art of Cooking*.

At seven o'clock, Malvina headed for the scramble of the markets. There she faced being crushed by passing carriages as she haggled with the stallholders. When it rained, water fell from the roofs onto the ragged piles on the stalls, where the best of the fruit sat next to the worst. Malvina wanted to buy the bright, sweet-smelling carrots, the beautifully shaped beans or the tender, curling parsley. But she was under strict orders from the count. 'Only buy what is repugnant! Only what is repugnant!' So she chose wrinkled apples, overripe pears and cabbages or any vegetable beginning to go mouldy. She would buy withered roots and rotten leafage. In the market hall, where the deleterious activity of bacteria knew no limits, putrefaction was so rapid that a lettuce could go off within hours, and courgettes, fermented by the heat, would decompose on being touched. The tripe butcher kept the cheapest scraps for her – offal, leftovers and the unwholesome saveloy meat he sold at eighteen sous a pound. She would never refuse the remains reserved for beggars nor the bones normally given to dogs. And at the fishmonger's she would likewise buy for a trivial sum fish heads and innards.

Malvina was expected to produce delicious dishes from these coarse, battered goods. She often thought of Hubertine when she was cooking. She now saw that her friend had been right when she said that many of the things considered unworthy could – once they did not pose any risk to the health – produce unexpected treasures. If one could discard one's prejudices, a whole new universe would open up to reveal new textures to be exploited and new, 'stronger' tastes to be explored. Malvina did not know why Dandora wanted her to undertake this curious exercise. But she was happy to carry out his wishes and worked hard in her dark laboratory to give birth to the most subtle of transmutations. Her spirit was dedicated to perfection, and she succeeded in taking the most humble of substances, sublimating them and extracting from them their very essence. She took what was small and made it big, the abject she made noble, she subtilized the coarser parts of foodstuffs, refined them, purified them, spiritualized them. And when she was finished, there would often be nothing to reveal the origin of her creation. Malvina became an intransigent priestess of the liturgy of taste. She found that even her own palate could now be fooled by her concoctions, when, for example, she realized that she could no longer tell the difference between thyme and marjoram or between asparagus and bamboo shoots.

The count would slip into the kitchen every day at around three o'clock, but he would always wait a few moments before letting Malvina know he was there. He loved to watch her move around the room, from one saucepan to the next, with her sleeves and her skirt hitched up so they wouldn't get in her way. She would constantly wipe her hands on the apron that covered her stomach. Two, three or four times on each side. It was as though she used this time to plan the numerous tasks she had to carry out. There was no lack of words to describe these duties. She had to braise, chop, mill, marinate and fry. Malvina had to become a magician, if not an alchemist, in her quest to transform the substances she handled. No sooner would she have finished extracting aroma from a mushroom than she would have to begin work on a piece of tough old meat. The count liked to surprise her, to see the exasperated expression on her face when he asked if everything was ready. He came to the kitchen to analyse the *chefs-d'œuvre* of culinary ingenuity the girl was creating.

The master and his pupil would also engage in blind tasting. They sniffed each dish, tasted it, dissected it and then wrote down their observations in a special notebook. During their subsequent discussions they soon began to digress and in their digression wandered so far from their original path that they would often arrive at some startling destinations. Dandora was at pains to impress upon his new ward the importance of memory. 'Memory is the curiosity cabinet of the gourmet,' he would say. He made Malvina carry out mnemonic exercises and then tested her progress every Thursday. She would memorize the tastes of various foods by linking to them a story, a fact or a person. Blindfolded, she then had to taste whatever her employer put in her mouth and tell him what it was.

'Of the five senses that we normally talk about, taste is the most neglected,' declared the apothecary. 'The idealist tradition prioritizes sight and hearing. It is true that these two senses have the advantage of mediation, but they deal only with images and sounds, which have little to do with substance. Taste, on the other hand, involves the entire body. It involves chewing, swallowing, digesting and excreting. I share this opinion with materialists such as Diderot and hedonists like La Mettrie, who accord to each of the senses an equal dignity.'

These learned words showed Malvina that men of science shared what she felt instinctively. They told her that those who concerned themselves with taste would never be remembered as satraps. The quest for a rare spice or a precious flavour might not be a noble end in itself, but the infinitely large field of taste was as worthy an area in which to explore the future as was poetic or musical creation. Indeed, it was not rare at the time to see important persons at court holding forth on what they called good and bad taste. Fashion required one to be a lover of fine food, and it was not those who were hungry one felt sorry for, but those who ate badly.

Malvina loved to listen to or read these speeches. But for her, taste remained a question of nature, of sensations and emotions to touch the heart and soul. She compared taste with an abyss whose depths could be fathomed only by leaping into it. At dinner, which was now taken in the kitchen, she always made sure that Alcibiade sat opposite her so that she might observe the slight contortion in his mouth. She loved the disturbing, irresistible curl in the middle of his upper lip. There was no beauty in the dwarf's body. But he had a seductive quality that came from the ambiguity of his face, which alternated between surprise and affection, and from which were absent any signs of physical desire or greed. His infirmity raised him above other men. He was at once lover, father and brother.

Malvina loved to watch him eat. She was convinced that each of his gestures was the expression of a feeling. Education had refined him, but this did not explain the extreme delicacy and sensuality with which Alcibiade nourished himself. His mouth had forgotten the barbarism of ancient times. It neither gobbled nor ground its food, but seduced it in a game of love.

'Have you revised your lessons on the different phases of taste?'

The count was testing his pupil, as he did every evening. His obsession amused Malvina.

'Are you listening to me?' Dandora repeated irritably.

Malvina's attention had indeed been focused elsewhere. Did the count really think that talk of papillae, of bitterness or of acidity could be more interesting than looking at Alcibiade? She had changed over the last few months. One summer's day she had felt the heat of the sun on her skin. It had been caressing her for fifteen years now, but this was the first time she really felt it. And she understood why. Or, at least, she thought she did. Its intensity reminded her of the miracle of light that was Alcibiade's smile. If Malvina spent long hours watching the crackling embers in the fireplace, it was because she believed the little man's lips would burn her in the same way. An ardent, unrestrainable desire had been born in her. A fire had been lit in her flesh, had set her body ablaze and was moving through her veins like a flow of lava. She was faced with an absolute, shameful temptation.

In her dreams, Malvina would go to Alcibiade as he slept curled up in a ball. Without waking him, her eyes would caress each of his features in turn before coming to rest on his mouth. She was fascinated by the delicate design of the tender, appetizing and generous lips whose sensuality made her forget the disability of his body. She felt an irresistible desire to take him in her arms, to kiss him, to touch the skin that was as soft as a summer fruit and feel its warmth against her body. She gently took the child-man's hand and led it towards her expectant, ready-to-be-devoured breasts. She felt his tongue and his breath on her chest and then his sharp teeth on her nipples. Alcibiade was playing with her flesh as he consumed it. He found no maternal milk – nature refused him that – but he was able to taste and to absorb a single substance, a musk-perfumed pulp. But the bites he inflicted with a furious voluptuousness left no marks. Malvina did not suffer in any way as she submitted herself with total abandon to the dwarf's advances. She was offering herself up to be tasted, but was also an equal participant in the scene for she was infusing life into Alcibiade. The more he drew from her, the happier she became. There was neither victor nor vanquished here. A vital and reciprocal link united them and carried them away to the outer edges of madness.

'What are you thinking about?' asked the count. 'Your cheeks are quite red!'

'The tongue, master. I'm thinking about the tongue!'

'One must concede that it is nothing less than a masterpiece!'

'It is like a strip of velvet,' said Malvina.

'You are absolutely right. There are thousands of papillae, yet each one has a distinct role.'

The girl stared at the apothecary's mouth. In her mind she saw him chewing his food, saw it move into his throat, then down his digestive tract before finally making a triumphant entry in his stomach.

'Is there a stain on my jacket? Why are you looking at me like that?'

'I am trying, master, to look inside you as though your skin were made of glass.'

'A very peculiar idea, mademoiselle. Do you not find it somewhat insolent, Alcibiade?'

The dwarf rarely spoke, but this evening he did not hesitate to respond.

'The senses are linked to the heart and one should not contradict them. I understand very well what Malvina is trying to say.'

When the girl withdrew to her room and began to think about her new life, she realized it was making her very happy. Now, when she thought about the world, she felt that she too had a part to play in it. In this new role of hers, in which she used shoddy ingredients and simple criteria to produce the most delicious of dishes, she had begun to glimpse a different destiny for herself. She now had no adversaries to fight off. There was no longer a vacuum to be filled. Perhaps the pact she had made with the lizards and snakes that summer on the Gramat plateau, and the nightmares when death appeared to her, perhaps these were of a time now gone. She could now envisage a life that would be tolerable. She could see an existence for herself that would be like the rustling of wind through leaves, as airy as mist descending on the fields in the freshness of dawn.

When everyone in the house was asleep, Malvina got up, lit a candle and opened the door to a phantom visitor. 'Come into the drawing room. Do you find me to your liking, my dear friend? Splendid? Thank you.' She had recently become much concerned with her physical appearance. The count had given her a few measures of powdered brick to scrub her teeth with and some alum and nut bark to give a sheen to her hair, and she had now decided to make use of these gifts.

*

One day Malvina was working on a 'pure' taste when Dandora marched into the kitchen brandishing a pretty box tied up with a ribbon.

'It's a dress,' he declared as he put the package down on the table.

'A dress?' she repeated, astonished. 'But I couldn't accept it!'

'I am satisfied with your services. But as I don't think I should have to pay you a wage, I thought this present might please you. One has to place one's order with Mlle Bertin at least a week in advance because these days it is so fashionable to wear theatrical gowns.'

'May I open it?' she asked impatiently.

'I fear we'll have to make you wait a little! You shall open it when I decide there is an appropriate occasion to wear it.'

Although he was intransigent in his dealings with her, Malvina was growing more fond of her employer as each day passed. She had begun to learn what the love of a father was. There were few displays of emotion or tender gestures, but his trust in her filled her with joy. What she loved about him was his ability to poach inventions, to avoid taking any paths that had been marked out in advance.

'I don't know how to thank you,' she said. 'But let me tell you something which I think will please you.'

'Speak quickly,' said the count as Malvina went back to work on her mixture, 'M. Turgot's doctor has sent for me! The minister of state and controller of finances is being tormented by gout. It appears they are carrying him to council, where the King has let him sit in his own chair, the only one there.'

'When you return I shall have the honour of letting you sample a taste that existed when the world was but a few hours old. It is the taste of the Garden of Eden.'

'A paradise that the corruption of the world has not sullied? How marvellous! I shall return as quickly as I can,' he said, and kissed her on the forehead.

The count was proud of his pupil. She had learnt to extract from each substance its essence and its quintessence, to tame the taste of food and take from it its vital juices, its telesm.

It was her work on meat, all those hours spent at furnaces, which had led her towards the necessary formula. She had spent innumerable nights improving on what had gone before, eliminating the inessential, making fresh starts. Her research demanded that she accumulate much knowledge and experience. She had to do endless sampling, make countless preparations, classify the substances she used and reduce them to basic components. Doubt would often discourage her and make her gestures feverish. It was no easy matter to pluck out the tiniest fragment of purity from the most repugnant of substances. She felt she would never discover the supreme taste, the osmazome of the alchemists. But her tenacity and will pushed her on. She discovered 'pure' taste the day she decided go against logic and putrefy and mortify flesh before purifying it. This proved to be an indispensable step, one which took her work into the darkness before bringing it back to the light again. It permitted the necessary liquefaction to be carried out and thus enabled a better dissolution of the substance. The heat of the water in the saucepan bloated the muscular fibres of the meat and broke up the gelatine that was locked inside. The tastiest part of the meat would then make the broth unctuous and the albumin would expand and rise up to the surface as a light froth. Her hand would bring the wooden spoon a hundred times to her mouth so that she could taste the precious liquid. Her mouth, anaesthetized by the heat of the dishes she cooked, was no longer capable of recognizing that which she had initially thought she had identified. All her papillae had been burnt, but she still was able to achieve a result. She had made a sauce so perfect, of such finesse, that she felt it was comparable to an elixir that would grant long life to whoever imbibed it, to a panacea, to liquid gold. By drinking it, people would find themselves glorified.

*

Malvina could have further refined her invention. But she preferred instead to profit from the count's absence by preparing in Alcibiade's honour the most magnificent of dinners. She set out the kitchen table in the manner she had seen in the cabarets and restaurants of the Palais Royal. On it she placed an embroidered tablecloth, silver cutlery, a Bohemian crystal carafe and two candelabra. She wanted nothing to appear in her creation that might seem banal, so she decided against serving Bayonne ham, cooked tongues from Vierzon or the exotic almonds that could be bought at the Aligre market, that temple of sweetmeats. She instead prepared perfumed, puréed chestnuts. And she remembered the dwarf's predilection for milk and decided to serve this instead of wine.

The evening they spent together was punctuated with exquisite moments of emotion. The dwarf was faced with a barrage of questions from the girl. She admired his ability to overcome his hatred for a world that had marked him out from his fellow man. Instead of revolting, he had chosen to tame his emotions and develop a strong intellect and a burning curiosity. He used the microscope and the telescope to study things that were infinitely small and things that were infinitely large. He loved to observe the stars, those tiny pinheads picked out in the night skies, to wonder about the origins of comets, the movement of the planets and the pull of gravity. All of which gave his reflections a metaphysical bent. This passion for the sky had taken hold of him at an early age. He was born on a summer's night under a pure sky spangled with stars. A blessed day it was! He was no different to any other fragile, innocent baby, for there was as yet no sign of his deformity. 'A lovely six-pound boy,' the doctor had said as he held the child out at arm's length. Had he not noticed something? Did he say nothing because he knew he could do nothing? He continued to deny any infirmity as the child grew older but no bigger. Anatomists might have found a rewarding field of study in this nascent monster, but the boy's mother, a simple flower-seller, saw in her son a source of shame. When he reached his eighth month, she abandoned him to the care of a wet nurse, and each birthday saw Alcibiade become more of an orphan. The hump in his back had begun to swell and soon formed an excrescence that unbalanced and humiliated him and whose weight caused him to limp. The looks that people shot at him were like arrows penetrating his flesh. He wanted to become so tiny that he could no longer possibly be a cause of displeasure. But while his body continued to fail him, his heart and his mind began to develop an extraordinary sensibility. He had a thirst for knowledge and, in his quest for a surgical solution to his condition, had while working at the Hôtel-Dieu acquired the rudiments of medicine. Science was his ultimate hope. And if Jean-Baptiste Dandora de Ghalia failed to realize his dream for him, Alcibiade at least found in the count a sympathetic master and a reason to carry on living.

Thus it was that Alcibiade and Malvina were drawn together by a shared feeling of having been abandoned. Why had God marked them out? Malvina would have liked to tell her new friend how distressed she was that she could not leave behind her the sins of her parents. She wanted to tell the dwarf about the suffering that never left her, but fear prevented her from doing so. She could not easily talk of her feelings, so she chose to speak in metaphors that may not have been subtle or elevated, but which at least had the advantage of being clear.

'Do you think that the heart is like a chestnut whose prickly burr hides the delights of its delicious pulp?'

'Your comparison does not lack originality. But perhaps you are wasting your time trying to elucidate the mysteries of nature when what really interests you are the secrets of love?'

'No,' she said in a barely audible voice. 'I merely seek to know what a woman needs to know.'

Alcibiade smiled. What could he say? He had no experience in such matters.

'This word "love" is a very obscure one,' he said prudently.

He waited a moment before continuing, 'Love is a distant and wondrous island which one dreams of visiting without knowing how to get there.'

'An inaccessible paradise?'

'You might say that. In the beginning, love is discreet. It is merely hinted at. It is pearly and hollow like a shell held up to the ear. Then one day it suddenly becomes dense, pervasive. You feel it, you live it, but words are never enough to describe it.'

'Could it be possible that I have not yet loved?'

'We are all looking for the same thing on this earth – to be fulfilled by life. Love does not come about just by thinking about it. One either finds it or one does not. But surely you loved your parents?'

'I have never loved a man,' Malvina replied. 'Not my father, nor any other. I have hated them all, except for the count, for whom I have a profound respect.'

'Do not seek to hide from the divine dawn that is love.

Nothing is more precious than being bathed in the light of a loving look. To love is to live, Malvina!'

'If you were right, then I would not be here. Love frightens me. It means no more than duties and claims over another person. It alienates us, makes us dependent, makes us perpetually seek comfort and attention from our lovers. It reduces us to slavery. Love is unhealthy and lecherous. And it is mendacious, for it suggests that in the eyes of the loved one can be seen the face of one's own perfection. I refuse to be held prisoner, to suffocate in the grip of love, to be at the mercy of human instability! I can assure you, Alcibiade, my lack of emotion gives me a serenity that would be shattered by the passion of love. I intend to fulfil all my ambitions and no man, however handsome, intelligent or loving he may be, will thwart my determination.'

'But where does this hardness stem from? Your soul is so bitter and so full of disappointments, it is poisoned by an insidious violence. You must have an extremely low opinion of men to reject them in such a way. The greatest existing strength is not that of money or power, but of seduction. The person loved by the world possesses the world. If you refuse to be loved, then you will have nothing! You will be nothing more than a doll with a rag for a heart. You will be condemned to endless solitude.'

'You seem to know so much about love. But have you ever loved?' Malvina asked.

Alcibiade was silent. Women had always rejected him, mocked him. He frightened them. If they looked at him at all it was to wonder at his deformity. The dwarf's heart was made to give and to receive love, but his appearance could only arouse feelings of horror or sympathy.

'One must follow one's star,' he said. 'That is the only rule that counts.'

Malvina, disturbed by his piercing stare, got up and put some logs onto the hearth. The fire crackled and seemed to spread into her body, creeping into her veins and stirring up her heart. She wiped her brow.

'Do you love me a little?' she asked.

Alcibiade looked carefully at her as she bent over the fireplace. He observed the delicate curve of her neck and the hair twisted into a bun on the top of her head. From the first day he had seen her, she had seemed frighteningly beautiful and mysterious. He had often dreamed of such a woman, but was it not sheer madness to think that this creature could seek love from someone like him? His hope was reborn each morning, but his day always ended in disillusion. He finally decided to keep this love locked deep inside his heart, to imprison it by never admitting to it. And now here she was pushing him to make a declaration just to test him, as part of a little game she was playing. He was sure she merely wanted reassurance from his words, that she had no desire to requite his emotions.

'Could you love me?' repeated Malvina as she turned her face towards Alcibiade. Her rapid breathing caused her breasts to heave under her light dress, and her mouth trembled.

The dwarf lowered his eyes. It was a crime to say these words without believing in them.

'I do not love you! And you do not love me!' he cried.

Malvina was nonplussed. This ugly, twisted creature was rejecting her! She clenched her fists as if to crush her disappointment. She had never felt so humiliated, so brutally confronted with failure.

'Listen, Alcibiade. Listen well to what I have to say,' she said angrily. 'From now on I will treat you as nothing more than a male and I will seduce you using the base manoeuvres so beloved of your sex – meanness, subterfuge and sham. You will be outraged but I shall rejoice. My indifference will heighten your desire, and when I so choose I shall whistle and you shall come running just like all the others. Do you hear me? You are no better than any of the others!'

Alcibiade looked at her stoically, trying to hide his confusion.

'I hate you!' she cried.

'You have violence in your soul and it is worming its way through your flesh,' he said. 'Be careful, for it is a malady that will affect your spirit all the more since you refuse to fight against it. Your hatred for men is like a mad queen who has conquered all lands and has nothing more to subjugate. It is in every recess of your being. You think it has been stilled, that you have mastered it. But in fact it is reawakening, is endlessly repeating its curses. If you do not resist, it will once more take hold of you.'

'There is no one who cannot transform himself. Look at me, at how I have changed! I can create sublime dishes from nothing, can make them come to life. This work has metamorphosed me.'

'You are satisfied but you are not fulfilled,' said Alcibiade, a trifle mockingly.

'Do you mean with respect to love?'

'Of course I do, for loving and eating go hand in hand.'

'You are so right! The first ensures the survival of the species, the second the preservation of the individual.'

'I fear you have not understood me, Malvina. The true nature of the heart lies elsewhere.'

'Ever since I arrived in this place, I have wanted to give. But do not speak to me of love when in the next breath you reject me!'

'Yes,' said Alcibiade. 'You really do frighten me.'

Chapter Seven

Malvina barely said a word over the next few days. The count wondered what had provoked the girl's sad looks, her sudden melancholy. But she would tell him nothing. Her humiliation, like a chain tied around her neck, prevented her from speaking. As soon as supper was finished she would go to her room and spend hours in front of the mirror. The looking-glass revealed a tormented image, a face that bore no expression. She would grimace and distort her mouth, and then pull her hair down over her eyes as if to make herself disappear. She would laugh nervously and then weep in desperation. The emptiness she felt inside was like a dark and bottomless well. She drew closer to the mirror, placed her hands on the image she saw there, and kissed it. The kiss returned by the glass was cold. There are words that lips can pronounce only when they touch other lips. This mimed reconciliation reassured Malvina. She began to kiss herself madly, almost painfully, with an ardour that delighted her soul. No one else loved her, so she would love herself all the more.

One evening when it was already dark, Malvina threw a cloak over her shoulders and quietly left the house. A dense and humid fog hung over the streets. All colours except those of the garish cabriolets seemed faded and weary under this thick veil. She was almost knocked down by a carriage as it rushed past. Her heart began to beat faster and her muscles grew tense as she quickened her step. She threw back her hood with a sudden gesture of the hand and shook her hair free of the bun that had held it together. Why had desire suddenly entered her life, her life that had only just begun to become ordered? Why must happiness always elude her? Only God could have decided that things should be this way. Alcibiade was too good, too weak, to have found the strength to reject her without help from other quarters. She was sure the Lord was seeking to punish her. She should not have wished for Rougemont's death, should not have felt such cruel joy when Sister Clotilde died. But she had. She had tried to play fast and loose with God, with sin, with hell.

Her feet carried her towards a confrontation she knew was unavoidable. The façade of the church of Saint Roch rose up in front of her. Through its open door she saw a soft and trembling light. She went inside. Candles illuminated the altar and the front rows of the seats, but nothing else could be seen in the darkness. A few silent figures crouched in prayer. It was Saturday evening and they had come to confess their sins in preparation for Sunday mass. A priest bearing a long-handled snuffer moved along the right aisle, extinguishing candles as he went and casting the vaults into even deeper darkness. This growing darkness protected Malvina from curious eyes. She sat down on an empty pew and closed her eyes.

She sought to banish all thoughts from her mind and concentrate on the sole purpose of her visit – to prove to herself that she was evil. It had required much courage to come and confront God here in his church. If he really existed, then let him show himself now, let him manifest his anger.

The sounds in the church grew louder – the murmur of prayers, the faint click of rosary beads, the sigh of a woman as she knelt beneath the twelfth station of the cross. Suddenly it seemed to Malvina that God was revealing his presence. The statues of the Virgin Mary, of Christ and of the saints all turned in her direction. Their lifeless profiles, their fixed stares and tense petrified hands were imperious and menacing. She felt they were interrogating her, accusing her as if they were a jury about to condemn her. She wanted to scream out her hatred but the words stuck in her throat. The trembling in her legs became uncontrollable. She was scared. It was too early for any judgement to be made. There was no evidence, there were no facts. A mortal sin had to be committed consciously and with full consent. She had merely had the misfortune to be witness to other people's evil intentions. Malvina shivered. She pulled her cloak closer over her shoulders, tightened its collar, and got up. The worshippers had by now left the church and the priest was extinguishing the last of the candles.

'I do not wish to chase you from the house of God,' he said as he approached the girl. 'But . . .'

He stopped short when he caught her eye. In it he saw an extraordinary mixture of violence and total despair.

'Can I help you at all?' he asked. 'Is there something you'd like to talk to me about?'

'No.'

Her reaction did not surprise him.

'God has within him both pity and anger, but his mercy is great. Whatever wrongs you may have committed, you must never forget that the more repentant you are, the more you will be able to trust in God.'

'It is too late. Too late!'

'The Lord has infinite reserves of greatness. Those who do not admit their sins are lost, for the truth is not in them. And to lose God is the greatest misfortune that can befall you!'

At these words Malvina ran like a hellcat out of the church. The priest's words had given her an idea, an idea that delighted her.

The rain had stopped. All lights in the streets had been extinguished. It was late, and Malvina began to run. She was excited by her new plan and forgot to notice when she was out of breath. 'If it can be imagined, then it can be done,' she told herself. 'Everything can be done.' She climbed up the staircase that led to her room. Without even taking off her cloak, she lit a candle and went to her chest of drawers. She took out the box the count had given her as a present and whose contents she had never seen. She opened it and saw a carefully folded cherry-coloured dress. The delicacy of the cloth, made of tussore imported from China, and the richness of its embroidery told Malvina that she had in her hands a garment of rare quality. She slowly let the dress fall down over the length of her body. It was lined with white taffeta and the sleeves were trimmed with white lace. A velvet corselet, whose sides were held together by a complex set of laces, imprisoned her waist and held up her pert breasts. Malvina loosened the neckline to reveal skin the colour of candle wax. She perfumed it with sandalwood, then brushed out her hair into a cascade of satiny curls. She took one last look in the mirror, and imagined he was admiring her. 'Do you love me?' she asked of her reflection. Yes, he would love her, for it could not be otherwise.

Her heart beat fast and her legs almost gave way beneath her as she moved slowly down the stairs. Through a half-open door she glimpsed Alcibiade beavering away inside the laboratory.

'You haven't gone to bed yet?'

The dwarf swung round to face her. His eyes fixed on the silhouette moving in the darkness of the room. Her breasts and her hips appeared to blossom in her stunning red dress. She was like the serpent in the story of the creation of the world. She was majestic, supremely confident, almost haughty in her sovereign beauty. She knelt down at his feet and raised up to him a look of infinite sweetness. Then, in a voice which she barely recognized as her own, she asked:

'Do I still frighten you?'

Her hands were held out before her as though to pray. Alcibiade felt insignificant next to her. He was incapable of moving, overwhelmed by this vision.

'Do not speak,' she told him. 'I am going to undress. I shall give you no more than my body and the memory of my body. And if a woman ever refuses you, if the woman you desire rejects you, then you will be able to remember the young virgin who shamelessly gave herself to you. I have nothing else to say to you. Now, look.'

Alcibiade was stunned. He could not believe these words would become reality. He knew too well the mendacity of language. He knew the promises made to sharpen desire, and he knew such pledges were rarely honoured. But Malvina had already begun to remove her clothing, to undo her corselet. She slipped off her dress. Her magnificent, imperious breasts, whence came the scent of an oriental perfume, sprang out from inside a mass of lace. She triumphantly, proudly offered them to him as she continued to take off her clothes. Alcibiade's penis swelled when he saw her naked. His heart missed a beat and his face reddened. Malvina took his hands and guided them towards her hips, towards the coomb of her stomach and breasts. Then she began to undress him. She quivered at the touch of the hands that gauchely felt their way along her shoulders and face. He caressed her timidly and gave her a tender kiss that drew a frisson of pleasure. She felt the warmth of his body on her skin. He kissed her again, then took her nipples in his mouth and licked them as though they were about to melt over his lips. His tongue played on her flesh, savouring its taste of milk and honey. The two bodies became one, like a mother with a baby at her breast. Their hesitant hands suddenly gripped firmly, wildly, and their lips clashed. They were taken by a madness that was at once sweet and violent. Malvina closed her eyes and banished all thoughts from her mind as she succumbed to the exquisite agony. She arched her back and coiled up like a siren around a mast, and gave herself to the sacred rhythm of pleasure. She then took the dwarf's penis in her hands, caressed it with her cheek, and cupped her lips around it as though to swallow it whole. Alcibiade stared at her, overwhelmed by emotion. He half closed his eyes to better savour this carnal bedazzlement that was like the collision of two comets. A heart-rending cry of bliss sprang from his lips. He felt as if he had been sacrificed and had come back to life again. Orgasm overcame him. But not his partner.

For Malvina wanted to flee from this man whose virility was now reduced to inutility. The warmth of their united bodies had become unbearable to her. She detested him for having submitted so readily. He disgusted her as he sat there buttoning up his yellow satin trousers. He didn't even have the decency to hide himself. He was far too cocksure of himself.

She stood up brusquely and was about to return to her room when Alcibiade, seized with anguish, clung on to her with surprising force.

'Don't just walk off like that! Don't leave without saying something! What am I to do now?' he murmured.

'You must go with other women. And never forget that you are able to make them happy!'

'But I love you! I loved you yesterday, I love you today, and I will always love you!' he said in an almost inaudible voice. 'All I want to do is love you, even if you don't love me back.'

She smiled a smile that came from another world, a

dark and powerful world. Alcibiade could do nothing to hold her back. The bang of the door left him in solitude. Distraught, Alcibiade returned to his worktable, where he lowered himself down into a chair and buried his head in his hands. He closed his eyes to try to overcome the pain of having had his dream shattered. He tried to remember the sweetness of its first moments. But the ecstasy, the precious intensity of its final seconds, predominated his thoughts. He took a deep breath to drink in what remained in the room of the perfume of Malvina's skin, the inebriating sweetness of her hair, the burning taste of her lips and neck. He wanted to shake the memory of this carnal explosion as though it were a perfumed cloth that would thus release its fragrances. If only she could imagine what he felt! He had glimpsed happiness. And even if he were now about to spend the rest of his days in the torture of hope, this evening would always remain with him. The dwarf began to cry at the thought of it. His tears were the tears of gratitude that come after solitude.

Just as Alcibiade had expected, their encounter that evening altered nothing in Malvina's behaviour. The only perceptible change was that she seemed a little more sure of herself, and perhaps even a little arrogant. The following morning she passed by without apparently noticing him. She appeared unaffected by the previous evening. But the dwarf had been utterly changed by their union. Hope had reduced him to total submission. He was intoxicated with the idea of being a slave in both body and soul to a woman who received tribute as though it was her natural right. He had never before felt such emotions. This luminous energy inside made him forget past sorrows and effaced the dark ghosts of his infirmity.

*

'Malvina, I have noticed that your enthusiasm has cooled a little in recent days.'

Comte Dandora had slipped quietly into the kitchen, where he found the girl standing staring into space.

'You seem very distant,' he went on, 'lost in your thoughts. Is your work beginning to repulse you? Or is it perhaps a more personal matter?'

Malvina panicked for a moment. She assumed Alcibiade had said something to the master. But perhaps it was simply a trick to get her to confide in him? Her uncertainty led her to feign indifference and carry on with her work.

'You see,' he said, 'you're not even listening to me. Tell me what is going on.'

'Nothing is going on,' she replied. 'I've just been thinking about everything.'

'Tell me more.'

'Well, I've been working for you for the last eight months and I still have no idea why you are so interested in this question of taste. What's it all about? You never tell me anything.'

'But I did congratulate you when you discovered your "pure" taste. Now you just need to continue along the same lines!'

'I cannot continue if I don't know the ultimate destination. Your research must have some goal. You must tell me.'

Dandora had expected this reaction. He made her sit down.

'Be reasonable,' he said. 'Look at me. I have devoted my life to study but still do not claim to have all the answers.'

The old man's humour did not amuse Malvina. Her enthusiasm for her quest had abated. This cuisine, this strange cooking that involved the use of the most repugnant of ingredients, no longer held the same interest for her. Her progress had led her only to boredom. A boredom born of her great talent and of the rapid progress of her apprenticeship. 'A prodigy, a true prodigy!' Dandora had cried when one day he saw that she no longer needed to refer to the many books she had used for reference at the start of her studies. She had quickly learnt to make the most delicious of dishes from the most repugnant of products, thus fully satisfying all her employer's expectations. In fact, she had done even better. In just a few months, she had succeeded in creating what amounted to a laboratory of taste. All imaginable flavours were to be found there, classified into various categories. To each taste corresponded a musical note: *do* represented acid tastes, *re* was for insipid flavours, *mi* for sweet things, *fah* for what was bitter, *soh* for the bittersweet, *lah* for what was salted and *ti* for pungent tastes. Now she needed only to learn what use it could all be put to.

She had almost given up hope of ever finding out. But the count now decided to answer her question.

'From now on, I want you to use your knowledge in the service of medicine.'

Malvina jumped up.

'You want me to become a doctor?'

'What enthusiasm, mademoiselle,' said the count, amused by her naivety. 'I see the child in you is still alive!'

Malvina was ashamed of herself for having got so excited. She didn't like to lose face in front of Dandora.

'I think I expressed myself incorrectly,' he explained. 'It is because of your ability to make any substance pleasant to the taste that we are going to revolutionize the world of pharmacology. Do you understand what I am saying to you?'

Malvina did not. She was perturbed, and her face betrayed her perplexity.

'So this is why you made me spend months cooking rotten food?'

'You had to undergo this test. The difficulty of your task enabled you to surpass yourself. I could never collaborate with a person who is mediocre. What I seek is the exceptional, the rare. For what you are about to undertake is truly inconceivable.'

'Tell me, then. Tell me all.'

He paused as if to rehearse what he was about to say.

'You have discovered pure taste. Now you must discover a taste which will relieve the ill.'

Malvina burst into laughter. She had never heard such inanity. 'A taste to relieve the ill' could never be found. There were simply too many different people with too many different complaints.

'This taste would apply to remedies which, because of their repugnant nature, are never used,' said the apothecary.

'You would never, for example, think of eating precious stones because neither their taste not their texture appeal to you. Yet you know as well as I do that they are effective remedies.'

'Alcibiade is convinced of it.'

'Pulverized metals and minerals,' the count continued, 'are used in numerous health potions. Alcibiade would be able to sell twice as much hematite or topaz if, like Marbode agate, they gave off that sweet, pacifying scent of myrrh.'

'I see. You want me to work on tastes that flatter the palate, tickle the stomach, caress the mind and prepare the way for remedies that have a less pleasant taste.'

'You are simplifying matters a little. But you are not far wrong.'

Dandora made a little gesture to tell her not to move.

'I have prepared a little something for you that is most amusing!'

Malvina followed the apothecary with her eyes. He went into the back kitchen, then emerged bearing a tray whose contents were masked with fine cotton serviettes. He carefully placed the tray on the table.

'It's all here!' he said. 'One last test to measure what you have learnt. And then I will show you my curiosity cabinet. Are you willing to undertake this trial?'

She nodded. Her master handed her a sheet of paper. He gave her simple exercises to begin with, then gradually they became more difficult. She had to identify dishes the apothecary himself had prepared.

'I don't recognize this at all,' she said. 'The spices mask its aroma.'

'Go on.'

'I can't define the acidity, the bitterness of its aftertaste,' she said. 'Even its texture baffles me. I'm wavering between white meat and fish. Perhaps it's tuna!'

Malvina sniffed and tasted all that was presented to her. She offered a reply, then moved on to the next dish. Each time she tried to be ever more precise in the terms she used.

When Dandora decided that her senses were sufficiently sharpened, he placed in front of her a plate, bearing a silver-plated cover, that would reveal the secret nature of his ambitions. He removed the lid and she saw its revolting, unbearable contents. On the plate lay an entire heart, a heart that was much too big to be that of a fish or a bird. It could only be a pig's heart. Or a human heart! Dandora confirmed that it was.

'Go on, eat it! You cannot turn back now that you are so close to our goal. Eat!'

Malvina could not hide her disgust. She held her hand up to her mouth and insisted he stop this nonsense at once. She tried to tell herself that the count was playing some sort of joke on her.

But his next sentence showed her this was no jest.

'Does this disgust you?'

One could perhaps eat this 'food' in a moment of distraction, but to consume it with a clear mind was unthinkable!

'I am not simply asking you to eat it for its taste,' the count said. 'What I really want is for you to overcome your prejudices.'

Malvina felt her stomach contract. She dared not look across the table at her employer. Her trust had once again been betrayed. First Rougemont had revealed his ignobility, and now it was Dandora's turn. How could she have believed in him, how could she ever have thought he could help her achieve greatness?

Malvina turned away from the dish that lay before her on the table and cried out in despair. 'No, no! I won't do it! It's foul, and so are you! You're no more than an old madman with unacceptable and immoral interests!'

The apothecary smiled at her anger.

'Man can assimilate some of the virtues of the thing he eats. You are wrong not to try. This heart could give you strength and generosity. It is only the idea you have in your head of eating a heart that makes it unbearable to you. It is because you can see the heart lying there on the plate. But everything else you have just eaten is made from the very same thing you see before you.'

Malvina thought she might have misheard the count, and made him repeat himself.

'The fear of eating repugnant substances, of consuming bodily excretions and secretions, is generated by disgust. It is a very natural instinct which must, however, be overcome!'

Malvina looked frantically around her in all directions. She tried to make herself vomit, but succeeded only in retching. Her disgust was evidently not strong enough. She then tried to calm herself down by not thinking about what she had eaten.

'Perhaps it is me you now find repugnant?' asked the count.

Malvina pulled herself together. She must not weaken, must not give in to panic.

'Do you feel you are ready to learn more or should I conclude that I was mistaken about you?'

She clenched her fists, furious. It was not the reply that was difficult for her but its consequences.

'I am your pupil,' she finally said.

'Life,' he explained, 'is a vast world of experiences which can open up to us unexplored perspectives. Because your spirit is sufficiently strong, I will allow you to follow me. Come along, I will show you my curiosity cabinet.'

*

Dandora took a firm hold of Malvina's arm. A candle lit the stairs that led to the cellar. The steps shook under their feet and the wood of the walls soon gave way to the damp, oozing earth of a subterranean gallery. A shiver ran through her. It was first time she had been in this place. She had often, of course, tried to find out what secrets the cellar held. But each time she had asked Alcibiade, the dwarf had became nervous, almost hysterical. And now, as Malvina followed her master as though she were his shadow, she knew she was about to discover a hitherto unknown part of his life.

Her fear had left her by the time they arrived at the door to the forbidden room. She could see no lock. The count removed a stone from the wall and pulled on a chain that hung behind it. The door swung open and the count instructed the girl to enter the dark chamber.

'Go on, there's nothing to be afraid of.'

'But I can't see a thing.'

'In just one moment you will see, Malvina. You will see everything.'

But it was the stench as much as the formless darkness that held her back. It was worse than the reek of a dead and rotting rat, worse than the fetor of a grotto that has been sealed for centuries. What could be stored in this secret, inaccessible place?

Dandora lifted his candle up to shed light on the cellar's vaults. Malvina could see things hanging from the ceiling, but could not at first make out what they were. She thought they might be hunting trophies, but slowly began to realize they were in fact human skins. Some had been tanned and showed the contours of a face or a gaping hole where an eye had once sat. Others had been covered in pitch and cut into strips of various dimensions. Malvina was not entirely surprised by this as she knew that the apothecary sold mummy for medicinal purposes in the form of powders, ointments, plasters and electuaries. Her astonishment was due more to the other objects she was slowly beginning to discern in the chamber. She felt as though she were inside an abattoir. On the shelves were ranged jars containing monstrous foetuses. She saw body remains and countless bones. There were tibias, skulls and scapulas, all ordered according to size. There were dozens of human organs of all sorts laid out as though to form an exhibition. There were even rows of teeth that were clearly destined for use in dental appliances. Nothing seemed to be missing from this catalogue of the human body.

'Man is a panacea when his flesh and the flesh of the world are not entirely separate,' confided the count.

Malvina was not listening, for she was too shocked by what she saw. Her curiosity had, however, been aroused. Dandora noticed this and decided to speak no more as he let his pupil familiarize herself with her new lair. He did not want to rush things. What he required was patience and psychological finesse.

Everything in the room shocked Malvina, even the walls with their giant frescos. The candlelight revealed the paintings' themes – skeletons piled bodies into fetid trenches already packed with skulls and ringed with men being quartered or hanging from gallows. A large bell sounded the death knell for this hellish, burnt landscape.

Malvina held the candle up higher to discover yet more horrors on the walls. The fall of the angels was depicted, with the poor creatures being flung down into a sinister chaos peopled with feasting monsters. Even the ceiling was covered with macabre compositions as though it was part of a cathedral erected to celebrate death. Malvina was almost delirious. The room began to sway in front of her eyes and she felt as though she was about to fall over. She covered her eyes with her hands to escape the suffering depicted all around her.

Dandora chose this moment to lead her towards a thick red velvet curtain which covered the entrance to a second room that served as an anatomist's chamber. The count entered first. Bodies were laid out across the room. The organs that had been plundered from their flesh were displayed in glass cases and their skeletons were stored in recesses of the room closed off with black drapes. In the centre of the room, on an immense zinc table, lay a corpse that was slit down the middle. The contents of its stomach and ribcage were on display as was the tangle of its blood vessels and nervous system.

Malvina looked at all this without being able to utter a single word. Her ever slower steps revealed the ambiguity of her thoughts. These bodies did not seem to have dried up. They had no wrinkles, their complexion appeared healthy and their limbs supple. It was as though they had come back to life. Their vital organs were of course missing, but it seemed they were only asleep, that when they woke up they would be able to walk or talk. Malvina had never suspected that the count had an interest in anatomy, she had never imagined him dissecting or wielding a scalpel. To rummage through a dead body, even in the name of science, required a certain genius that Malvina admired. Like Leonardo da Vinci or Ambroise Paré, Dandora had no other ambition but to better understand life and death, mutilation and restoration.

'It must be quite extraordinary to act like God,' Malvina murmured.

'I have to admit to you that—'

She interrupted him.

'What you do clearly does not leave you unscathed,' she said. 'You must have enormous control of your emotions to be able to tolerate such unsavoury work. It's a little like what I do in my kitchen! I think I see now why you brought me here.' The young woman appeared transported by the realization. 'Are there any women in Paris who work as anatomists?' she asked.

'The best known is perhaps Marie-Catherine Biheron. She specializes in ceroplastics. She has created a device which enables one to visualize childbirth. It is used to examine the various problems that a woman can encounter when she is bringing a child into the world. Her practice is on Rue Saint-Jacques. I'll take you there some day if you like.'

Dandora stroked his chin, smoothing his beard as though this would produce the words he was looking for.

'I am merely a tenant here,' he confided. 'What you see around you is not my work.'

'Then whose is it?'

'This is my son's workshop.'

'Your son?' she repeated in surprise. 'You never speak about him. Yet I can imagine him here, working on these bodies, trying to understand life.'

'He went away several years ago, as I have told you already.'

'Do you have a portrait of him?'

'What's the point in keeping souvenirs if one is trying to forget?'

Malvina was troubled. She wanted to find out more about Dandora's son. She was fascinated by the work he had been doing in this chamber. She felt that finally here was someone who would be able to explain to her the mechanisms of human nature, to tell her what caused anger, hatred, attraction or repulsion. Only an anatomist could answer these questions.

'Let us get back to what we were discussing earlier,' said the count. 'If I have had you devote your time and energy to producing extraordinary tastes from the most unlikely ingredients, it is because I believe it may lead to a new type of treatment.'

'You want me to cook corpses?' she asked. 'Is that it?'

'Just listen and stop interrupting me,' he said firmly. 'The corpse is a great reservoir whose contents are largely unknown to us. A redoubled vitality can come from those bodily ingredients touched by death. There is nothing more precious than the remains of the flesh, nothing more propitious for healing. The sacred nature of the body confers great powers on such a use. It is the principle of *homo homini salus*, which means that man is the best remedy for man.'

'So your idea is to have the invalid, who is suffering from a complaint in a particular part of the body, eat the corresponding part from a corpse?'

'That's exactly it!' he replied. 'Dried body parts, when applied to the problem area, heal by symbolic affinity. Skin, for example, is good at treating spasms of the hands or feet. A bandage made of skin and wrapped around the wrist stops convulsions. Because such a substance has itself gone through illness and death, it can offer strengthened resistance to the patient.'

'But how can one eat one's own kind, even if it is in the form of a remedy?'

'Have a look in the *Pharmacopoeia universalis*, edited in London in 1747.'

Dandora took the book down from a shelf and handed it to Malvina. She skimmed through the opening pages, totally absorbed by the lines that almost burned her eyes. All the parts of the body were described here, and their symbolism and properties were discussed at length. On one of the plates was depicted a contorted Tibetan divinity, Mahakala, the terrible guardian of the law who wore a string of miniature skulls around his neck.

'Strange,' whispered Dandora. 'Rosary beads have a striking similarity to his necklace. You see,' he went on, 'there is nothing immoral about it.'

'Do you think this is the future of medicine?'

The apothecary was surprised by the girl's insolence. His face reddened with anger.

'Does the Academy of Medicine support you in your endeavours?'

The question provoked further irritation.

'Ever since the King and the comte de Artois had themselves inoculated,' he replied drily, 'they can speak of nothing else. Inoculation, inoculation, inoculation!'

'I didn't mean to vex you.'

'They're all idiots, do you hear me? They understand nothing about my work. I am trying to make the first medicine which will be as pleasurable as it is effective. I am going to create health pastilles the whole world will talk about!'

'So what you want to develop is a medical cuisine which uses human flesh and is pleasant to the taste?'

'Why do you speak so cruelly? What is wrong with the term "health pastille"?'

'Nothing, master.'

'We shall have a tremendous victory. The osmazome is nothing compared to what I am planning!'

Dandora calmed himself, and his reassuring smile returned to his face as he led her to the door.

'Don't worry. If you agree to help, the work you carry out will be known only to you and me. And you alone will know the formulas.'

'So Alcibiade will be kept in the dark?'

'Just as Alcibiade and you have your secret, so shall you and I have our own.'

This last sentence both troubled and seduced Malvina. It troubled her for it revealed that the count knew of her relations with the dwarf, and it seduced her because it showed that the master had great trust in her. Now he had told her about his project, she had become his accomplice. The idea of participating in such elitist work flattered her and lessened her doubts.

Success, celebrity. These were the words that ran through Malvina's head as she walked back to the kitchen. She was almost euphoric as she considered the new direction her life was about to take. She threw her head back, whirled her body around and flung her arms out in a gesture of total abandon. She was beautiful in her sudden happiness. A feeling of power almost lifted her off the ground. The life she had been leading until now was about to end. Her years of humiliation would be forgotten, and Rougemont's horrible predictions would be rendered null.

Society did not regard a woman of science as a mere cook. She would change from being an object of disdain to one of admiration. Belonging to this new world would place her above all suspicion.

Chapter Eight

Malvina told Dandora the next day that she would accept his proposition. She did not know exactly what her collaboration would entail, but then there had been so many events in her life that she had never fully understood. She wondered just how much longer it would be before she could join the closed circle of the eminent. What other mentor would she need to give new impetus to her life? She at least knew what her guiding principles should be. She knew she had to decide exactly what it was she wanted and then do whatever it took to achieve this. With this in mind, she came to give the count her answer. She majestically drew herself up to her full height as she stood before him.

'Although I know I should have considered the question for much longer before giving a response,' she said with just a hint of irony in her voice, 'I have decided to work for you.'

The apothecary was amused at her audacity, and pretended to hesitate before accepting her offer. Malvina was relieved, but could not yet rejoice for she had a request to put to her employer. She asked him to tell her about his son.

The count could not hide his perturbation. He sat down and with a brusque gesture took from his pocket a string of beads which he began to fiddle with nervously. He began to describe his son. He was, he said, a great libertarian. He was excessive, had a sharp intelligence and unbridled ambition, and was supremely skilful in business. The count acknowledged his son's achievements in the world of commerce which, while not comparable to success in the field of anatomy, were nonetheless admirable. He had become the biggest importer of minerals to France and the quality of his stones was such that he had made a name for himself among the jewellers and goldsmiths of the court. The count was proud of him for this. But there was something which had been a cause of sorrow for years, something of which he never spoke and of which he could now only express the pain it provoked in him. It was not due to the difference in generations which often estranges a father and his son. No, the matter was more serious, the wound deeper.

'Matthieu and I have been strangers since the death of his mother.'

'Where does he live now?'

'He's an adventurer, always departing for some distant land. He rarely returns to France. But when he does come back, he is always kind enough to pay me a visit.'

'Is he married?' she ventured, a little embarrassed.

'Matthieu married? Lord, no! He is horrified by love. He has felt like that ever since—' The count suddenly stopped. 'I shall not continue, for I risk disappointing you. Please do not insist.'

Malvina understood. She left the room after promising not to importune him further on the subject. She would think about Matthieu in the intimacy of her dreams, and would perhaps obtain further details from Alcibiade. He had been unforthcoming the last time she had asked about the count's son, but she would keep at him. His jealousy rendered him silent, but with time it would ease.

In the meantime, Malvina would have to prove she was up to the task she was being entrusted with. The young woman worked steadily for weeks to find the precious formula for the 'health pastilles' Dandora wanted her to make. It was in the King's gardens, among the exotic plants, that she came across a berry perfect for her purposes. Its macerated pulp produced an oil sufficiently pungent to hide the stench of the corpses used in the fabrication of the pastilles. The oil turned the odious reality of the product into something apparently quite pleasant. Bitterness and rancidity were banished, giving way to a slightly sweet taste. A taste that comforted and calmed, a taste that came from a very natural ingredient science had turned into a wonderful tool.

When Malvina treated the corpses she would first give them a thorough scrubbing to eliminate any undesirable elements. She would then extract the brain through the nostrils and fill up the skull with herbs. She would remove the stomach and the entrails and fill the empty space they left with a stuffing similar to the one she used with rolled veal or roast chicken. The cadavers were then washed with distilled vinegar and alcohol before being left to hang for four hours. When they were taken down they were sprin-

kled with quicklime, alum, myrrh, spikenard, green rose-
mary, musk and amber. And finally, once the flesh had
been seasoned, it was dried and made into powder. Malvina
would also grind down the skeletons and grate some of the
skins. She now had to discover in what proportions she
should mix the powder produced in this way with other
substances to make a preparation pleasant to both taste and
smell.

The young woman learnt the art of carving up human
bodies just as others excelled in embroidery or poetry. She
applied herself to the task with almost no show of emotion.
For her, a corpse was no more than a sort of shell, a
substance to be used. But she still shivered a little when
she looked at a skull, and distilling liquors extracted from
the skull bones continued to repel her. To overcome her
nausea, she would remind herself that she was above those
who felt disgust at such things. She felt the hideous
spectacles that were part of her daily routine set her apart
from the rest of humanity. Survival for her meant making
herself exceptional. It did not matter how she achieved
this. One had to play the cards one was dealt as a child. If,
here in her laboratory, she daily encountered the stench of
death, then this was not due to mere chance. Her daily
combat with horror enabled her to take revenge on life.

And it let her take revenge on the world. For Malvina
was not just aiming to make scientific discoveries but also
to find ways to dominate her fellow creatures. She wanted
to dupe them, for their own good, of course, but also to
manipulate them. Nobody, apart from the apothecary,
knew the true origin of the health pastilles. Indeed, the

mystery surrounding them contributed largely to their success. When a customer entered Dandora's dispensary, he would be offered tiny white dragées as smooth as Sèvres porcelain. The pills all looked identical, but the jars they were taken from bore a variety of bizarre names sprung from their inventor's imagination. The patient had an enormous range of flavours to pick from. He had only to communicate his choice to the count who would then retire to a back room where enormous copper pots bubbled with syrup impregnated with flavours such as strawberry, bergamot, apricot, musk, honey, jelly, chocolate or coffee. Coating the pills in these syrups was one of the count's favourite activities. And he was delighted at their phenomenal success, the key to which lay in the fact that the dragées revitalized the mind as well as healing the body.

Never had such a stimulating medicine been produced in Paris, nor indeed in the whole of Europe. Catherine II of Russia and Maria Theresa of Austria sent their emissaries to bring back supplies of the new drug, and such was the demand that they were kept waiting an entire month before their orders could be filled. And at the French court, the princesse de Lamballe, the head of the Queen's household, became an advocate of the product after it succeeded in calming her nerves. She had been devouring the pastilles ever since Panckouke, in his *Journal de politique et de littérature*, hailed them as heralding a new pharmacology to rival the work of Mesmer.

In short, Malvina's discovery had in just a few months carried Jean-Baptiste de Dandora's reputation to its peak. These new pastilles that cured all ills seemed to be the sole topic of conversation in the capital, and the dispensary had great difficulty in meeting demand.

*

One day, the count decided to tell Malvina of his plans to develop their business. It was the hushed elegance of the restaurant that dazzled the young woman. Its refinement was evident even in its smallest details. The immense mirrors on the walls reflected the light of a hundred candles, and the ceiling was decorated with a motif of floral garlands. The skilful play of light and the marriage of silk and velvet seduced her eye. Between the long lines of tables scurried waiters bearing trays laden with meats, fish and pyramids of fruit.

Dandora and Malvina's arrival caused a stir of excitement to ripple through the dining hall.

'What a magnificent place,' said Malvina as she sat down.

Like a child who has forgotten her manners, she stared at her fellow diners in the hope of reading on their lips words of praise for the wonderful medicine she had created.

But the apothecary was in a hurry. He handed her the menu.

'The word "to feast" comes from the Latin *festinare*, which means to hurry! Choose your dish, if you please.'

He paused to look again at the menu.

'Would a Condé soup be to your liking?'

'There are simply too many things to choose from! Do people really eat petits pâtés à la Mazarine or Chambord pike?'

'There is no need for you to imitate the Queen in her rejection of the rich cuisine of the Bourbons. You must simply pick whatever pleases you.'

She examined the menu again.

'Do not worry about the cost,' he told her. 'As you know, our business is doing rather well.'

Malvina smiled ironically at the count's words. Apart from the expensive dress she was wearing and the meagre savings she had managed to make, she had not financially profited from the success of their venture. She ordered what she believed would be the most expensive dish on the list – lamb chops grilled with a salpicon of foie gras, truffle and mushrooms.

'Your choice does not surprise me,' said Dandora. 'It is the choice of a woman of taste.'

He paused for a moment.

'I have brought you here to tell you that I plan to enlarge the dispensary. You are the first to know of this. I also have a proposition to put to you.'

Malvina moved her chair closer to the table and cupped her chin in her hands.

'You understand that it would be difficult for me to place you at the head of the entire business. But I would like to set you up at the court as an expert on taste. Louis le Désiré has an irascible appetite and an inherited penchant for the very finest foods. Your charm and your talent cannot fail to seduce him. But you must be careful not to reveal the composition of our health pastilles. Just yesterday I barely escaped an inspection by the medical authorities. They have no doubts about the medicine's effectiveness, but they are beginning to wonder what exactly it is made of.'

'I am flattered by your offer,' said Malvina. 'But how could I ever establish a reputation? You would need quite a lot of gold to hide my humble origins. Please do not laugh. I can't bear to be the object of your derision.'

The count did not respond to her tirade. 'May I speak now?' he asked when she had finished.

She nodded.

'It is the pleasure of conversation that brings together people of wit. A young stranger who has spirit and gaiety and one or two daring ideas has every chance of being accepted. It is by no means impossible to overcome the social handicaps one is saddled with at birth! Grace, finesse, charm and verbal dexterity can help achieve such a transformation.'

'But how could I ever know which subjects are of interest to them? I've heard that at Fontainebleau it is those stupid donkey races which the court finds most amusing!'

'These ladies confide in Alcibiade. They tell him of their fears and worries, and sometimes they ask him for certain potions. I shall not tell you what use these preparations are put to, but will simply note that a prescription can often tell you a lot about a person.'

Malvina gave him a knowing look.

'Alcibiade will help you,' repeated the apothecary. 'Unless you do not want him to.'

It was clear to all that relations between the young woman and the dwarf had changed. A heavy silence hung in the air at supper, the only time they ever saw each other.

She would act as though he were not there, while he became ever more withdrawn.

Alcibiade was pained that Malvina could be so hard, so insensitive with him. There was not a single tender gesture from her, no sign to give him hope that a renewal of their friendship might be possible. She did smile at him occasionally, but this was only when she wanted to ask him a question about Matthieu. Indeed, the subject had become an obsession for her. She wanted to know everything about his life in Paris, the reasons why he left, the women who accompanied him on his trips. She even began to believe that she was like him, that she might be his female equivalent.

'As you will have noticed, Alcibiade is not particularly talkative at the moment,' she told the count drily. 'But his advice will doubtless be useful.'

Then she added breezily, 'So when is my first outing?'

'Madame de Balendard's salon is next Tuesday. I will accompany you. It will be a pleasure to play, for the first time in my life, the role of chaperon! But you should begin to think about taking a husband, for that is what a young woman is expected to do.'

Malvina was touched by the count's attentions. But she knew that no man of rank would ever ask for her hand, for she had no dowry.

'You know, of course,' the count went on, 'that I have great affection for you.'

She smiled and placed her hand on his. 'I promise I will become the lips that say the words you want to hear,' she murmured.

Dandora was moved. He looked at Malvina's blue-veined and almost translucent eyelids, at the faultless white shoulders and neck emerging from her low-cut dress. She seemed so haughty, so untouchable. He regretted that he was old and she was young. But in his mind, he saw himself draw closer to her, caress her, undress her. He did this not to possess her, for his pleasure did not lie there. He wanted simply to see her free herself, to drop her guard for a moment. He felt no guilt at these thoughts. There was no morality could forbid him to taste this flesh that nourished his soul. He neither ate nor drank during the meal. He was simply happy to watch Malvina consume food as delightful as she was delicious.

*

Within four days, Malvina had learnt to present herself as well as any lady. She did not like the fashionable hairstyles or heavy make-up, for they seemed too unnatural to her. But she was willing to experiment with a whole range of ointments and perfumes such as Eau de la Reine de Hongrie, which Mme de Polignac was so fond of, Eau de Cordoue or Parfum de Vénus. She would place several drops on her lips just as others put them on their wrists. Why should the tongue remain the slave of the other parts of the body? It was far more sensitive than any other organ. Malvina became so enraptured by these new smells that she spent over an hour deciding which one to buy. It was her penchant for both sweet and hot tastes that led her to finally choose perfumes made from amber, cinnamon and sandalwood.

In the Grand Mogol, the famous boutique run by Mlle Bertin, the count bought her a cashmere fitted coat with metal buttons and a lawn petticoat. Her outfit was completed by a black hat decorated with pink ribbons, pink shoes with black rosettes and a bamboo walking stick with a golden pommel. It was thus dressed, with a number of set phrases on the tip of her tongue, that she entered, on the count's arm, the duchesse de Balendard's salon.

A group of lackeys in saffron livery, whose necks and sleeves were bursting with lace frills, awaited them on the steps. The duchess's husband, who had died some ten years previously, had built himself a home that would make clear to the whole world just how much luxury a farmer-general could afford. There was a main building, between the courtyard and the garden, and two side wings, one of which was reserved for the private apartments of the owner, the other for hosting receptions. Malvina was impressed as she passed through a succession of chambers before arriving in an immense circular room painted a luminous, light pink. In this abundance of beauty, wealth and rarity were gathered some thirty people. Servants increased their numbers by almost half. Malvina had never seen such an assembly. Shimmering harmonies appeared and just as quickly disappeared as the silk dresses rustled and floated around the room. There was a mass of guipure lace and a cloud of intoxicating perfume. Iridescent jewels reflected the lights of the candelabra. And yet in the midst of all this bedazzlement, the silhouette of the duchess could not be missed as it floated from one group to another.

Despite her forty-two years and her generous curves,

she was still a very beautiful woman. She wore a brightly coloured dress, and her bare shoulders and diamond- and pearl-draped arms were magnificent. She made no effort to hide the fact that the bloom of her youth had long since faded. Indeed, she was proud of her maturity. It was with great dignity that she went to receive her visitors.

'M. le comte Jean-Baptiste Dandora de Ghalia, what a pleasure to see you again! You haven't changed a bit since the days we used to spend together in the pursuit of pleasure.'

'It has indeed been much too long since those wonderful times. But I must say that my work has helped keep me from boredom.'

'It is just as difficult these days to be granted some of your time as it is to get hold of your medicines!'

'Please know that I shall always be your humble servant! And accept this present, which I give to you as a sign of my repentance. These pills will bring you comfort that soon you will not be able to do without.'

'I am more grateful than you can imagine!'

'How can one resist such charm, madame.'

The compliment delighted the hostess, who directed a conquering look towards the count's youthful companion.

'Let me introduce Malvina Fournier,' said Dandora. 'But perhaps you have already heard of her? She is a specialist in the fine art of taste!'

'Tonight I already have the privilege of playing host to M. Grimod de la Reynière, the most wicked tongue in Paris. And now I have the honour of receiving the most expert as well.' She smiled at Malvina, who replied with a curtsy. 'But please, my dear friends, let us take our places and begin the debates.'

The men were kept apart from the women. This was the wish of the countess, who wanted the representatives of the two sexes to engage in unbridled oratory jousts. But the battle was nevertheless so constructed that the men would always win.

The duchesse de Balendard always picked the most idiotic and talkative women as team-mates, for she could not bear to face any real competition. But when the count obliged her to accept Malvina, she did not seem overly concerned. She would quickly put the newcomer in her place if she began to shine.

This meeting was due to centre on events affecting the life of the country, and so the conversation turned first to the war that was threatening to erupt between France and England. The assembled wits spoke first of the celebrated Doctor Franklin, who was making increasingly frequent visits to various government ministers. They then began to discuss reports that the King was counting on the enemy being exhausted due to her engagements with her colonies.

'Our old foe believes she can still subjugate the Americans,' said the duchess. 'What naivety!'

'But we must not wait,' interrupted the duc de Jazamet.

'It is now that we must punish the insulting arrogance of the English! Yet our leaders are in a state of worrying immobility. We should follow your example and go on the offensive!' he cried as he pointed to the duchess's hair.

She had what was known as an 'insurgent' hairstyle,

which was some four feet tall and had at its peak the form of a serpent which represented England.

'I cannot hide my opinions. You know that!' she said as her dark eyes flitted about the room.

'Your opinions serve only to augment your beauty, madame.'

There was a short silence before the conversation continued.

Malvina listened attentively. She knew nothing about politics. She would have been happy to simply observe proceedings if the count had not, shortly before they arrived, given her a piece of advice that now terrified her. 'Those who hold their tongues are idiots, and idiots are nothing!' he had said. The words ran through her thoughts like a chorus. The minutes passed and she found nothing to add to the conversation flowing around her. What could she do? What topic could she begin to speak about? Dandora noticed her pale and tense face and, with a discreet gesture of the hand, moved to ease her anguish. He had often seen people's reputations shattered in salons such as this one. A badly chosen word or an inappropriate attitude was enough to make a person look ridiculous, and this was something it was nigh impossible to recover from. Dandora knew also that patience was vital. One had to unite strategy and talent to win over such an assembly.

In the end it was the duchesse de Balendard who enabled Malvina to participate in the conversation. She had, for the second time, raised her eyes to the ceiling to remind her friends that uninterrupted eloquence could be such a bore. The apothecary seized the opportunity to make an opening for his young friend.

'What a thoroughly indigestible conversation!' he said. 'The news of impending war makes us morose, and all we can do is add to the gloom by fuelling it with our pessimistic commentaries! Would you not prefer to taste of lighter, sweeter subjects?'

'Sweeter?' repeated the hostess. 'But we are talking about sin!'

'A vitally important subject!'

'Enough mystery. Speak, for we are eaten with curiosity.'

'Eaten is a very apt word,' said Dandora. 'For it is of the sense of taste that we are about to talk.'

'I see now where you are leading us,' said the duchess as she looked at Malvina.

The dice were thrown.

The young woman stood up, walked to the centre of the room and bowed again to the gathering. 'The honour is mine, madame.'

'Enough pleasantries, mademoiselle,' the duchess interrupted. 'What have you to tell us?'

Malvina smiled at each person in turn.

'The mouth is my favourite subject. If you are willing, I should like us to wonder at its mystery, its power, its magic.'

'The mouth holds no surprises,' remarked the duchess.

'Everyone knows,' said the comte de Boisrenard, 'that it is neither through the head nor the heart that women rule us, but through their talent at taming our stomachs.'

He laughed at his witticism and then scratched his wig with the help of a long red and black needle that had a miniature finger carved at its tip.

'You are doubtless thinking of Mme de Mainteron,' said Malvina. 'It was thanks to old Douillet's famous ducks that she became so beloved of Louis XIV. We must admit that there are few who had such influence over a king!'

Her tone and her bearing were magisterial, as though she had just made an important theological point.

'We are but paltry things, messieurs. But how pleasant it is to let ourselves be tamed by a woman,' added Dandora.

The remark amused the guests, each of whom felt obliged to make some clever response. But the conversation slowly came back to the subject of the mouth.

'Is the mouth really the interpreter of the heart and the spirit?' asked the duc de Jazamet.

'It can reveal, both when at rest and in the infinite variety of its movements, many facets of the character. When you meet a person for the first time, I am sure you have often paid more attention to his mouth than to his eyes.'

The guests looked at each other with amusement. There were gathered here many sensuous mouths bearing an excess of make-up. There were luscious mouths, mouths like ripe fruit, carnivorous mouths resembling the snouts of animals and tight-lipped mouths. The duchesse de Balendard spoke of the mouth as an object of pleasure, full of sensations, while the count preferred to view it as a device which served to transmit knowledge.

Malvina was jubilant. For it was her mouth, with the

aid of the words emerging from it, that directed the conversation. 'A generous upper lip is the sign of goodness, and a slightly protruding lower lip reveals a pleasant nature. But lips that are too thin show avarice, severity or baseness.' Everyone wanted her to come and say what their mouths said about them, and she spent over an hour passing among them. She did not seek to flatter, but would pick out the most promising aspect of each person and avoid any mention of negative traits. And when there was something she deemed too intimate for public consumption, she would lean over and whisper her words in her subject's ear.

The originality and insolence Malvina displayed quickly seduced her audience. The evening came as a welcome change for them, for they were used to salons where the tone of the debates was one of unrelieved harshness. Even the duchesse de Balendard had just one word to say to the count as he was leaving with his young ward: 'Marvellous! Quite simply marvellous!' She had no other desire than to invite them back again as soon as possible.

*

The success of her first salon filled Malvina with self-confidence. She lost her natural discretion and reserve and became jovial and talkative as soon as she found herself in society. Her company was soon requested by Mme de Genlis and by the princesse de Chimay. Mme Helvétius, who appreciated the simplicity and spontaneity she displayed in her conversation, introduced her to Bergasse and

Chamfort. The talk could turn from literature to music to philosophy, and the young woman would not be flustered. She could now juggle with ideas or words, and was not afraid to touch on the most delicate of subjects. She drank in everything she heard around her and her ignorance was soon left far behind. She was able to nourish herself on the spirit of the person she was speaking with. And when she spoke of the science of taste, her conversation was unparalleled. Her measured tone and her even-handedness enabled her to establish a bond with people. Thus when jealous wives began to make barbed remarks about her – 'She has clearly used some elixir to enchant poor Dandora de Ghalia' – Malvina would simply smile and promise to bring them a powerful aphrodisiac the next day. They would rave about, for example, mummy tincture that warmed their stomachs, or dried stag mixed with wine that awakened desire, or honey-coated badger that guaranteed conception.

Within just a few months, Malvina had gathered around her many suitors. This may have been due to her love potions but was more likely to have been thanks to her womanly charms. As she never did anything half-heartedly, she had soon claimed as many victims as all the campaigns of the English armies. The Comédie Française actor Vincent Bailly was the first to fall. At society dinners he would blend his acting skills with his talent for seduction. It was at a dinner given by a friend of the count that Bailly, adopting the voice of Figaro, made a public declaration to Malvina. 'My looks will already have spoken of my feelings for you. You must respond, but let me first assure you that, whatever your sentiments, I will love you until my dying day.' She did not hold this fiery statement in great esteem, but was happy to let Bailly continue courting her simply to reassure herself of the effect she could have on men.

She had barely got to know Bailly when Armand de Laville turned up. Or perhaps the two arrived at the same time, for it was the fashion of gallants to chase after the same beauty and to share in the spoils if she fell. De Laville made much the same approach as Bailly – impassioned declarations, jealous rages and transports of emotion. It was all so well done that Malvina was truly impressed. She was proud to be the prey of an aristocrat who was desired by so many high-society ladies. She spent much of her free time with him, and would often go walking with him of an evening in the Jardin des Tuileries. Their relations, however, came to an end when Mlle de la Mayelle announced that it was inappropriate for her fiancé to continue with such dishonourable activities.

But carnal relations were for Malvina a regression to a primitive state, and she sought out a victim who would demand from her nothing more than friendship. This she found in the comte de Peyssac. He was old, married and did not pester her as the young men did. Their relationship was cemented by regular correspondence. The count fancied himself a poet, and would send her pages and pages on the subjects of love, friendship and faith. 'You would no longer exist, my sweet, if you ceased believing in these eternal values for which one must strive all one's life.' His letters touched her. She felt great tenderness towards this man whose culture and benevolence she greatly admired. But the count had a weak chest, and his death in the month of May 1777 left Malvina in a state of profound distress.

She quickly tired of the conquests that followed. Triumph was always followed by tedium, and she quickly came to feel contempt for the men who pursued her. Her face, which until now clearly expressed the exaltation of her discoveries, began to show melancholy. She left her laboratory only to go to the dispensary. All dinner invitations were rejected. Word soon spread among her former suitors. Their love, the idol with the brilliant smile and the quick wit, no longer had any friends. Malvina now lived as a recluse.

*

Alcibiade, who was more learned than most in the sciences of the heart, understood his friend's trouble. He had kept himself informed of her activities, and had vainly tried to protect her from others and from herself. He was forced to look on as she became involved with men for whom she had no love. He remained convinced that she was incapable of love, and his suspicions were confirmed when she came to talk to him one afternoon.

'I have neglected you recently,' she said. 'Please forgive me.'

'We don't even see each other at supper.'

'I had to stay away from you.'

'But was it really necessary to break the bond that united us? Without any explanations?'

'Do you hate me?'

'You inspire many emotions in me – love, hate, admiration, contempt. But what matter?'

'I didn't want to vex you further. I thought I could spare you further upset by keeping away from you.'

'Are you at least happy?'

Malvina did not reply. She had not expected such a simple, straightforward question.

'These conquests,' said the dwarf, 'that you have been wasting your time on . . .'

'You are jealous!'

'I cannot be jealous of nothing,' he said, and laughed.

'What do you mean by that?'

'You know better than I do. You are only attracted by what you can't have. The master's son, for example. They say that you ask about him everywhere you go.'

Malvina's face stiffened.

'What one wants has little to do with love,' said Alcibiade. 'You cannot just decide to be loved, especially by someone you have never seen!'

'He will love me, you just wait! But it is true that I cannot explain why I am so attracted to him.'

'Is it the father or the son who interests you the most?' asked Alcibiade aggressively. 'And what sort of love are you talking about? The type you dream about but can never have? You are too full of doubt to be able to take on something real. You even doubt . . .'

'That somebody could love me? I know.'

'Forget about Matthieu.'

'I find you just a little too pretentious if you think you can judge me with such certainty.'

'You are mysterious, enchanting, strange. He will be attracted by these qualities, but he will later come to see them as faults.'

Malvina used to be comforted by the dwarf's talk of love, but now his moralistic ranting exasperated her.

'I simply must meet him.'

'If I prove to you that you are misguided, will you then stop this madness?'

'And just how would you do that?'

'Stella will tell you.'

'Stella? I don't think I know her.'

'She holds the key to all dreams.'

'Does she live in Paris?' asked Malvina. 'I have money. I can pay whatever she asks. When can we go to see her?'

Alcibiade was not sure he had done the right thing, but he nevertheless kept his word.

*

As night began to fall the next day, they took a coach to the Faubourg Saint-Antoine. Malvina sat looking out the window and did not say a word. Her face revealed no trace of the excitement the trip should have provoked in her. Her agitation was however betrayed by the piece of blue cloth she held pressed against her stomach. The whiteness of her knuckles contrasted sharply with the impassivity of her face.

They arrived in a lane that bore the name Basse-du-

Rempart. It was on a much lower level than the street they had just turned off and it was poorly lit. Indeed, it rather resembled a cesspit, and it was whispered that the Devil had made his home here. The windowless houses were darker than the night sky. The coach pulled up outside one in a state of advanced dilapidation. Saltpetre had invaded the dank walls, from which large chunks of plaster had tumbled off onto the ground below. On the water-logged cornice could be made out the faded forms of winged and horned creatures. A judas hole was suddenly flicked open.

'Who's there?' a voice asked.

'Alcibiade. I'm with someone.'

The door was unbolted and a man, whose face was as pale as his hair was black, looked the visitors up and down before saying that he would have to ask his mother if she could receive them. The door was shut once more. The dwarf gestured to Malvina not to be afraid. Moments later the door was flung open again, and an enormous turbaned black-clad woman greeted them.

'In the name of all the saints!' she cried out in a voice full of mock reproach. 'How many years has it been? I thought you were dead!'

'Forgive me, I just never found the time to come and see you.'

'Are you going to wait till I'm about to die to keep your promise?'

'But of course not! You know only too well, my dear Stella, how fond I am of you!'

The old woman's face took on a sceptical look. All her

incantations and her potions had not managed to make Alcibiade grow to the size of an adult, and she wondered sometimes if he could ever forgive her for this failure.

'I have brought a friend along,' said Alcibiade.

'And a fine-looking woman she is too! She could easily turn a man's head,' said Stella. 'You have love problems, is that right?'

Malvina stared down at the ends of her shoes.

'I see. Follow me. We shall have to seek the help of the spirits.'

They went into a tiny room that was furnished with only a pedestal table and two chairs. A strong smell of grease and burnt roots came from the fireplace. Malvina was invited to take off her coat and sit down. The man who had opened the door brought in a sheet of paper, a quill and some ink. These he placed on the mauve table-cloth next to a candle and a basin filled with water. Malvina was impressed by his theatricality.

'You are a little nervous, but that is to be expected. But just try to relax. Breathe deeply. That's it! Shall I put you to sleep or do you want to remain awake?'

'Put me to sleep?'

'With just a few words I could plunge you into a deep sleep. And no harm would be done to you.'

'I think I'll stay awake. Please tell me what you see.'

The clairvoyant cleared her throat.

'The equations of chance will reveal to us who you are. Can you please tell me your name and your surname.'

'Malvina Fournier.'

Stella took the paper and drew on it sixteen irregular

lines of dots. 'Malvina Fournier,' she repeated. 'M. A. L. V. I. N. A. F. O. U. R. N. I. E. R.' She then grouped the lines into fours, and made four small figures on the right of the sheet. These were the 'mothers', she said. And in a rapid gesture she made a further ten figures of the same type which she called 'daughters', 'nieces', 'witnesses' and 'judges'.

'The form the figures take will tell us whether the message is good or bad. These five points that form the Y shape symbolize the head of the Dragon. And there we can see the sign of Inconstancy, which means you are in love. Is that correct?'

'Go on. Please go on!'

'I see another person, a woman who has your first name and looks so like you that she could be your sister.'

Stella lit the candle and handed it to Malvina.

'Look at the flame,' she ordered. 'What do you see?'

'Nothing.'

'Look again and then close your eyes.'

'I see violent bursts of colour and fleeting, luminous forms.'

'Do you see a face?'

'No.'

'Hold the candle over the basin.'

A few drops of wax fell into the water and as they solidified Malvina saw new visions.

'The event which you have been waiting for,' said Stella, 'is about to take place.'

Malvina thought immediately about meeting Matthieu de Ghalia. She smiled.

'He will be in Paris in October.'

The drops of wax had by now formed into the shape of tiny waterlilies.

'Will fate bring us together?'

The old woman looked at Malvina through eyes red-rimmed with concentration.

'Look, there are three drops that have formed into rings. This means you will meet at a dinner.'

'Am I right in believing he will love me?' asked Malvina in a choked voice.

Stella held the candle back over the basin. This time, the wax drops exploded onto the water before taking on a crimson colour and sinking like lead.

'Death! I see violent death!'

She pushed the basin away.

'Let us stop there.'

Her son ran to her side and blew out the candle. He, too, paled when he leant over the basin.

'It's over,' he said. 'Please leave.'

'But you must explain! Speak to me!'

'Death!' he said. 'Do you not understand? You are marked with the sign of death!'

Malvina realized that this mad old woman's supernatural gifts had enabled her to glimpse her bloodstained past.

'You're mad!' she said. 'You can't know!'

'Go, mademoiselle. Go! You are like fire inside, my child,' murmured Stella. 'It won't be long. It won't be long till that other woman comes for you, and for him.'

Malvina took her coat and stormed out. Alcibiade, who

had been waiting for her in the next room, quickly said his goodbyes and followed her into the street.

'What did she say?' he asked.

She turned away from him, pretending not to hear.

'You are deathly pale! Are you not well?'

'I hate you!' she hissed.

Alcibiade thought that Stella had simply warned her to forget her designs on Matthieu. Yet for an instant he considered going back inside to find out what had really happened. But Malvina had already clambered into the coach and was sitting hunched up like a child, with her knees up to her chin and her eyes staring blankly ahead. No one could understand the vacuum she felt inside her. A fire was burning her entrails while at the same time a deadly cold made her shiver. The cries and screeches in her head were the sounds of the past returning to haunt her. Only the damned died and died again. And Malvina, like them, was dying.

She slowly held up her hand to her breast to feel the pulsations of her heart. She began to cry. Spasms contorted her mouth and tears burnt her eyes. Alcibiade took from his pocket the blue cloth she had dropped as she fled out of the clairvoyant's house. He handed it to her and asked her to forgive him. She looked at him and bit her lip.

'I am marked by death,' she said in a whisper.

'What are you saying?! Who put that idea into your head?'

'You cannot understand. Your heart is too pure.'

'I'm too nice, is that what you are saying?' he retorted.

'I'm nice like idiots and weaklings are nice! Do you think being nice excludes being lucid or cynical?'

'I can't explain it to you. And I don't want to.'

Her voice became more strident.

'Stop! I'm getting out here.'

'I can't leave you alone in this state!'

'Don't worry. I just need to walk a bit.'

Alcibiade looked out of the carriage window and saw they were passing a block of houses on the Rue Saint-Honoré. He told the driver to stop.

Malvina got out and began to walk with no particular destination in mind. She soon arrived at a cemetery. She had been fascinated by graveyards ever since her mother had died, and even more so now that she rubbed shoulders with death every day in her laboratory. Wandering among the tombs helped her calm down. She stopped in front of a bed of earth that seemed ready to receive her body. She lay down on her stomach and, with her face to the ground, stretched out her arms to form a cross. She was hypnotized by this other world, which teemed with smells, embrocations and fumigations. She closed her eyes and entered the infinity that was beckoning her. She felt her flesh disintegrate and her limbs crumble into powder. Already she felt she had become one of the creatures of the dark. 'Take me!' she screamed at them. 'Take me before I do a wrong that is irreparable.' They appeared as if from nowhere, their gait heavy and mechanical. Some were no more than fleshless skeletons held together by mere shreds of muscle, while others were more recently departed and had just begun the rotting process. Hundreds of them, thousands of them came and stood around Malvina. But none dared take away her life. Her body heaved with sobs. Bitter memories of childhood and the sorrow of a deserted heart fed her anguish. She did not understand that death was denied her because she had not yet chosen between good and evil.

Chapter Nine

Malvina fell ill. All her senses seemed to have been dulled and she withdrew into complete silence.

'You must take one of our remedies,' Dandora told her. 'At least drink this primrose infusion.'

She pushed away the bowl he held out to her.

'Alcibiade cannot replace you in the laboratory, our customers are crying out for more pastilles and our stocks are dwindling!'

His words angered Malvina. How could he think of such trivial matters when she was engaged in a battle with the accursed part of her soul? When she was tormented by her belief that death would take her soon and that something terrible would happen if it didn't?

Alcibiade sat by her side every night and tried to soothe her. He had never seen anything like this before. Her ash-grey eyes clearly expressed her agony and from her mouth came sounds that spoke of terrible suffering. Invisible creatures taunted her and their liquid voices echoed through her thoughts. The entire room seemed to be filled with their birdlike cries.

The dwarf whispered soft words of affection in her ear, but to little effect. He knew the meeting with Stella could not be the sole reason for such a disturbance. He rebuked himself for not having realized how fragile his loved one was and felt partly to blame for letting Malvina be pushed over the edge.

It did not ease his conscience, but Alcibiade felt that his master harboured similar feelings of guilt. And he was right. The more time Dandora spent at Malvina's bedside, the more he realized that he had only seen in her an assiduous and talented pupil, a seductive and troubling woman. Her self-assurance and her strong will had blinded him to her fragility.

He kissed her hands and rubbed them as if to pass on some of the warmth of his own body. She must forgive him and not leave him, he pleaded with her. He would lighten her workload, would even take on a new apprentice to handle the corpses. She opened her eyes while he spoke, to see if he meant what he said.

'I will call in the most eminent of specialists,' he said. 'I'll even get Mesmer if I have to!'

But the next day when the doctors came to examine Malvina, they found not a trace of any recognizable condition. Even when they bled her, the only conclusion they could come to was that she was suffering from a mysterious lassitude. She was breathing normally and her organs did not appear to be suffering from any lesion. They confirmed that the problem was rooted in her mind and added that such problems were infinitely more difficult to resolve. Each day she would fall into a sort of coma, and hours would pass before she became lucid again. And thus it continued until early October, until the day the count came to her and announced that he wanted to adopt her.

'Love is what you need, my child,' he said. 'You must accept my offer. My line is already assured, so between us it is simply a question of emotion.'

Malvina's breathing quickened.

'I know now that giving brings much greater happiness than receiving,' the count continued. 'Please accept this offer, in return for which I ask only a little solicitude.'

Malvina sat up in her bed.

'Do you really think you could love me?' she whispered.

'I will take you as you are. Matthieu is due to visit us at the end of the month. We shall break the news to him as soon as he arrives.'

'But he would never accept me.'

'Accept you? But he is so looking forward to meeting you. Our letters have recently been full of talk of you.'

Malvina closed her eyes again, pacified.

'He wants to protect and care for you. He will love you better than any blood brother.'

'And shall we have a dinner in his honour?' she asked.

The words she spoke seemed to resuscitate her.

'Please let me organize the reception,' she begged. 'Alcibiade can help me, and we shall hire a whole team of cooks. I will make the occasion so special that not even your fertile imagination could conceive of it.'

'Good, good,' said Dandora. 'But are you not a little too weak?'

'I have a mission to carry out on this earth. I must find love. My survival depends upon it!'

The count looked at her. He did not understand what she meant by this. He was about to reply when Malvina sat up and kissed him. It was her first ever spontaneous gesture of affection and it surprised her as much as it did the count.

*

The following weeks were spent preparing for the dinner. Invitations were sent out on cards bearing in gold letters the name of M. le comte Jean-Baptiste Dandora de Ghalia and the words 'Grand Banquet des Illusions'. Malvina wanted the guests to expect a totally original experience where dreams and reality would merge. The Greeks had their symposia and their Dionysian feasts, the Romans their bacchanalia and their orgies. And now Malvina was inventing something new – a theatre of the senses in which the senses were freed from their usual hierarchy.

It was left to the celebrated designer Jean de Beauvoir to create delights for the eye and the sense of touch, while the count chose the music, which had a distinctly Italian flavour. Malvina meanwhile took charge of staging the meal. Between courses, doves would be released into the air, sprinkled with the smells of the dishes that were about to arrive. She realized that both gustative and olfactory excitement was necessary for the success of the evening. She decided that violets, whose scent was of velvet dipped in sugar, would be a perfect accompaniment for the sweetmeats. She sought a more daring note for the poultry and game dishes. She peppered them with a red secretion from the intestine of a stag, oil from the blubber of a sperm whale and castor from a Russian beaver. She relished the ability these musks had to waver between the beautiful and the disgusting. A tiny error of dosage and the faecal odour of a civet would nauseate, while if the correct amount were used, it could transform a dish into a powerful aphrodisiac.

Astounding the sense of taste would, of course, be the most delicate operation of the evening. Nobody knew until the very last moment what was being prepared.

'Why so much mystery?' asked the count, who had just insisted on being allowed into the kitchen. 'My house has been like a building site for the last week and you've even banned me from entering my own kitchen.'

Dandora's nervous movements revealed his concern. He moved around the room lifting the lids of various pots and pans, but found nothing to reassure him. Quite the opposite, in fact. He was dumbfounded to discover bubbling barbel entrails, thrush brains imprisoned in thick grease and caviar made from mullet eggs. Further investigation revealed spits bearing parrot heads, sows' vulvae, pig throats and nightingale tongues.

'It seems to me that our guests are invited to a festival of the carcass!'

'Yes, but with the word "carcass" taken in its most disconcerting and evocative sense,' she replied. As she spoke, her hands were plunged deep inside a container filled with a slimy substance the count had no difficulty in recognizing. He had never been able to understand how anyone could bear to handle a substance as disgusting as tripe. Certainly, it was at his instigation that Malvina had for the last few years been engaged in such sordid work, but he was now for the first time struck by the fact that she took a real pleasure in rummaging through the bloody, open belly of an animal. She would rip open a carcass and remove its marrow as though she was simply breaking eggs to make an omelette. The sloshing blood provoked not even a hint of reaction or revulsion in her. She operated with the coldness and precision of a machine.

Dandora, holding a scented handkerchief up to his nose, moved closer to her. 'You are working like a true anatomist.'

'Had you forgotten that such base tasks hold no horror for me?'

'I'm getting a little worried about what you're planning for the dinner. Liver, tongue, heart, lung, stomach. Nothing but innards! Have you nothing else planned?'

'So you're turning up your nose at it now, are you? You who until now made me cook meals using the most unwholesome of ingredients?'

'Are you trying to reveal the monstrous nature of the human body?'

'But the body is monstrous! You cannot deny it!'

'I do not have the time to get into this argument,' he thundered. 'Our guests should be treated to the most wonderful of foods, not fed with offal and other such rubbish!'

'There is magic hidden under the skin and in the

entrails. Every organ has its own secret. It was you who told me that. The fat of the brain is the substance of thought, the thymus and the kidneys are rich in purine, and the liver gives strength and vitality. These are your teachings!'

'Your fantasies could cause us to lose everything, Malvina!'

'These are the only dishes which can bring about the heightened emotions and strength of mind and body that I want our guests to experience. I want these brilliant people who are coming to our dinner to eat flesh that, were it not for my culinary talents, they would normally refuse to swallow.'

The young woman had invented recipes which enabled her to make delicious dishes with the basest of products. She used ginger, cinnamon, cardamom, poppy and saffron to delight the palate, and the food was to be presented in such an imaginative fashion that it would dazzle the mind. She disguised ram's testicles in ambergris dragées, wrapped intestines in cardoons and stuffed truffles with the flesh of wild fowl.

Thus it was that Alcibiade paid a small fortune in the Hôtel de Provence for a dozen black truffles from the Lot. He had never seen such monstrosities. The words parasite, tumour, blister, black sperm and excrement ran through his head as he looked at them. What magic properties could this verrucose mushroom have to make people spend so much on it? He could not say. But he saw his friend's face light up when he placed them on the kitchen table.

Watching her brush them carefully and slowly sniff them, he realized there could be few things for which she cared so much.

Malvina was in transports of joy. The scent of the truffles had brought thoughts of her past flooding back to her. Sounds, colours and people returned to fuel her happy nostalgia. When she wandered in the country as a child, every year between the months of January and March, she sniffed the heady, musky, sulphured smells of the truffle. Her mother prepared them for the more wealthy travellers, the rich merchants who wanted to treat themselves to this black delicacy with its bark bevelled like the point of a diamond. Gabert rarely allowed his wife to enter the dining room of the inn, but he would do so to let her cook truffles in ash before the guests' admiring eyes. Marie would sit on a stool in front of the fireplace and dip them in wine before placing them in the dust of the fire. Malvina would never miss this magic moment, for she felt so proud to see all the men's eyes turning towards her beautiful mother. How sweet it was to bathe now in this past happiness! She wished her mother could see her the following day when she made her debut as the worthy heiress of this tradition. And not in a mere tavern at the order of some merchant, but in one of the most fashionable salons in Paris and before a plethora of important people.

Dandora, who could not guess what thoughts were passing through his friend's mind, continued with his gloomy predictions.

'The whole thing will fall apart! I'm telling you, it will

collapse! Have you gone mad? Do you really think you can act like Tantalus?'

Malvina knew well that because Tantalus, the King of Lydia, had served the tender flesh of his son to the gods of Olympus, he had been sentenced by Zeus to hang on the branches of a fruit tree above a stream. Whenever he reached for a fruit, the branches would swing away from him, and when he tried to drink, the water would recede.

'This meal will deliver a message clearer than any speech could ever be,' said Malvina. 'Not one of your guests will be able to identify what he has eaten. The food will have been metamorphosed to such an extent they will be dumbfounded and the evening will resound with their compliments. They will want to know what has so enchanted them, but the secret will remain with you for they will not be told. At least not until the following morning, when they will each receive a copy of the menu accompanied by a personal letter. Does this idea appeal to you?'

Dandora could only agree. It was a dangerous project, but a most interesting one.

'You really are a strange woman,' he said.

Malvina smiled. She took up one of the birds laid out on a block on the table. It was a bustard, a bird which has the peculiarity of seven different meats of varying colour and texture. Some are white like chicken, others almost black like hare or mutton. She chopped off its legs and plucked it before slicing open its belly with a knife. Her great skill impressed her master. She then seized the bird's lungs and wrenched them along with a tangle of innards from its body.

'You must never forget,' she said, looking Dandora in the eye, 'that insolence and danger are always an integral part of the boldest enterprises!'

*

The evening of the magnificent dinner came and for several hours the house and the guests therein were given over to magical and voluptuous pleasures. The doors of the oriental drawing room opened onto a spectacle the like of which had never been seen. The great table was illuminated by a multitude of candelabra and precious stones. Immense mirrors reflected a hundred times the iridescent Baccarat crystal, the bright red colour of the plates, the Dresden china and the fine silverware. This splendour contrasted sharply with the austerity of the black velvet draped over the walls and the grey marble of the supporting columns.

Between each column stood an automaton in livery with a black rose in his hand. They bowed and the spectacle began. Burning ribbons suddenly lit up the room's architecture. From the shadows sprang fountains of water and the eyes of statues began to glow. Giant chandeliers descended from the ceiling and from the walls emerged bronze arms. These released into the air dozens of doves to sprinkle the room with appetizing fragrances, spicy aromas and sunny perfumes. Four sideboards then rose up out of the ground. On each stood the statue of a unicorn whose open flank displayed a range of culinary delights. The scene as a whole was intended to intrigue the assembly as well as to whet their appetite for discovery.

Very few of the dishes on display were recognizable. Most had lost their names and origins for the sake of this excessive and extravagant show. Unknown meats had taken the form of Anubis, Cerberus, Hecate and Hermes. They lay on beds of chestnuts, pea mousse, olive pâté, artichokes, courgettes and aubergines.

After this seduction of the eyes, it was the turn of the taste buds. Comte Dandora asked his guests to take their places at the table. The duchesse de Balendard and her sister, the duchesse de Burgeade, sat on either side of him. Then came Messieurs Ancelot and Leblanc, two eminent members of the scientific community, followed by M. de Fayet, the apothecary's financier, and then the count's son, Matthieu, who had arrived that very morning from Constantinople. He had heard much about his father's pupil, but far from enough to satisfy his curiosity. He insisted that Malvina join them at the table.

'I have come to meet my future sister!' he cried. 'Why has no place been reserved for her?'

'Your sister?' asked the duchesse de Balendard.

'I am planning to adopt Malvina,' said the count as he lightly stroked his neighbour's hand.

'Malvina prepared this entire meal herself,' he went on before the duchess had time to formulate a response. 'So I would ask you to honour her by appreciating the dishes that will be placed before you.'

At these words an iron door opened in the middle of

the table and eight silver dishcovers appeared, shining like the helmets of emirs. The assembly was amused. Inside the covers lay chocolate croissants perched on sugar loaves in the shape of swans. The guests glanced at each other in embarrassment, perturbed at the thought of eating them as a first course. But soon they were won over by the sweet smell of cacao, a scent enhanced by hints of jasmine, vanilla and cinnamon, and even had second helpings, for they were even more surprised and delighted by the discovery that the chocolate was simply a coating for the meat that lay inside.

'One could live off the aroma alone.'

'Apicius would be green with envy.'

Words of appreciation flowed from every mouth. All admitted they had no idea what the food they were eating had been made from. Someone suggested pork and cacao stuffing. Someone else said it was flavoured giblets. Matthieu turned the food over and over on his plate as though he were conducting an anatomical inspection. He missed not an ounce of flesh, yet could not find the answer. He begged to be told what it was, but the count merely smiled.

The element of surprise was an essential ingredient for the success of the evening and it was sustained for the second course, which provoked a wave of exclamations. 'Parnassian rocks' emerged from the ground. Water gushed over them and kept fresh the immense azure shells in which turbot, trout and char were bathed in a sea-blue sauce. Orchids and lotus floated on the surface, which was sprinkled with crushed pearls and golden powder. There were fillets of meat with an exquisite hazelnut taste and woodcocks in unctuous coral cream, and a multitude of tiny translucid eggs that crunched between the teeth and burst onto the palate, liberating a bouquet of iodized scents.

The conversation, which had until now consisted of mere verbal jousting aimed at describing the magnificent meal in the most eloquent fashion, now began to fragment. Nothing distinct could be heard above the concert of voices. Comte Dandora sighed in relief, for here was clear proof that the evening was a success. A superb feeling of well-being had entered bodies and minds and had freed the guests from their inhibitions. The apothecary was happy to watch his son's amusement at the gastronomic quarrels going on around him that opposed Voltaire to Rousseau, or to pepper his conversation with epigrams, anecdotes and riddles. The guests made light of all subjects. The men of science forgot to be serious and talked about things customarily discussed in the boudoir. The wealth of words was, of course, not hindered by the constant flow of champagne.

Dandora announced the third course – black truffles in champagne and silver ash. A drum began to beat and its rhythm was joined by the frail melody of a flute. Three loud drumbeats, and a heavy curtain was raised to reveal a hearth in which blazed a fire. In front of it sat Malvina, proud and imperious. The heat had reddened her cheeks, and drops of perspiration made her red taffeta dress stick to her body. The generous and suggestive curves of her body were silhouetted by the animation of the flames. Her delicate neck, her slim waist and the firmness of her breasts escaped no one's attention. An ecstatic silence accompanied her steps as she walked to the table. The damp mass of her curls fell down over her cleavage. She wore on her forehead a purple stone which mirrored her rosy cheekbones and added to the impression of a supernatural apparition. All the guests complimented her unreservedly as she moved around the table to serve them. Their praise quenched Malvina's thirst for revenge.

But her attitude nevertheless changed when she arrived at the last guest. The man sitting opposite Dandora was eyeing her with the same intense interest he had earlier focused on the other guests. Two jade irises, accentuated by the black line of his eyebrows, drank in her every move. Their colour seemed to vary with the flickering of the candles. The nose below them was short and narrow, and a discreet smile played on the well-shaped mouth. A dimple in the chin was the only trait that did not correspond to the canon of classic masculine beauty. The thick hair was tied back in a ponytail with a green velvet bow, and the body was clothed in a short light-tan tailcoat.

Malvina knew from portraits she had seen that this was Matthieu de Ghalia. The years had changed him little. He was exactly how she had imagined him – self-confident, almost haughty, but devilishly seductive.

'Join us,' he said.

Malvina blushed. She was so nervous that she wanted only to run away and hide.

'I cannot,' she answered. 'But please do try this. I call it the "Black She-Devil" and it is intoxicatingly succulent.'

'And it is exceptionally evocative,' said the duchesse de Balendard as she swallowed a mouthful.

The count insisted that Malvina sit down with them, but she again refused.

'Are you trying to anger me? Stay, I beg you,' said Matthieu in a stern voice.

Malvina turned to look at him.

'Do you not want to hear what we think of your cuisine?' he asked her. 'Do you not want to know what sort of effect your preparations have on those who consume them? You say you are an expert in the realm of taste, do you not?'

His tone was now one of insolence and it was clear that he was trying to make her look ridiculous.

'That is correct, monsieur.'

'And your talent is no doubt as strong as your reputation. But perhaps you could tell me to what use such a branch of knowledge may be put?'

Malvina moved closer to him.

'My talents have helped your father develop a new pharmacology,' she said.

'His famous research!' smiled Matthieu. 'Men simply cannot get used to the idea of death. Fear makes them naive and idiotic. I do so wish that this accusation were groundless, just as I wish that Joseph Balsamo had never taken advantage of his patients' credulity and sold them a potion of sugared oil! For I can give you the recipe, if you want – two eggs mixed with sugar candy!'

Matthieu's comments spread unease among the guests, who began to look at each other nervously.

'Ladies and gentlemen,' continued the count's son, 'appearances have deceived you. And your palates.'

'What do you mean?' asked a worried duchesse de Balendard.

'Do you know what ingredients went to make up what you have just eaten? I doubt it, for if you did, you would not have touched the food.'

All faces were now turned to the cook.

'Was it not delicious?' asked Malvina, whose chin had begun to tremble.

Honesty obliged them to agree that it was.

'Well, then,' she went on, 'this merely proves that all that is false is not necessarily bad! But please, be not afraid, for I have not sought to poison you.'

A frisson passed through the crowd. The apothecary stood up in his fine clothes and sought to dispel the apprehension.

'One must take pleasure whenever it is offered to us, and this is what we have done this evening,' he said in a loud voice. 'It is true we do not know the origin of the food we ate, but we have all been delighted by its novelty. This theatre of the senses has enabled us to go beyond our prejudices, to leave behind our taboos. And since our century is one of revolutions, I am only too pleased to tell you that this very evening we have been engaged in a revolution of our very own!'

Everyone, except for Matthieu, applauded. The ability to create an illusion was just as worthy of admiration as any technical invention.

'You have dazzled us,' said the duchesse de Balendard

as she raised her glass in Malvina's direction. 'You are a virtuoso, a true artist, mademoiselle.'

'Thank you,' she replied. And then, remembering her anger towards Matthieu, she added cuttingly: 'M. de Ghalia undoubtedly sought to displease me. But I fear he shall be disappointed in this, for I shall willingly debate with him at a future occasion on the science of taste, a science which he clearly underestimates.'

'I do appreciate,' replied Matthieu, 'that in a relationship it is sometimes necessary to sacrifice superficiality for the sake of more long-term aspirations. We shall see each other again, have no fear, my dear sister. I leave at dawn for Constantinople and before then I have some matters to discuss with my father. But I pledge here and now, in front of these witnesses, to speak with you upon my return about this new science you have created.'

Malvina smiled at him, then slipped quietly out of the room, leaving the guests to continue their feast. Dates from the Levant and scalded figs from Marseilles were being consumed with relish when it was announced that a concert would soon begin in the music room. The revelry went on till late in the night, and it was three o'clock before the guests began to ask for their carriages to be prepared.

Malvina sat in the kitchen and stared into the crackling fire as she listened absentmindedly to Alcibiade.

'You were magnificent! They were like blind people who had suddenly regained their sight. They couldn't take their eyes off you! I have to admit I was jealous.'

'It was a humiliating failure!'

'You mean Matthieu?'

She turned to her friend and, with the look of a child who is about to misbehave, begged him to help her.

'What am I going to say to the count? There were important people from the Science Academy at the meal. Our wonderful project will be ruined if they start to believe the accusations that have been levelled against us.'

'But the apothecary's son has no qualification whatsoever in the field of pharmacology. He is merely a diamond merchant. Listen,' said Alcibiade as he took her hands in his, 'Matthieu is simply the type of person who likes to stir up trouble. The rumours will stop once he leaves.'

'I want to seduce him and he responds by making a fool of me! Could he not see that this meal, this theatre of the senses, was simply a way of warning him of the dangers of trusting too much to appearances?'

'Too complicated. Much too complicated,' said Alcibiade. 'You like to manipulate people, to dominate them. But this time you got it wrong. The object of your attention is a person who uses the same methods that you do. In his book, as in yours, there is just one way of fighting, and that is to be the victor!'

'But he will have to see me again if he wants to truly defeat me.'

'There is little doubt that he will want to learn more of the person who is to share his inheritance.'

Alcibiade stood up and began to walk around the room. The kitchen was a shambles, with dirty pots and pans piled up everywhere and enormous pyramids of plates on the tables.

'Shall we start to tidy up?' he asked.

'Leave it until the morning,' she said. 'I'm exhausted. I think I'll wait until tomorrow before talking to the count.'

'Don't worry, he will forgive you.'

Malvina gave him a sad smile. The evening would stay in her mind like a dream that does not stop when the dreamer wakes up. She only had to close her eyes to see Matthieu as clearly as if he were standing at her side. Never had she had such strong feelings for a man. She was no longer angry at him for being unpleasant to her, for he was the one she had been waiting for and she had to accept him however he was! She had never let the thought of failure enter her plans and she saw no reason why her designs on Matthieu should not come to fruition.

Chapter Ten

The only subject of conversation in the whole of Paris the next day was the banquet held by Jean-Baptiste Dandora de Ghalia and his pupil. 'What a devilish good dinner!' they said a hundred times at court. 'What a marvellous idea! I do hope there will soon be another episode of your theatre of the senses!' said Mme de la Ferté-Imbault when she invited the apothecary to join the select few who met regularly in her salon. Her request was quickly repeated by Mme de Polignac and Mme de Genlis. No mention was made of Matthieu's little outburst. None of the people who had been present at the meal dared question the value of the health pastilles. And the dinner had served only to reinforce their faith in Malvina, for whose talents they found only praise. The duchesse de Balendard was so taken with the young woman that she soon asked her to become her adviser. From then on, each and every one of the gatherings she held bore the mark of Malvina.

A springtime dinner Malvina organized for the duchess was a particular success. She presented, on a bed of rose petals, the roots of daisies prepared in the manner of salsifies, borage soup that tasted of oyster, peppered nasturtium pies and crystallized poppies. Each banquet consisted of at least four courses. A 'baroque' dinner she organized later in the year consisted of rotting meat, amber and musk-scented gelatine, saltpetred capons covered in wort biscuits and sausages made of the viscera of slaughtered animals. All the dishes had a whiff of death about them which should have shocked, but did not. On the contrary, the libertines were delighted to amuse themselves with something that was just as scandalous as the practices they normally engaged in.

The acolytes of the marquis de Sade helped Malvina discover food that excited the brain and heightened desire. There was an abundance of fine foods and sumptuous wines from Bordeaux, Champagne and foreign lands. The scenes of true debauchery came only late in the night, long after the orgies, when the guests would give themselves over to acts of rare violence. Malvina would never forget the look on the face of a countess who had lain down naked and let her body be used as a tray for burning hot plates. Her friends poured the hot food over her and began to jab her with forks as they ate it off her skin. 'Cannibalism always gives me such an erection!' said the comte de Pressac as his mouth twisted into a hideous rictus.

God must have been both deaf and blind to have remained indifferent to such atrocities. The Devil revelled in this place of lust. The libertines, on the pretext of proving their ability to rise above their prejudices, loved to build up the most elaborate of arguments. To listen to them, one would think that man was no more than something to be consumed. Death, they said, could not touch them because, on the molecular level, the creative acts of killing and giving birth were the same.

Malvina was enthralled by their talk, which, if it did not convince her, at least reinforced her convictions. What differences were there between these eccentrics with their unbridled morals and a vulgar torturer? Could one excuse such depravity by saying it was merely an expression of individual liberty? The more she frequented these decadent people, the more they lost the right to judge her. Their example pushed her ever closer to freeing herself from any fear she still had of the laws of man or God. Her taste for anatomy and dissection could easily now lead her to choose the pleasures of the flesh over those procured by fine food. She began to be preoccupied with things she had never even dreamed of before. How could someone want to feed on saliva, vomit, sperm or excrement? Yet this was exactly the type of thing the libertines engaged in.

Malvina had made her fortune after just a few months in her new position as culinary adviser. She not only earned enough to achieve financial independence, but could now afford to take on an apprentice. Dandora, meanwhile, was attentive to her every whim. He even offered her an apartment in the heart of the Palais Royal. He had promised to treat her like his own daughter and Malvina no longer doubted his word after seeing her new abode.

The best part of the building was reserved for the comte de Durange, but the apartments on the first floor were vacant. They consisted of a drawing room illuminated by four huge windows, a large bedroom and a kitchen. The garden could be seen from every room. And it was a very pleasant sight indeed, with its double row of century-old trees and the giant chestnut known as the Tall One ever since a group of writers had gathered underneath it to brag and tell each other tall tales. Malvina was delighted to find two white marble fireplaces and a modern set of furniture made from mahogany and lemon-tree wood. And she was overjoyed to have, all for herself, a bath with hot and cold running water. And the drawing room, with its beautifully curved furniture and peaceful colours, promised to be the most comfortable of nests.

'Am I worthy to live in such a place?'

She walked back and forward across the room with her hands on her forehead as though she were about to faint.

'Why are you doing all this for me?' she asked.

'You dare to ask me that?'

'Will your son not be angry? Maybe he's still annoyed with me for having taken advantage of his trust? I fear he did not quite see the point of the dinner we organized in his honour. He was so hostile towards me!'

'The boy is a perpetual rebel!'

Malvina smiled. The first time her master had spoken of Matthieu, it was his contradictory character that had immediately appealed to her. She complimented the count for having brought up such a fine son.

'You must be proud that you enabled him to remain in touch with his whole being. Too many children are ruined by too much discipline.'

'I wonder just what you are seeking to obtain with your flattery,' said Dandora.

'Master,' she admitted, 'I know that to run after a man

in the manner I am pursuing your son is a sure way of displeasing him. But I cannot hide, either from you or from your son, the feelings I have for Matthieu.'

She said the name as though it were a familiar word she had been using for years.

'Alcibiade has kept me informed of your attachment to my son,' said the count, 'which I believe to be most unrealistic. Matthieu is incapable of making you happy. He cannot love a woman: he can only desire her. He never asks for something: he demands it. And I must admit that I am partly to blame for the way he is.'

'I find that hard to believe. You are undoubtedly demanding, but you are far from being a tyrant.'

'He suffered from having an overproud father who had to excel in all things. I so wanted to make my name in medicine that I neglected those people closest to me. Only success mattered and emotions served only to scare me. It is so easy to be consumed with the egotism that comes when you absorb yourself in your work. Alas, yes! I abandoned the countess for my research. I should have protected her. I should have seen her desperation and need.'

'What did you tell Matthieu about his mother's death?' interrupted Malvina.

'For a long time he thought she had succumbed to some illness.'

'He never blamed you?'

'He loved his mother and admired his father. At least until the day he announced he was giving up his anatomical studies and was leaving for England. I knew then that he understood. He never confronted me, but he made it clear that he no longer wanted to follow in my footsteps. I know now that what he really wanted was to talk about what had happened.'

'Perhaps it is not too late.'

'When we meet now I always hide behind the mask of forgetfulness. Seeing the consequences of my cowardice is an unending punishment inflicted on me by life.'

'But why should you continue living this life of remorse? Help me make Matthieu happy!' Malvina pleaded.

Dandora took her hands in his and looked her in the eye.

'Forget him, I beg you! It is not good to be so obsessed with an image of a person rather than with the person himself. I must ask you to forgive me if my talk helped you fall in love with him.'

'But you do love him, don't you?'

'He is all I have left.'

'And me, what do I have?'

The count thought for a moment. Women were superior to men because they never liked to lose an argument. He admired her tenacity and so responded favourably to her request.

'When he returns to Paris in six months, I shall do nothing to prevent you from meeting him. He has said that he does not object to my adopting you, so the matter is now for you to decide. But you must give me your answer soon. For as Montaigne has said, "Age brings more wrinkles to the spirit than to the face." If you accept, then I shall instruct the notary to change my will accordingly.'

Malvina was touched by the count's offer, but she was also aware of the consequences if she were to take it up.

'Please give me a little more time to think about it,' she said. 'But does the affection we have for each other really need to be formalized by legal documents?'

Dandora cleared his throat. 'Whatever you decide, I shall always be there for you in times of trouble.'

Unlike the last time, waiting for Matthieu now seemed to Malvina a delectation, and one that gave her ample time to plan how she would go about conquering him. She would first listen carefully to all that he said, then ask him questions that would lead him to confide in her. For she wanted to see into every corner of his soul, to possess him. She became more and more obsessed with the man as time passed. She thought she recognized him one day as she was out strolling on the boulevard. When the stranger crossed her path, she stared at him and followed him with her eyes as he moved off into the distance. She had been deceived by the man's gait, by the way he held his head. She thought day and night about Matthieu. Every evening she would go to his room. In the cracks in the parquet floor she thought she could make out his profile, and in the oak posts of his bed she saw his silhouette.

*

Matthieu announced his return from Constantinople. The Academy of Science was expecting his report on the mineralogical work he had been carrying out, and the court jewellers were keen to place their orders with him. The ladies of Versailles prided themselves on their collections of gemstones and knew that Matthieu could provide the finest examples. To celebrate his return, he invited Malvina to accompany him on a visit to the duchesse de Bragnac, who had promised to take them to a secret ceremony. Matthieu might have been expected to see Malvina privately, but he preferred instead to show her something she would not quickly forget.

Malvina looked at herself in the dressing-table mirror. She wore a white lawn camisole with a plunging neckline, a drawstring waist and puffed sleeves ending at the elbows. A bodice pushed up her breasts and held in her waist. It was so tight it made her breathing difficult, but she considered it a sacrifice worth making. Her petticoat was hitched up to reveal crossed legs sheathed in silk stockings held up by embroidered suspenders. But all this was lost on the hairdresser, whose thoughts were entirely taken up with the job in hand.

'Ah, madame!' he cried, proud of his creation. 'You look ravishing!'

Malvina watched in fascination as he pranced around her, manipulating his oils, brushes and combs. He had made her hair shine like satin. It was parted in the middle and moved in waves down her face to fall in curls onto her bare shoulders. She held up a mirror and moved her head from side to side to admire the man's handiwork.

'Good,' she said. 'Very good. Now I need to do something about this face of mine. But you must stay close to me, for I shall be needing your advice.'

She darkened her eyebrows, powdered her eyelids with violet-coloured ash and reddened her cheeks. Then she picked up a long, thin brush, dipped it into a bluish ointment and marked out the veins on her neck and chest. She drew a beauty spot on her right breast. Her refined taste and sureness of touch amazed the hairdresser, who was dumbfounded at the young woman's metamorphosis.

'Do you like it?' asked Malvina.

'I cannot find the words to describe your beauty,' he replied.

'But is there not something missing?'

'Perhaps a little more make-up on your cheeks. Aha! I know what it is. The crimson of your lips needs to be touched up a mite.'

Malvina drew closer to the mirror. She ran her fingers over the tender flesh of her mouth. Her lower lip was the more generous of the pair, while the upper was almost severe in its discretion. If the woman's character were to be read from her mouth, one might have concluded that she had a split personality. She nibbled at her lower lip, as she often did, then sucked it in to make it disappear. She could not explain to herself why she was wont to do this. Nerves, perhaps. But it mattered little, for it made her delicious mouth seem all the more beautiful.

'Good Lord!' cried the hairdresser. 'Your mouth is even more attractive than your eyes, and that is no easy matter.'

Malvina smiled at his flattery. She checked her hair one last time, put a drop of lemon juice in her eyes to make them shine, then applied her perfume. She paid the hairdresser for his services and accompanied him to the door. As he left, he made her promise to relate to him in great detail the effect she was about to have on her victim.

'You don't need me to help you dress?' he asked.

Malvina declined his offer, said goodbye and went to her bedroom, where a large gilded wooden box awaited her. She solemnly lifted its lid and took out a dress which she held at arm's length to admire. It was made of dapple-grey taffeta and embroidered with flowers and was the most beautiful piece of clothing she had ever bought. Its flared sleeves served to accentuate its fragility. The outfit was completed by black satin shoes and a lace fan.

Ten minutes later Malvina had transformed herself into a woman of high society. She swished back and forth in her room, smoothing out creases and adjusting her sleeves. She stood before the cheval glass to make sure no faults remained. She experimented with numerous postures to show off her figure and dress. She smiled and practised her pleasantries.

'No, I just can't manage it,' she repeated to herself. A terrible anxiety had suddenly taken hold of her. She may have looked fresh and relaxed, but her heart was thumping and her hands were damp with perspiration. She was terrified that he would not be impressed with her new look. The one and only time he had seen her was when she appeared to him as a she-devil against a background of flames. It would be difficult to live up to that vision, which was no doubt greatly enhanced by the festive atmosphere of the evening. Fear of failure now made her unsure of herself. What would he think? What was this mysterious rendezvous all about? She knew, however, that she must not let herself be overcome by fears, for this would tarnish her beauty.

As she sat in the carriage she tied her mother's scarf around her wrist. It felt soft against her skin and lightened her heart. Whatever happened, she told herself, she would forgive Matthieu. The simple fact that he existed was a source of incomparable joy for her. Even if he spurned her, this would not change the fascination she had for him, since she was sure he merited even the greatest of sacrifices. She had lost any sense of prudence and wanted only to abandon herself to mad love.

Malvina felt as though she were floating on a cloud when the lackeys opened the door of the duc de Bragnac's mansion. She walked into the magnificent building like a goggle-eyed automaton. A servant invited her to wait in a small antechamber, where she checked her hair one more time. She was admiring herself in the mirror when the duchess and Matthieu made their entry. He wore a green morning coat, an embroidered waistcoat sporting polished metal buttons, and a batiste jabot and sleeves. Malvina froze at the sight of such elegance. She suddenly felt clumsy and awkward, and was angry at herself for this. She worried that she wouldn't be able to put two words together. The count's son was touched by the malaise he had inadvertently caused.

'I am so pleased to see you again, my dear. Let me introduce the duchesse de Bragnac, an old friend of mine.'

The elegant woman standing next to Matthieu smiled. She appeared to be of foreign extraction. Her distinguished face had the look of a gazelle, with its long narrow nose, its plump lips and its dark complexion. She was not at all like the other ladies at court. She had a distinct air of mystery about her.

'I have heard so much about you, mademoiselle! All my friends are jealous of your talents. Your dinners are all the rage, it seems.'

'I am ready to offer you my services at any time.'

'She can tackle any type of cuisine,' said Matthieu, looking Malvina in the eye. 'I think she will find this evening much to her liking. But are we not a little early?'

'Yes, it is not done to be on time,' said the duchess. 'Let us wait a little.'

Malvina looked at her but saw in the deep blue of her eyes nothing to elucidate the point of the evening.

'Shall we go into the drawing room?' she asked.

Matthieu replied that he preferred to visit the laboratory.

'Our hostess has a thousand secrets to tell you,' he whispered in Malvina's ear. 'She has a passion for chemistry and for alchemy.'

'Alchemy was my first passion,' confided the duchess. 'My husband taught me the rudiments. The poor man died last year.'

When Malvina asked if she knew the philosopher's stone, the duchess replied with a gracious smile that she already possessed it. She invited them to follow her to a room where, for the last fifteen years, she had kept heating in an oven a powder that could transform any metal into gold.

'To calcine mercury is child's play,' she explained. 'At

least, when one has the secret, as I do. Everyone thinks that Telliamed died in Marseilles in 1748, but I can assure you he writes to me regularly.'

Malvina could taste the smell of burnt wood and the rancid damp of old papers. It was a powerful, ambiguous, disturbing taste. She wondered what game her companions were playing. Why hadn't Matthieu chosen to meet her in a more intimate place? The duchess, as though she had read Malvina's thoughts, supplied an answer.

'You are, it is said, interested in mortuary cuisine?' she asked as she closed the door of the laboratory behind her.

'Taste is my passion! I fervently believe that refined senses are the expression of a refined soul.'

'Matthieu, you did not mislead me. Your friend is truly exquisite. I think she will find our Mass highly amusing.' Then she added, after looking at the clock, 'But let us go now. My carriage is waiting.'

Malvina wondered what their destination was as they raced along the dimly lit quays. She saw the imposing silhouette of Notre-Dame set against a leaden sky, then spotted the fortifications on the edge of the city. The carriage rushed on at full speed and soon they passed the first trees of the countryside. Their bare branches were like claws ready to pounce on a passer-by. An irrational fear took hold of Malvina, a fear heightened by the silence of the night. Malvina was about to say something when Matthieu placed his hand on hers. She was comforted by his gesture.

'Don't be afraid,' he said. 'I am not trying to shock you, simply to surprise you.'

She looked first at him, then at the duchess.

'You are free to leave us at any moment,' the latter said. 'Matthieu told me that you wouldn't be able to stay very long. And to see you together now, I well understand his impatience to be alone with you.'

The coach came to a halt.

'We have arrived,' announced the duchess. 'Be sure not to speak to anyone, and above all do not respond to any questions. They would see immediately that you were not one of their own.'

She handed a domino to each of them and told them to put it on.

*

The building they now entered looked like an abandoned church. The stained glass had long since disappeared and the windows were bricked up. Wrought-iron chandeliers hanging above the side aisles lit up tables piled high with food. The masked guests wandered from one buffet to another and then on to the altar where they were served with chalices of wine and liqueurs.

A servant in livery approached Malvina and her companions. The duchess took out of her purse a tiny selenite stone which she handed to him. It caught the reflections of the candlelight as he turned it round in his fingers before inviting them to join the assembly.

'Follow me,' said the duchess. 'Sister Eleonore is about to prepare mass.'

There was no longer any doubt that this was a place of black magic. For although the rituals of religion appeared to be respected, they were merely subverted. There were phials instead of a ciborium, and eggs took the place of a host.

'The eggs,' explained the duchess, 'are mixed with the bread and wine. But the thirteenth egg is always cut in two, powdered and stirred into a jar of vinegar.'

'What is the significance of this ritual?'

'To remind us of Judas. The vinegar is the symbol of the lees of the world. All the disciples here must drink of it.'

'I knew that convulsionary cuisine would arouse your curiosity,' said Matthieu. 'The Sister is a regular at convulsionary masses. She was a humble disciple for many years before becoming a priestess.'

Malvina stared at him in surprise.

'Let me recount some of the scenes I have seen here,' he went on. 'Do you see, for example, that wretch sitting on the steps of the altar?'

She looked at the adolescent he was pointing out, who wore a simple white linen blouse and held in her hand a glass into which she vomited an opaque substance.

'Mlle Lepaige,' explained Matthieu, 'has for months lived only on excrement and urine. She claims she can no longer feel disgust after attending the sad feasts that take place here. Her mouth would now just as readily accept tea or milk as it would the vile things she pours into it now.'

'I find it hard to believe what you say,' said Malvina.

The duchess asked them to be quiet, for a ritual was about to take place.

'We must leave now,' said Matthieu.

'Please let me stay a few more minutes,' Malvina begged. 'I have never been so fascinated in all my life!'

'So it pleases you to watch a re-enactment of the tortures faced by the martyrs?'

'But you yourself have taken part in this!'

'The unhealthy pleasure you are displaying goes far beyond mere curiosity!'

How could she have been so stupid? He was testing her. If she showed her attraction for the morbid, then all would be lost. Matthieu had finally been repulsed by the macabre side of anatomy and would clearly reject a woman who did not also reject it.

'Let's go!' she said.

They nodded at the duchess as they passed and quickly left the building.

'I couldn't bear it any longer,' he said as they climbed into the coach. 'Do you know how these masses finish?'

She did not.

'When they are not inflicting pain on themselves, convulsionaries delight in eating the most repugnant things possible. They imitate Francis of Paris, the deacon of the parish of Saint Médard, who died in 1727 after leading a life of piety, charity and austerity. These people gulp down human vomit and think that by doing so they can save their own little group from eternal damnation.'

Malvina did not know what to say. She turned and saw that Matthieu was smiling broadly at her.

'I have been haunted by your memory since I last saw you,' he said. 'You intrigue me!'

'Do you mean that you are intrigued by my cuisine?'

'By the way you practise your art,' he said, and moved back into the shadows of the fiacre in a bid to make her talk more easily.

'I live for my cooking. Is that an acceptable answer?'

'So why do you look so serious now? You seem to be forever battling against something. The first night I saw you, you were staring at the guests as though you wanted to follow each and every mouthful they took right down to their stomachs to see what effect it produced. You were like a hangman revelling in the rising emotion of the crowd as the time approaches for him to carry out his task.'

Malvina's breast began to rise and fall as her breath quickened, the blood surged to her fingertips and her cool arms suddenly seemed on fire. Yet she was pleased that Matthieu had thus confronted her. He had pointed out her scars just as another might have complimented her on her beauty. She was impressed.

'Forgive me for being so blunt,' he said as he took her hand, 'but you are different from any other woman I have ever met.'

His flattery brought a smile to Malvina's lips.

'I like cooking much more than you might think,' said Matthieu. 'Is it not magical to be able to seal dozens of hams or legs of lamb in a flask no bigger than your thumb? I love extracting the divine essence of things.'

Malvina feigned confusion, then added, 'I, too, think there is nothing more beautiful than essence.'

*

Neither Malvina nor Matthieu dared speak as the journey neared its end. Their emotions wavered between apprehension and desire. Their gestures were measured so as not to spoil the moments to come and the looks they exchanged were bursting with expectation. Matthieu was radiant. He was ready to do anything to please her. Malvina was both impatient and perplexed, for her lucidity appeared to have abandoned her for the first time in her life. He could ask for the impossible and she would give it to him.

He whisked her through a brightly lit porch and up three flights of stairs to his apartments. He lit a candle to conserve the intimate atmosphere they had created. Then, without speaking, he took her wrists and turned them over as though to examine them. He ran his fingers over her cool, pink, velvety skin, tracing the blue of her veins up along her arms as far as the inside of her elbows. Malvina quivered at his touch, but she held his fingers tight when he went to take them away.

'For months,' she said, 'I have desired you with more passion than it is possible to bear.'

Matthieu savoured her languorous tone and touching sincerity, and the mouth and the body that so eloquently said to him, 'Come!' He had never before felt such a combination of respect and burning desire. He slowly took her hands in his and drew her to him. The curves of her body were so clear under her tight dress that she appeared almost naked. The muslin covering her shoulders slid down over the small of her back. Matthieu held her ever closer as he undid her dress. He shuddered with desire as he exposed her breasts and felt their warmth. He began to caress her wildly. Their teeth and noses collided before their lips united. Malvina closed her eyes as she felt the intensity of desire rising within her. This was what she had longed for. She was so overcome with emotion that she dared not move. She was like a hunted animal frozen with fear. Matthieu was bewildered. He realized that his conquest must be a gentle one. Letting himself be guided by his mistress's sighs, he penetrated her with a brusque movement which he then alternated with gentler thrusts of his hips. Malvina was soon no longer afraid to give herself over to him. Her entire body quivered with delight and her consciousness was floating high above her by the time ecstasy made her cry out.

The morning found them asleep in each other's arms. Malvina woke and observed her sleeping lover. She breathed in the scent of amber that is left after lovemaking and brought her lips close to his face so that her perfume would melt in his mouth. Then she ran her fingertips lightly over his tender skin. She felt no repulsion this time, no desire to flee. She placed her head on his chest and in this position they lay for a long while. Outside the city was waking up and the rumble of carriages on the paving stones grew ever louder. A sunbeam lit up the room. The heat of the day swathed the couple in their peaceful, motionless slumber. The only movement was the rising and falling of their chests. They slept the sleep and dreamt the dreams of lovers.

Chapter Eleven

Malvina would visit her lover whenever she was not busy preparing her society dinners. Their relationship was one of pure passion and they preferred to express their emotions through sensual jousts rather than words. They vied to outdo each other in daring, and discovered penchants they had never even dreamed of. They would whisper the most shameful of desires and then gleefully satisfy them. They would dress up in each other's clothes or don masks to heighten their unbridled passion. Malvina soon became so inventive that no two of their lovemaking sessions were ever the same. And how could he not succumb to her when she was ready to do anything for him? The art of subjugation came naturally to her. Prudence and hesitation were strangers. She was galvanized by the terrible power of domination.

Matthieu slowly became aware of the hold his mistress had on him. His pride would not let him admit to his docility, but he nevertheless secretly rejoiced to have found a woman who was more than a match for him. Her mystery seduced him: her extreme sensitivity touched him. He loved to watch her in the moment of ecstasy, when her face was lit up by a joy so violent it could be expressed only by tears and screams. Malvina knew better than any other woman he had been with how to deploy her weapons to captivate him. There was not a single inch of her body she did not let him explore.

When they were not making love, they liked to walk in the park and watch the chess players or go to the Café de Foy. Malvina loved the sparkling trays there overflowing with pastries, petits fours and jars of chocolate. Matthieu noticed that she always chose a table from where she could discreetly observe the rest of the room. A mirror enabled her to watch how he reacted when other women were present. Matthieu would play up to this by teasing the girl who served lemonade, who would respond to his flattery with an enticing smile. But he would never truly test his mistress's jealousy, for he did not want to shake the complicity that united them.

'Tell me about yourself,' she ordered him one day as they sat in the café. 'Help me to know you better.'

She then spent hours listening to him, questioning him, looking at him. After the Academy of Science had given his work its seal of approval, Matthieu had travelled to the four corners of the earth for years on end to carry out his research. This pleased him enormously, for he hated being confined to the musty rooms of the Louvre just as much as he loathed the incessant disputes with the intendant of the Jardin Royal des Plantes. Malvina feared he might soon go off on another expedition, but she nevertheless became fascinated with the obscure world of mineralogy to which her lover dedicated his life. It was perhaps her jealousy that pushed her to discover what it was that so preoccupied him. She knew something of how precious stones were used in pharmacy but nothing of how they were formed nor of how they were extracted from the earth. Matthieu's explanations employed much imagery and colour so as not to dampen her enthusiasm with technical jargon. And he readily used terms from the science of anatomy, for he knew this was an area she was familiar with.

'The earth is simply an immense body. Its surface, just like the skin that envelops us, is full of signs of what lies underneath. A yellow vein streaked with red signals a deposit of copper, and sedimentary rocks or schist may hold opal or turquoise. Once you have read the signs, you then begin the dissection. You dig, you make cuts, you rip open the tissue to get inside the endless organ, then you hunt until you reach what might turn out to be the tiniest of seams.'

One day, while he was telling her about a deposit of emeralds discovered by the English in the Indies, Malvina dared ask him about the particular attachment his family appeared to have for the stone. Matthieu was a little taken aback by the question. He knew it was impossible to work with his father and not be let into some family secrets, so he felt that his mistress's question was more knowing than it appeared to be.

'The countess loved the mystery of emeralds,' he explained. 'There was a story she told almost every evening when I was a child. She would tell me that in the mines of ancient Egypt, each and every stone had a certain power. The most beautiful would be shaped into scarabs and kept for the pharaohs. And when a pharaoh died, they would replace his heart with one of these scarabs before they mummified him. The emeralds were thus a sign of immortality.'

'The emerald is green like the plants in the field. It speaks of nature, life, youth, hope,' enthused Malvina.

'And do not forget the Grail,' responded Matthieu. 'The vase that held the blood of God, the vessel that was a symbol of love and sacrifice, was made of emeralds and green crystal.'

The word 'sacrifice' suddenly made Malvina think of something Dandora had confided to her – the real reason why his wife and Matthieu's mother had taken her own life.

'Love can lead people to carry out all sorts of acts,' she said. 'But do you think that one can die of love?'

Matthieu knew she was alluding to his mother. He never spoke to anyone about her for he suffered both from his great love for her and from a sense of having been abandoned by her. In her final years she would frequently spend entire days locked up in her room and her perceived betrayal of him was compounded when she left him for ever by ending her own life. It was to escape his despair that he fled abroad. From such a distance he was able to nurture an illusion that she was maternal perfection.

'Life,' he said, 'must use its pleasures as weapons to oppose the cold monster of death. The other world does not attract me. I hate suffering and want neither to impose it on anyone nor to submit to it myself.'

Malvina looked at the emerald embedded in the silk of his shirt.

'This stone,' he said, 'is just like my mother – beautiful, inaccessible and enchanting.'

'It is iridescent like a preternatural light illuminating the night sky,' said Malvina.

He was moved by her words and took her hands in his. 'Would you wear it for me?'

'I couldn't wear something so precious!' she said, enchanted.

'So you would refuse me a favour?' he said as he undid the emerald. 'Please honour me by accepting it.'

He placed the stone in the palm of her hand, where it shone so brightly it might have been a living thing.

'Even if it is polished or plunged into acid, this emerald will keep its magnetism. My mother was certain that it would cause profound malaise for the wearer if he or she did not know how to love. Take it,' he said with just a hint of sarcasm in his voice. 'It will let you test the depths of your emotions.'

He seized her hand and closed it tight over the jewel. She said nothing, but knew she could not refuse such a gift.

'Does its power frighten you?' he asked with a burst of laughter.

'No, it is more the power of my own feelings that terrifies me!'

Matthieu did not respond. To wander down this path would be to enclose their love in banality. The unique, incomparable nature of their union must take them far beyond the vapidity of promises and plans for the future, of talk of marriage or children. Words could not describe the link that bound them.

Malvina could not sleep that night. Countless thoughts and images filled her mind. Her happiness was so new it was almost painful. She looked at the man sleeping next to her and knew he was unaware of how he had become the unhoped for light in her life, the light that would put an end to the darkness of her past. Should she tell him? The truth would shock him, but perhaps it would also be a test of the depth of his feelings for her. Maybe it was better not to say anything, to simply be happy to have this hand to hold, to kiss its silken skin.

How could she not taste this lover whose epidermis was quivering with rising desire? She wanted to mark his body with a sign that only she could read. She began to run the tip of her tongue over his humid skin, over his neck, his chest, his stomach. Matthieu soon became fully aroused and wanted to enter her, but she stopped him and instead climbed on top of him. What she wanted went far beyond mere copulation. She took her lover's head in her hands and pressed his mouth against hers. She nibbled his lips and then in a long and languorous kiss sought out the taste of his saliva to savour the exquisite melange of their fluids. Then she raised herself up so that her breasts were even with his mouth. She wanted to nourish him with her flesh. As he sucked on her glistening flesh, she revelled in this reversal of roles where she was brought to a climax by being inside him. Ecstasy washed in waves over the writhing couple. The emotion that filled Malvina was far beyond anything she had ever experienced. And she knew this was what she had always wanted – to abandon herself to a cannibalistic love.

*

The next day, Malvina decided to visit comte Dandora. Matthieu went to see his father regularly to discuss business, but Malvina had not dared enter the pharmacy for some weeks. Alcibiade had taken over her duties, but she felt bad about abandoning her former master without thanking him for all he had done for her. 'Surely he will be only too pleased that his son has found happiness!' she told herself as she pushed open the door of the boutique.

The apothecary stood up and moved towards her. He had the same gestures, the same elegance, the same refined voice as when she had first seen him all those years ago.

'Can I help you, mademoiselle?' he said with a note of amusement in his voice.

'I am thinking, monsieur,' she replied.

'An apothecary's shop has never been noted as a place where people come to think, but please do carry on, mademoiselle, do carry on. The smell of narcotics is undoubtedly most intoxicating.'

Age had slowed him a little physically, but his wit was as sharp as ever.

'Sit down here, my child,' he said, offering her the comfort of his armchair. 'So you haven't forgotten our first meeting either?'

'How could I forget my arrival in Paris?'

'How you have changed since then! Your success has given you the confidence of a lady of the highest society, and love has made your beauty radiant.'

'I love Matthieu and I am glad this is clear to the world.'

His voice took on a mockingly authoritarian tone. 'But was it really necessary to abandon your old friends?'

Malvina lowered her eyes. 'Forgive my ingratitude,' she said. 'Happiness makes you selfish.'

'Alcibiade misses you. He is forever tired and has lost a lot of weight. In fact, I am quite worried about him.'

'Is he in a bad way?'

'It is clearly not healthy to spend too long in the company of corpses. The morbidity of his work makes him sad. He only carries on making the health pills because it helps him feel closer to you. You do know that he loves you dearly, don't you?'

'He has always refused to accept my relationship with your son! What am I to do about such pig-headedness?'

'He is hurt and you know it. You lacked the courage to talk to him. I'm not judging you, but you should at least admit your error.'

Malvina pursed her lips and clenched her jaws. 'Do you want me to take on an apprentice to help him out in the laboratory?' she asked drily.

'That will not be necessary,' the count replied. 'I am thinking of retiring from the business.'

'You mean you plan to give it all up?' she asked in surprise. 'You can't do that, not after all the effort you've put into it.'

'We are no longer selling as much as we need to.'
'So you just have to develop a new product!' she said. Her eyes glistened with ambition and excitement. 'This time all we need to do is create a drug that will act not on the body but on the mind,' she said. 'Just yesterday in the market I saw a charlatan selling viper flesh which he claimed would calm anxiety.'

The count ran his finger nervously over his upper lip. 'You do not understand,' he murmured. 'There is no man who does not begin to feel the bitterness and mould of age. I have lost my taste for life, Malvina.'

'You astound me! You of all people should want to taste of the final pleasures that life has to offer.'

'Yes, but I want to do so without having to worry about my affairs. So I have decided to go and live in Saint Malo. Alcibiade will stay on at the pharmacy for as long as it takes to tie up the loose ends. And, as you already know, I plan to bequeath you a share of my fortune. I do not know if Matthieu and you plan to marry, but whatever happens, I want to be sure you will never be in need. I want to be your adoptive father, the one that I should have been for your mother.'

Malvina's trembling hands revealed her disarray.

'You shall have an allowance every month double your current salary. That should make us quits,' he said as though he had just clinched an important business deal.

The count went on to explain in detail how he would pay the money to her. Then he got up to fetch a bottle of orange liqueur and a couple of glasses. He poured out the scented liquid and downed his glass in one go. Malvina did the same. The alcohol burned her throat, made her eyes shine and helped hide the strong emotions that were running through her.

*

It was after nine o'clock when she left the Rue Saint-Honoré. As she hurried home she decided to try on several dresses before choosing the one she would wear when Matthieu arrived later in the evening. She would place a few logs on the fire so that the hearth would be at its most intimate when her lover came. And she wondered which of her many perfumes would be the most enchanting for this particular evening. For she knew that love needed a thousand little touches to keep it strong. These were the happy things she was contemplating when she heard a voice behind her.

It was a forgotten whisper from the darkness of the past, a strident whisper that had the name Rougemont imprinted upon it, a whisper that made her choke with fear. She saw once again the storm that had raged the day her parents were hanged. She heard once more Sister Clotilde's poison glass crash to the ground.

She looked round and saw an empty street. But when she walked on, a different set of footsteps echoed her own, slowed when hers slowed and quickened when hers quickened. She began to run, and ran until she had no more breath to run further. A pair of hands suddenly gripped her shoulders like a vice and whirled her round. She screamed when the hawker began to drag her along the ground, but her screams were in vain for there was no one to hear them. Rougemont's face was pressed against her own, his mouth just millimetres from her lips. His stinking breath was so repulsive she felt as though she was suffocating, as though her heart had stopped beating. She thought she saw blood everywhere, on her face, on her hands. Something inside her was about to explode.

Rougemont let her fall onto the pavement. She crouched on the dirty ground and looked up at him as a child would look at a giant.

'Why now?' she managed to say.

'I got ten years in prison for handling contraband,' he said. 'Hubertine looked after you better than you could have imagined. She died shortly after your departure. And you killed her with your weasel words and your evil eye!'

The words burnt into Malvina's soul like acid poured on naked flesh.

'I've been looking for you for the past six months. It was the name on that book of yours that led me to you in the end. Dandora de Ghalia – I spotted it in the newspapers. "For sale", the advertisement said. I waited there for weeks for you to show up.'

'What are you after?'

'Me? Nothing. I just wanted to be present at your downfall. The Devil in you will soon take you, Malvina. I have paid for my crimes and it is only right that it should be the same for you. I have lived through the hell of prison, and now am faced with sickness. Look! Gangrene has set in on my leg. But I plan to hang on just long enough to see you fall. It's the one thing that keeps me alive.'

'You are mad!' she cried. 'Totally mad!'

'You haven't forgotten!' he said, holding out a cheap rag doll. 'I'll bet it's just like one you had when you were a child. Every little girl had one.'

Malvina snatched the doll out of his hands. Yes, she did remember. Her father used to say it was just like a sister for her. 'No flesh, no heart, just a bundle of misfortune,' he would say. She had repeatedly tried to rid herself of it, and once even buried it in the garden. But the cursed thing kept coming back to remind her that she was bad.

'You can never escape your childhood,' said Rougemont. 'It just don't go away, the past, eh? Me, I wouldn't know how to stop myself thinking my thoughts of revenge.'

Malvina was petrified. She thought of Matthieu. She thought of their love, their love that the blood of her past was about to stain.

'I will pay for your silence,' she said.

He snorted with laughter, and his belly rocked in and out like the flank of a fevered beast. 'Your wealth will not save you!' he said.

'You are no more than your venality, so just take this money and be gone!'

Rougemont limped forward, weighed the purse she gave him in his hand, and pretended to bow. 'Let's look on this as a down payment.' He smiled, then disappeared into the night.

Malvina wandered aimlessly for hours through the city, looking up from time to time at the dark skies. Her unbalanced gait suggested an inner struggle, an incessant interior monologue. It was almost midnight when she reached home, exhausted. A worried Matthieu met her at the door. Instead of throwing herself into his arms as she usually did, she went straight to her room.

'What's wrong?' he asked.

Malvina took a seat by the fire. She was like a child as she sat there holding her doll. Matthieu suddenly realized that she was delirious.

'I hate him!' she repeated nervously. 'I hate him.'

Her armchair began to sway as though the earth were shaking the foundations of the house. She swung back and forward on it as she sucked the thumb of her right hand. With her other hand she squeezed the doll until it burst into a shower of porcelain shards and cut open her skin.

'Don't touch me!' she screamed at Matthieu as he went to help her. 'I am not bad! Do you understand? That was long ago, a long time ago.'

He wanted to hold her, to stroke her hair, but he feared this might upset her even more. 'I'm going to clean that wound,' he said, and got up to fetch a jug of water and a cloth. Malvina held out her hand. Her eyes had suddenly taken on a look he had never seen before. She licked her cut and asked him to do the same. He pressed his lips to her hand and stroked the wound with his tongue.

'What does my blood taste of?' she asked him. 'Tainted blood tastes different. You have pure blood, you should know that.'

'You don't really believe this rubbish, do you? Malvina, look at me! I don't recognize you any more.'

'Blood is the expression of the soul. Tell me what you see.'

Matthieu did not reply. He concentrated on bandaging her hand, then took her in his arms and carried her to bed. But she had barely lain down when she was once again overcome with anguish. Matthieu was becoming seriously concerned for her.

'I surely can't be bad if I am capable of love, can I?' she asked plaintively. Her dark eyes glistened with tears and her long hair lay tousled on the pillow. 'My love for you will save me from hell!' she muttered.

'I don't know what got you into this state, but believe me when I say nothing is going to happen to you.'

'Take me!' she begged. 'Take me!'

He penetrated her brutally.

When the fire of desire burned brightly in her stomach and in her chest, Malvina hoped it would bring with it a death to free her from all suffering. But she knew this was not to be. When the act was over she lay on the bed and caressed her lover as he slept. She ran her fingers over his body as though to recapture the ecstasy of their union. They moved gently at first, then more firmly. She suddenly began to scratch at the skin which she now found repugnant. She wanted to wrench the epidermis from its body and roll it up into a ball which she would bury deep within herself. This was the only way to erase the bruises and scars of her childhood! She must eat this skin that tormented her!

*

Matthieu asked her again the next morning what it was that troubled her, but she would talk only of his father.

The count's departure for Brittany, his inheritance and his remarks on ageing had all given her a sense of urgency, she said. She insisted that Matthieu spend all his time with her before he went off on his next voyage. Thus they became caught up once more in the fury of their relationship and spoke no more of Malvina's trouble. She did all she could to hide her fears from him. Her desire took on a renewed vitality. The assassin's blood flowing in her veins took possession of her body. It was only with sexual exhaustion that she found peace of mind.

Their lovemaking was always preceded by a meal. Not an ordinary dinner, but a series of dishes designed to enable them to prolong their congress. Matthieu was always enchanted by the noise of clattering saucepans, the smell of game roasting on a spit and the sweet voice of Malvina singing as she cooked. She delighted him with her remarks on how the strength of the spices or the bitterness of the rocket would affect their performance in bed. Just as Rabelais wrote of his 'venereal' herbarium, Malvina liked to play with ingredients to produce the most prodigious of results.

When Matthieu brought her an enormous bouquet of roses one day, she decided she would use some of them in her cooking that evening. Their thorns cut into her hands as she held them and the pearly white of their petals was stained with the red of the tiny drops of blood that emerged from her skin.

'They are so beautiful!' she repeated.

Tears of joy ran down her cheeks. She was so happy she almost forgot the pain inflicted by the thorns.

'Give them here. You'll hurt yourself,' said Matthieu.

She removed the petals one by one and placed the darkest ones on a silver tray. She sprinkled a little brown sugar and water over them, then placed the tray in an oven. From another oven she took two thrushes which she promptly slit down the middle to reveal a stuffing whose scent Matthieu recognized immediately.

'Truffle!' he cried in delight.

'Rose truffle,' she replied proudly.

The dish was truly impressive, and had a positively aphrodisiac effect on the couple. They began to feel an intense heat slowly build up inside them. Malvina's blood had dissolved into the juice of the roses, into the flesh of the thrushes, into the wine and into each and every taste of the meal. Her being entered Matthieu's body with every mouthful he took. He swallowed her without resistance, let her penetrate him profoundly.

'I have never eaten anything as good as this in my life!' he said.

But how could it be otherwise, when Malvina had decided to be delicious?

They repeated this ritual endlessly. They lounged in the mornings after vigorous lovemaking, then made love again before taking a siesta in the afternoon. And if routine came to threaten them, they would chase it away with their love of the new and the unexplored. For their perpetual quest was to make the ultimate discovery.

*

When Matthieu announced that he must travel to Idar Oberstein in Rhineland-Palatinate, Malvina felt he was violating a tacit accord between them. She tried to dissuade him, but he insisted. He said the mission was of the highest importance.

'We can't live like recluses any more,' he explained. 'We are both of us brimming with vitality. But we can only be enriched by contact with others, not by wallowing in the void of our frustrations. We must nourish ourselves with the world outside, with travel, with discoveries. No man or woman alone can achieve this.'

'That's not true! I have enough ideas in my head to keep you amused for a hundred years!'

Matthieu would normally have been delighted by such flattery. But he had begun to suspect that the treasures of Malvina's imagination might soon begin to lose their charm. She had been for him what he had been for her – a shock, a fire burning everything that stood in its way. But he felt that such intensity could not last. Or that it could only be made to last if excess became the norm. Perhaps they were denying themselves true love by their endless search for the unknown and the unusual. He knew he should speak to her of his doubts, but cowardice prevented him. He kissed her and promised to return as soon as he could.

The separation was an ordeal for Malvina. She did not know what to do with herself and ended up spending entire evenings reading books on mineralogy. She began to wonder if Matthieu was suffering as much as she was, and a horrible suspicion began to gnaw at her. Perhaps her bond with him was not as strong as she thought it had been. Yet since her encounter with Rougemont she had given even more of herself to him, if that were possible. The hawker had not returned, but the very thought of him still terrified her more than if he came to her door every day. Fear left a horrible taste in her mouth. Her lips became dry and pale and her throat refused to drink in the air she needed to fill her lungs. Every single day she wished Rougemont had never used the word 'curse'.

She knew that only her love could save her. She had reached its heights and now had to learn how to slow the inevitable descent. To bottle up her true sentiments would be a sign of jealousy and weakness. No, if she wanted to keep her lover, she would have to risk losing him. It was with these thoughts in mind that she decided to host a Greek dinner to mark the night of his return.

Chapter Twelve

Each guest was given an elegant white tunic girdled with a golden sash. The lights in the dining hall were subdued and a penetrating scent of flowers mingled with incense and the vapours of provocative liqueurs. On the table were eels from the River Eurotas, partridges from Mount Taygetus, kids, olives, figs and honey cakes. Young African slaves served wine from Cyprus.

Malvina was no longer amused by the festivities and sought Matthieu's eye. She spotted him sitting like a sultan in the midst of a clutch of women whose cheeks were plastered with vermilion. They were not prostitutes but ladies of the court and they all turned to look at their hostess when she joined their circle. They wanted to assess whether she was a serious contender.

'Sit down, my dear,' said one of them, and offered her a seat on the edge of the circle. Malvina chose one nearer Matthieu.

'You are more beautiful than ever,' said another.

'You flatter me. It is to yourself that such compliments should be addressed,' replied Malvina.

Matthieu thought she would be angry to see him

surrounded by all these women, but she smiled calmly as she stood before him.

'Ladies,' she said suddenly, 'do you not think that M. le viscomte Dandora should recount for us his finest conquest, his love of all loves?'

'Yes!' the women cried in chorus.

'You must begin immediately before you have time to think about it,' said the comtesse de Sucy.

'But why should such things interest you?' asked Matthieu with the nonchalance of a man who knows that his audience is bursting with impatience.

'Go on, monsieur,' said Malvina. 'Dare to let yourself go.'

The train of her dress hung over her chair like a serpent choking its prey. Matthieu gave his admirers a seductive look and then sat back to think for a moment before agreeing to the request.

'Discretion shall prevent me from naming the person whose love has given me the greatest satisfaction.'

Malvina tensed.

'She was,' Matthieu continued, 'charming, intelligent and sensitive. She was the most tender of mistresses and the best of friends. I have never encountered more goodness or sympathy in a person.'

'Is she your betrothed?'

'The angel left me, madame, without ever having existed.'

The assembled women applauded, for the young man had thrilled them all with his tale and wounded none. Only Malvina did not respond. She was more sad and disappointed than angry. She got up and went towards the door. Matthieu caught up with her just as she was about to walk through it.

'Do stay! You know I was merely jesting.'

'Go ahead and have your fun, but do not treat me like that!'

'I thought you would understand. It was just a joke.'

'Then you do not know me well if you thought I would be amused.'

'Sometimes I think that you love me too much! Please forgive me – I was wrong!'

She looked deep in his eyes. 'Are you sure you do not want to leave me?'

Matthieu did not dare upset her further.

*

The memory of this evening perturbed Malvina for a long time. It was surely not insignificant that her lover had chosen to vaunt the charms of an unknown woman, even if she was merely the fruit of his imagination. This was not just a simple smile for a girl selling lemonade, this was a betrayal. He had made light of their emotions in front of people who knew about their relationship. Matthieu was playing on her jealousy and this was clearly a sign that he was beginning to get bored. This was the first time he had needed to use other people to rekindle the flame of their passion. If he continued down this path, their love would soon collapse into quarrels and then violence. To avoid this, she must once again prove that she was unequalled, that she was above the laws of men.

Malvina had not forgotten Rougemont's claim that she was the personification of evil. Why should she deny that she was faced with an unending internal struggle between darkness and light? Yes, she had watched and said nothing as the nun drank the poisoned cup. Yes, she had wished a hundred times for the death of the hawker. And she did not regret it. Yet her time with Matthieu had been a respite from the darker side of her character. At least until the day when she saw him begin to move away from her. She could have sought revenge, but this would merely fulfil Rougemont's predictions. And besides, she knew that the passion she carried in her heart for Matthieu would never be quenched. She knew that whatever fate had in store for her, she could keep evil at bay as long as she kept loving.

Yet she also thought that she had for too long tried to shut emotions out of her life. She had, for example, never once sought to get in touch with Hubertine, and now her old friend was dead. She tried to remember the details of her round and tender face, but they were gone from her mind for ever. Malvina did not want this to happen with Matthieu. She would offer him her flesh and blood to keep him. And she now realized that she must reconcile herself with God, whose presence she was beginning to feel for the first time in her life. It was as though he had opened a little door to let her approach him.

*

It was one sunny morning in the month of March when she finally walked through the door and marched up to the flower-bedecked altar of the church of Saint-Roch. She sat down on a bench opposite a statue of Jesus hovering in the light of the candles. She was alone in the silent church. She knelt down, joined her hands and contemplated the figure of Christ on the cross. He did not look like a bloodthirsty torturer. It was his love for mankind that led him to sacrifice himself for mankind.

Malvina prayed. The voices of the Sisters of Cahors rang out in her mind with the words of the 'Our Father' and the 'Hail Mary'. She began to say these prayers again and again and grew calmer with each syllable. Her past appeared to lose the bitterness of sin. On her lips she had the taste of her tears and in her heart she felt a new purity. A ray of light pierced the stained-glass windows and illuminated the nave of the church. She smiled when she saw this symbol of the peace that was entering her heart. She sat for a long time in this light that came from above, for all around her were shadows and dangers to be avoided.

When she finally left the church, she had just one thought in her mind. She wanted to suffer in every part of her body so that like the saints she could become an instrument of salvation. Matthieu was tiring of her body, so she would put it to new use. It was obvious to her that a truly pure love must refuse pleasure in all its forms. She remembered the hagiographies Clotilde used to read to her to frighten her. She thought of the hermit who resisted the Devil by chopping off first his fingers, then his hand and his arm and throwing them into the fire. She recalled the terrible sufferings that marked the life of Theresa of Avila. Yes, this was the price of salvation – privation and physical degradation!

Malvina's attitude towards men and her outlook on life were thus radically and suddenly altered. She had left jealousy far behind her. A frenzied desire for purity had taken hold of her heart. Yet she had not forgotten the vulnerability of the flesh nor the fragility of the soul. She could thus forgive Matthieu for his misdemeanours and would place their love beyond the habitual degradations of the emotions. It had taken her so many long years to realize that the violence within her was simply a desire for the absolute.

When she went to see her lover that evening, she went straight to the bedroom. She sat there with a serious look on her face and with her legs drawn up beneath her like a bird at rest. How could she explain to Matthieu this new way of loving she had discovered?

'Abstinence! So that's how you plan to punish me!' he cried.

'I am merely trying to love you even more than I already do.'

'You want to love me better by depriving me of something that brings a man and a woman together in the most natural of ways!'

'You don't see what I'm trying to do for us, do you? We have to find a way to escape from the routine of intimacy, from the vulgarity of the flesh. One must lose oneself if one is to achieve true love. I feel ready for any sacrifice to achieve this.'

'Including the chance to create new life!' he said drily.

'Are you talking about having a child?'

But she could never do this! The Virgin Mary herself

had never deigned to bless her womb by making it fertile. And why did Matthieu ask her this now when he had never spoken of marriage? He could not be serious. He was mocking her. He sought to wound her.

'How could I procreate when nature is against it?' she asked him.

'Is it nature or your mind stopping you?'

'My body cannot be shared. It must remain intact. You must understand that.'

Her reply confirmed Matthieu's fears. He scrutinized her face with his anatomist's eye. He saw under her skin a skeleton that lacked any generosity. Its angular bone structure revealed a cold hardness.

'I do not want a child,' repeated Malvina.

He could not think of a reply. This woman was refusing him the most elementary of gifts.

'What are you afraid of?' he asked after a long pause. 'Of seeing your body grow ugly? But a mother is the most beautiful of all women. She is beautiful because of the unique power she has to give life and because of the sublime love with which she swaddles her naked child. Mothers are the envy of all women.'

'I cannot have a child without taking a risk of which you can have no idea.'

'Tell me, then. I know nothing about your past.'

'I was brought up in a hospice. There is nothing to tell.'

'My father knew your mother when she was still a child. He has fond memories of her. Do you feel the same?'

'I loved her less than I love you. Are you not proud of that?'

'I am flattered, but I am also sad to see that you can be so insensitive.'

'Let us end this conversation here!'

Matthieu agreed. He needed time to take stock of his troubled emotions, to decide how he would deal with this bitter disappointment. For the first time in his life he was afraid of what lay ahead. He had always placed his liberty above all things. But now he felt like a prisoner.

*

It was around three o'clock in the morning when Malvina heard the church bells ring. She opened her eyes, or at least thought she did, and saw the silhouette of a woman against the dying embers of the fire. 'What a pleasure to meet oneself,' said the stranger without moving her lips. 'I have been waiting for this moment for so long and you have been resisting for so long. You have destroyed everything by seeking to keep him. You poor fool, you forgot that a single thorn is enough to burst a man's heart, to end his life. Your refusal to have a baby is so cruel that it will not be long before he rejects you! You made the wrong choice and now you must accept your failure. Just say the word and I am yours.' Malvina suddenly was wide awake and filled with nausea. She got out of bed and sat down on the floor with her knees drawn up to her chin. She must not give in. This vision did resemble her but it was only an impression, it was not reality. The spectre could not be herself because she had not lost her reason. Her mind was still clear. She was alone in the room with Matthieu. She would wake him now and he would tell her there was no one else here.

'Look carefully,' she begged him. 'I can still hear a sort of murmur, as if someone is talking.'

'But there is nobody else here!'

'I know that. But something is there without being there.'

Her face was the troubled mask of a frightened woman. He took her by the shoulders. This was not the first time she had woken him like this in the night.

'What's the matter? Please tell me.'

'The final decision will always be yours,' she muttered. 'Isn't that right?'

'What are you saying?'

'I will give you more than a child,' she said in a barely audible voice. 'When you have decided, I shall be ready.'

'Ready for what, in the name of God?'

'To pass into the other world, where I shall be able to keep intact that which we have created in this world.'

Matthieu released her and began to pace up and down the room. After a few moments he turned to her and said that he did not want her to die.

'But not now, of course!' she said brusquely. 'It is you who must give me the sign.'

'Have you lost your mind?!'

'Never say that!' she screamed. 'Never! Do you hear me?'

Matthieu stormed out of the room, slamming the door behind him. But a strange noise, the like of which he had never heard, made him stop before he had even got to the stairs. Never had Malvina's voice been so sharp. It was like the sound of a sharp instrument being drawn slowly over crystal glass. It was a howl that might have been heard in every corner of the world. Matthieu went back to the bedroom and found his mistress stretched out on the bed. Her tear-stained face was contorted with pain. She had bitten her cheeks so hard that they bled.

He sat down next to her and gently brushed the tousled hair from her forehead as her body shook with an enormous sob.

'My love for you is stronger than my soul or my body,' she said. 'If I lose you . . .'

'But why do you talk of losing me?'

'You must protect us by loving me. That is all I ask of you.'

'You must calm down,' he said.

He put his arms around her and began to stroke her hair.

'I can't live without you,' she repeated.

Matthieu was mesmerized by the intense look in her eye. The cold and determined woman he had been dealing with just a few moments ago was now a defenceless child. He rocked her in his arms until she fell asleep. He looked at her slumbering and told himself he could never leave her.

Over the following days Matthieu came to realize that their life together had entered a new, sombre phase. He could no longer see the woman he had fallen in love with. Her strangeness used to exhilarate him but now it began to perturb. When he was alone with her, he felt he was being spied upon. He sensed some heavy, invisible presence in the room with them. He tried hard not to let boredom come between them, but his love was not strong enough.

After seven months of intense passion, their relationship was now one of carnal friendship. Their embraces grew less frequent. At first he thought this might be some game of Malvina's aimed at rekindling the fire of their love, but he soon realized she no longer wanted him to touch her. She was also refusing practically all nourishment, arguing that food prevented clarity of mind and caused the soul to fall into a state of lethargy. Her body gradually grew thin and lost its youthful vigour. It came to resemble that of Matthieu's mother shortly before her suicide and he could not bear to look at her. He did not want to see Malvina sacrificed like this. 'If you love her, you must lift this woman out of her distress,' his conscience told him. 'Only you can undo the knots that tangle her spirit.' But he could not bring himself to action.

His cowardice led him to accept any business propositions that would take him away from the capital. And when he was in Paris, he spent most of his time in cafés listening to the new ideas spoken so enthusiastically by the young people. France was nearing bankruptcy and a series of impotent governments came and went again in rapid succession. The country was experiencing too many upheavals to leave any of its citizens untouched. Yet Malvina carried on as though these national traumas had nothing to do with her. She stayed locked in her room, looking out of the window at a Paris transfigured by events.

She shivered, for the icy winter air came through gaps in the frame. Both the cold and a deep despair had invaded her body. She no longer knew whether it was her soul or her body that ached the most. But she did know she had failed. How could she ever make him love her again? How could she stop this descent into the void? Her eyes had been damaged the day she had sat in the church and stared into the ray of light that fell through the stained glass and now she could bear the light of day for only a short time. She lay down on the bed, riven by nausea and violent headaches. She was like an insect pinned to a cork. God had mapped out her life with a chilling logic. He had made her believe that love would bring forgiveness and purity. How she hated him for having made her happy!

She was not at all reassured by the fact that Matthieu did not speak of leaving her. She knew that men lacked emotional courage, that they easily accepted a deteriorating situation. Her lover no doubt planned to leave her in the manner of a snake shedding its skin. He would cast her off knowing he had taken all the good things from her. She was desolate, but could not bring herself to fight against her fate. Yet she still harboured a wild ambition. She still planned to make her sentiments eternal.

But for now all that mattered were the rare moments she spent with Matthieu. She did not care that he had less and less desire to be with her. She would bring her lips close to his and say, 'Kiss me.' He would obey. 'Again.' Again he would obey. She wanted to insert her tongue in his mouth to explore it, to lick his soul and discover what he kept hidden there. One night, as they lay in bed, she gently took hold of his hand and without waking him examined the lines that marked its palm. By the light of the moon she studied his heartline and saw a long, delicate curve that came to an abrupt end near the base of his fingers. Yes, it was all clearly marked out here, she thought. Too clearly. She wanted to draw a new line that spoke of a happier future but knew this was a futile idea. She then imagined herself biting into the palm and destroying this destiny which tore her from the man she loved. Her decision was now taken.

She woke Matthieu and sat stiffly as she spoke in the darkness.

'We must leave each other, for we are no longer worthy of our love!'

He leant on an elbow and looked at her.

'I am no longer afraid of losing you,' she went on. 'I will be able to live alone again.'

He did not understand. 'Why this sudden sense of urgency?' he asked.

'There is nothing left to be saved. You must now let me regain the dignity I have lost in staying by your side.'

He took her hands in his. 'I am very fond of you, Malvina.'

'I have finally understood that you cannot save me from my life. I have come to see that there is a certain purity in darkness and an imperceptible light in evil. This lucidity enabled me to love you, for one cannot love if one does not accept oneself. This you know.'

Malvina had taken hold of his shirt and gripped it so tightly that she almost ripped it. 'I love you,' she sobbed.

'You must never forget that! But we must live apart for a time.'

'Are you sure?' He already knew the answer.

'Please promise me something,' she said. 'Please agree to dine with me every Tuesday.'

'You want me to dine with you?'

'I will be greatly distressed if you refuse.'

He agreed. He was horrified that she should think he could abandon her.

'I will be there,' he said as he took her in his arms. 'It will be a pleasure to see myself once again walking into a trap.'

Little did he know how soon this trap would ensnare him.

Chapter Thirteen

Malvina wanted Matthieu to regain his trust in her, she wanted him to look forward to their meetings. She appeared to regain her zest for life, but it was merely a pretence, for inside she still felt alienated from the people and objects that surrounded her. Walks through the city, visits to salons and sumptuous dinners contributed to the illusion of her rehabilitation. Each afternoon she would pay a courtesy visit to her old home at the pharmacy. There she would sit for hours on end with Alcibiade in his workshop. The dwarf had long ago forgiven his friend. She rarely spoke when she came to see him now, but he knew that she needed him just to be there with her. Sometimes he would rest his head in her lap. No words could translate the ambiguity of their emotions.

Malvina would often stand in front of her mirror to contemplate her desolation. Sadness had made her once striking face sullen and inexpressive. Cucumber water, which normally brought colour to any skin, could do nothing for her. She knew that her mask would soon begin to crack, so to precipitate the inevitable she began to mutilate herself. She sought out the sharpest edge of the emerald her lover had given her, ran the soft flesh of her thumb over it and then brought it up to her face. She first made a tiny cut in her neck and then plunged the stone deeper to make a bloody gash. She did not yet understand why she was doing this, but she did not let her ignorance stop her.

The sumptuous dinners she prepared for Matthieu soon took on an aura of magic and mystery. True to her penchant for travesty and for the distortion of genres, the dishes she created were unprecedented. And it was, of course, almost impossible for her lover to tell what ingredients had gone into the fare. Yet the exotic aromas wafting up into the air left no doubt that Malvina had made ample use of powerful aphrodisiac spices. Her meats were invariably scattered with cardamom seeds and her sauces were paprika red or the glowing yellow of Madras curry.

Malvina herself did not eat on these occasions, as though the sight of her lover was enough to nourish her. She would simply sit opposite him and watch closely as his fork moved between his plate and his mouth.

'It's good, isn't it?' she would ask anxiously.

Of course it was. Matthieu delighted in her culinary creations. But he always remained on his guard, for he knew the entire spectacle was aimed simply at showing her in a docile and reassuring light. And to remind him that it was their mutual love of food which had given them such pleasure throughout their relationship.

'Would you like some more?'

Now she was swathing him in maternal benevolence and from this role she moved into that of a child kneeling silently at his feet. This was too much for him, so he stood her up and put his arms around her.

She moved her hands over his torso, then placed her ear against his chest as though to listen to the food moving through his digestive system. She imagined it filling up this inaccessible body and enriching the blood that fed its soul. Her creation was conquering every muscle, every blood vessel. The intense pleasure this gave her was in every way comparable to any carnal delights she had known. This was Malvina's new way of possessing her lover. She was penetrating him like a man takes a woman.

This satisfaction gave her back some of the sparkle that had once characterized her. Her eyes no longer had the terrifying opacity that is the mark of the desperate. It was as if she had at last found a way out of a nightmarish maze.

'Are you at last seeing reason?' asked Alcibiade, who had soon noticed the change in her demeanour.

'Yes, you're right. I am feeling a lot better.'

The dwarf made her turn in a full circle in front of him.

'You are magnificent, madame!' he said, and bowed elegantly. 'But where has your wonderful dress sense gone? You wear nothing but black these days. One would think you were trying to disappear under all that material! Look at those sleeves! They go right down to your fingers. And your dress is buttoned right up to your chin. Have you forgotten that spring is almost here?'

'Is it not fashionable to have a milk-white complexion?'

'I hope it is not mere coquetry that has led you to shut yourself away from the world!'

'I have had a project in mind.'

'Yet another project you have not shared with me!'

'When are you leaving for Saint Malo?'

'The master expects me next week. We are to go through the accounts together.'

'He is still determined to give up his business interests?'

'I fear so. He wrote to me that his life of leisure pleased him well.'

'I am glad to hear it.'

'Why don't you come with me next week? The sea air and the Breton breeze will do you good.'

Malvina imagined herself spending long, happy hours contemplating the sea, but her dinners with Matthieu prevented her from leaving Paris.

'What date do you get back?' she asked.

'The count plans to close up shop in mid-June.'

'Promise me that you will come and see me as soon as you return. I shall be waiting for you.'

'Of course I will.'

Malvina's face lit up at his response. She got up to accompany him to the door.

Alcibiade took her hands and began to kiss each of her fingers in turn, when he noticed that her skin looked as if someone had tried to tear it off. Malvina quickly pulled them away.

'It's nothing,' she said as she hid her hands behind her back. 'Nothing, do you hear me? Let me go. I'm exhausted.'

Alcibiade did not dare insist. But as he walked down the stairs he was filled with anxiety. What if she was seriously ill? It was true she looked better now than she had done for months, but this might be a mere appearance. He could not bear the thought any longer and turned on his heel to go back to her door. But before he even had time to knock he heard her say:

'I'm fine, I tell you. What do I need to do to prove it?'

'Nothing,' he replied. 'I just wanted to tell you that when I'm in Saint Malo I will get some plants to cure your skin problem.'

She knitted her brows as though she did not understand what her friend was saying.

'Thank you. You're so kind to worry about me as you do.'

Her ailment was in fact much worse than the dwarf had suspected, for Malvina knew how to hide its true extent. Each morning she would place ceruse plasters on the scars that were spread across her entire body. Her arms, her stomach and the insides of her thighs were raw. Leprosy could not have marked her more. Only her face had kept its beauty.

*

Malvina made a point of being in good humour whenever she was with Matthieu. Yet sitting in his living room was an ordeal, for the heat of the stoves there caused her to itch and opened up her scars. She had to struggle to hold her tightly corseted body upright.

Her sacrifice appeared, however, to be paying off. Her lover was no longer wary of her. It was the end of April and when he came to see her every day, they would engage in endless conversations. Matthieu seemed to feel the need to justify himself, to explain why he had kept his distance.

'All I want is a simple, happy life,' he explained.

'Simple? What a bore! I thought novelty was what excited you most. So it was not weariness but the incandescence of my love that turned you away from me!'

'You did indeed frighten me, I have to admit it. Those years you spent working with my father and handling the vilest of substances affected you more than you might think.'

'The count is not responsible for my behaviour.'

'So why did our relationship become so morbid, so obsessional?'

'That is a lie!'

'I was enraptured by our lovemaking, by the sharing of sexual and spiritual pleasures. But all of a sudden I just felt that my life was reeling out of control and I needed to regain my equilibrium.'

'Why didn't you talk to me about it?'

'How could I? A whisper was a tempest in your eyes. The closer I grew to you, the more I felt that you were dragging me towards some dark abyss. You were forever falling, whatever I did for you! You were under some awful curse.'

Malvina was outraged. She screamed like a wild animal. Matthieu tried to embrace her to calm her down but she broke free of him.

'You have no right to treat me like this! Not you!'

Matthieu looked at her, powerless.

'But don't worry,' she said. 'I will take this burden from you. You are right. There is no point in trying to revive a love that is dead. Your happiness or sadness is no longer of any consequence to me, for I feel only indifference towards you! You have tried to make me a normal person. But it was an impossible task, for I am not nor ever will be a normal person. I am Death. Do you hear me?'

The entire world seemed to fall silent around them. Matthieu, bewildered, walked towards the door. But before passing through it he turned to her and said, 'I am sorry that I loved you so little, that I loved you so badly, that I did not know how to love you. Alcibiade told me you were not well. I shall always be there if you need my help.'

'You may have noticed that I have packed a few bags for a journey that I have been planning,' she said.

Matthieu turned and left the room.

*

Matthieu soon learnt that she meant what she said. He once again became obsessed with the thought of his lover. He tried to distract himself by seducing other women, but in vain. The more he thought about her, the more he believed he had not been patient enough, had never bothered to listen to her concerns. Only his pleasure had mattered. He cursed himself for being just like his father. The blame did lie partly with Malvina, of course, for she was a volatile woman. She was perhaps even mad. But no one had ever loved him like she did. She loved him with her every breath, her every heartbeat. He knew now that the main reason Malvina had left him was simply to tell him she too mattered in their relationship.

Matthieu was weighed down with regret. One evening in May he walked to her apartment and stood in a doorway opposite. A fine rain fell on the empty, silent street. It was dark, but no light shone from the building's windows. He crossed over and knocked on her door. No response. He still had a key, so he placed it in the lock and went inside. It seemed as though no one had lived here for centuries. The furniture in the drawing room was hidden under large white sheets. In the bedroom, the dressing table and its collection of combs and powder puffs were covered in a thick layer of dust. Malvina was well and truly gone!

The clock struck eleven. Its last beat resonated slowly through the dry air. Matthieu was turning to leave when he glimpsed a light in the kitchen. As he walked towards the kitchen door his nostrils were filled with the sweet aroma of cooking. He smelt the green freshness of bay leaves and marjoram and the sugared perfume of spices. A pot frothed and spluttered on burning logs. Malvina stood in front of it. She wore a red silk dress, the one she had on the day they first met. She did not turn around, and he was about to speak when a little, piping voice said, 'I have been waiting for you. Are you free to dine with me this evening?'

A table draped in a white damask cloth stood in the centre of the room. On it a porcelain dinner service was artfully laid out. On the right was a bowl containing cutlery, in the centre a soup tureen and on the left a bouquet of chrysanthemums.

'Take a seat,' she said. 'Dinner is ready.'

Matthieu did as he was told, unable to take his eyes off Malvina. Her face was a cadaverous white and the skin so thin he could clearly see her veins. Apart from her lips, which occasionally moved as she sighed, her features seemed inanimate.

'Do you want me to help you?' he asked.

He had noticed that she was not using her right arm.

'No, thank you. I have already finished.'

'Will you not eat with me, just this once?'

'Eat, or it will get cold.'

He smiled.

'But I came here to talk to you!'

'Eat,' she repeated. 'We can talk afterwards. I, too, have something to tell you.'

Matthieu liked her cooking too much to be able to resist, and particularly this evening for she had prepared lapwing eggs, one of his favourite dishes. The eggs were filled with a stuffing made of foie gras, truffles and chicken seasoned with pepper and grated nutmeg.

'You love this,' she said. 'Do you love me?'

'Yes,' he replied. He poured himself some more champagne and then accepted the cigar Malvina offered him. The halo of smoke he produced heightened his sense of being in another, almost unreal world. He watched Malvina watching him with her big eyes set in a face that was as still as a portrait. He was touched that she wore the emerald he had given her.

'I love you,' he murmured.

She stood up and walked around the table to stand behind him.

'Don't move,' she whispered in his ear. 'Please do not move.'

Her hands began to move up and down his torso, following the rhythm of his breath. They descended further and further before brushing lightly off his sex, which swelled with the pleasure that filled it. Matthieu let out a groan of joy, then threw his head back to receive his mistress's lips. Malvina sank her tongue into his mouth, still warm from the food he had eaten. She licked its insides, then began to dart her tongue in and out in imitation of a couple in the throes of lovemaking. He stretched out his arm to pull her towards him. She screamed out in pain.

'What's the matter? Did I hurt you?'

'You did say you loved me, didn't you?' she asked in a low voice.

'I did.'

'Are you sure of it?'

'There is no doubt about it.'

'Well then, look at this and remember that no woman has ever given herself to you like this.'

She moved closer to the lamp and began to remove her clothes one by one, slowly revealing a mutilated body whose entire skin was an open wound. Her right arm appeared to have been sliced open by a red-hot poker. Matthieu was staggered to think of the pain she must have suffered, but his words of consolation remained trapped in his throat.

'Do not cry,' she said.

'You poor thing!'

'I did it for you.'

Matthieu could not understand what she was saying. He went to cover her with a cloak.

'No. I want you to see.'

'We'll make you better. I shall look after you.'

'You just haven't understood, have you?' she screamed. 'I did it all for you! You have been eating my flesh for months now! I couldn't fill your mind, so now I flow through your veins, I feed your blood. That is why you have come back to me! Because you belong to me!'

Matthieu stared at her with bulging eyes. Surely not even an insane person would undertake such a barbaric sacrifice? He began to retch.

'You're not going to vomit me up, are you?'

So she was completely mad! She began to follow him as he lurched around the room.

'Stop right there!'

He ran out of the kitchen only to collapse in the corridor and throw up his dinner. The taste of Malvina's flesh burnt his throat as he felt every morsel passing once again through his mouth. What seemed like an eternity went by before he was able to struggle to his feet. He had to flee this cursed place, yet the closer he got to the door, the further away it seemed. Everything began to spin around him and he soon fell back onto the floor. It was no longer nausea but fear he felt now, for he was sure that some horrible poison was eating his stomach. His heart felt as if it were being spiked with a thousand incandescent thorns.

Malvina drew closer to Matthieu. She was filled with a demonic strength, and her face, with its jaw hanging open, was now that of a beast. She wanted to be the last thing he saw before he finally succumbed to the hemlock. And to ensure that the last thing he heard was her breath, she lay down on top of him like a spider on its prey. She planted her lips on his to suck the life out of him. Matthieu's body gave one last spasm before releasing his soul into the night.

A resounding silence filled the room, a silence that escaped Malvina, for she was taken by madness. Her head was filled with questions. Matthieu had died because he was not capable of giving of his worst to hold on to her. How could she possibly have disgusted him? She who now licked his dead body, who bit into it so she could feel his blood flow into her. The blood metamorphosed her, became her own. Already her heartbeat was his heartbeat and her brain had taken on a new identity. She no longer wanted to see, to hear, to feel. Her gesture of love had brought her the eternity she had always longed for.

*

When Alcibiade called on Malvina two days later, he found her door half open. He went inside and found the shutters in the drawing room closed. He fumbled in the darkness to open the windows to let in the soft light of the spring morning. Turning back into the room, he saw Malvina squatting in a corner with her knees tucked in against her chest. Her thin and scarred hands fiddled distractedly with a piece of blue cloth. She looked at him. He looked at her. Neither spoke. Alcibiade went into the bedroom and cried out in alarm when he saw Matthieu's body stretched out on the floor. The apartment fell back into silence after the dwarf's scream as he began to understand that Malvina was responsible for the death and that she would soon follow her lover to the grave. She had clearly neither eaten nor drunk for many days. Alcibiade offered her a glass of water and a little sugar, but she could take neither. She was visibly fading before him. He helped her onto the sofa where he placed a cushion behind her head. Her matted hair hung around her face like a dishevelled halo. She tried to speak but no sound came from her lips. Alcibiade gave her the gentlest of kisses, and then put his arms around her so she would not be afraid. So she would never more be afraid.

How long did he hold her? He could not say. The blue scarf had fallen from Malvina's hand. Death had come to her to unburden her tortured soul. It came as a groundswell that no reef could hold back. Its devastating strength crushed all hatred, all fury. Alcibiade picked up the scarf, then knelt down and prayed to God to forgive his friend's mad crime.

The late afternoon sun swathed the room in a dull olive colour. A probing sunbeam landed on the bouquet of white roses lying on a pedestal table. Its warmth caused one of the flowers to open up and free a bee that had been trapped inside. The insect crawled dizzily around the table before taking off and heading through the open window towards the blue of the sky. Alcibiade knew he could now leave.

A man crossed his path as he walked out through the porch and on to the street. Alcibiade would not have given him a second thought if the stranger had not caught hold of his arm.

'Evil comes to those who make bitter things sweet and sweet things bitter,' he said as he stared at the dwarf.

Alcibiade looked back in incomprehension. He pulled himself free and walked off down the street. A glance over his shoulder showed him the man limping up the stairs.

The sun had turned violet and a pale moon hung above the darkening rooftops. It would be a clear night, thought Alcibiade. This was surely a sign.